God knows my heart, He knows what is true. I'm praying and giving it all to Him. If the authorities won't believe me, so be it. I'll go wherever God leads, even if it is to prison.

Prudence Willard's Journal
July 18, 1863

SECRETS OF WAYFARERS INN

SECRETS OF
WAYFARERS INN

Red, White,
and True

LESLIE GOULD

Guideposts

New York

SECRETS OF
WAYFARERS INN

Red, White, and True

Be strong and of a good courage, fear not,
nor be afraid of them: for the LORD thy God,
he it is that doth go with thee;
he will not fail thee, nor forsake thee.
Deuteronomy 31:6 KJV

CHAPTER ONE

Tess Wallace stepped behind the front desk in the lobby of Wayfarers Inn, pushing her hair away from her sweaty forehead. She'd been running up and down the stairs all evening, trying to accommodate the Hines family.

It would have been nice if the entire family had gone down to the river to watch the Fourth of July fireworks, but the older adults and younger children had stayed behind. Most were on the back patio, enjoying time together playing board games under the stringed lights that criss-crossed the space, but Granny Hines had insisted on staying in her room. Nathan, her teenage grandson, had stayed in his too.

Tess sank onto the stool behind the desk, glad to give her aching feet a rest. She glanced appreciatively around the lobby at the red, white, and blue bunting that Janice had strung throughout the bottom floor of the inn, including the café. Tess was what Janice called "decoratively challenged." So she stuck to what she did best—finances and hospitality—while LuAnn, the third member of their Inn Crowd, kept them organized and up to code.

Tess's eyes lit on the curio cabinet that stood against a wall several feet away, and she groaned. She rose to her feet and, for what seemed the umpteenth time in two days, tried once more to get the bunting to stay attached to the top of the cabinet. The cabinet was a new addition to the lobby and housed an exhibit from the Marietta Underground Railroad Museum. It held a first edition of *Uncle Tom's Cabin* and a few other things, including a pamphlet, a shawl, an old pair of boots, and a knife.

As Tess collapsed onto the stool again, the phone rang. She glanced at the caller ID and groaned again. Nathan. Then she smiled before she answered it, hoping it would cheer up her voice, which otherwise would sound as exhausted as she felt. "This is Tess. How may I help you?"

"I need to speak with your IT department."

She sighed. Yes, it was Nathan. "I already told you. We don't have an IT department." He'd been complaining all evening about how slow the Wi-Fi was.

"You have to have someone who handles your technology." He obviously wasn't even trying to hide the exasperation in his voice.

"I'm not sure what else to tell you…" Tess raised her head to see Nathan's mother, Val, standing in front of her, reaching for the phone. Her husband was Granny Hines's son, but he wasn't able to come on the trip. Tess gathered, from what Val said, that he owned a start-up business that was struggling. Val seemed absolutely devoted to her mother-in-law and spent more time taking care of Granny than Granny's own daughters.

"I'll talk to him," Val said with a stern look on her thin face. Tess handed the receiver to her.

Val pressed the receiver to her ear, tugged at a heart necklace around her neck with her free hand, and said emphatically, "Nathan, leave Tess alone. She's been running around all evening trying to accommodate you. You're here to spend time with family—not play computer games."

Tess couldn't hear what the boy said back.

"We'll talk when I come upstairs. In the meantime, don't call Tess again. If you do, you'll need to come out on the patio with the rest of us." Val said goodbye and then handed the phone back to Tess. "I'm so sorry."

"It's not a problem," Tess said. She liked Val. She was no-nonsense. Not nearly as intense as her daughter Keeley, who was interning with Maybelline Rector, the curator at the Marietta Underground Railroad Museum. Keeley had put together the exhibit in the curio cabinet and had visited the inn many times to double-check something or to test the alarm. For a while it seemed as if she were on staff at Wayfarers and not the museum. The young woman, who was a junior in college and majoring in history, was the sole reason her family had chosen Marietta—and the inn—for their family reunion. She was in Marietta for the summer, renting a room with a local family. The extended Hines family had rented every room in the inn except one. Keeley was great to have around, but she definitely took her position at the museum seriously.

Val ran her hand through her short dark hair. "Between Granny and Nathan, we're quite a handful."

Tess hastened to reassure her. "We do what we can to accommodate our guests, although I'm not sure there's anything we can do about the Wi-Fi." No one had ever complained about it being slow before.

"Nor should you," Val said. "In fact, please don't. Maybe it will get him off his laptop. I didn't even know he'd brought it along until we got here. He hates to travel and wanted to stay home alone, but I forced him to come." The boy was probably sixteen or so and was sharing Woodsmoke and Pine with his cousins, Chad and Chet, eight-year-old twins who made Tess's four-year-old triplet grandchildren seem like the calmest children in the world.

Tess could understand not wanting to leave Nathan home alone. The Hineses lived in California, in a San Francisco suburb, if she remembered the address correctly. It wasn't as if they lived in a small, sleepy town.

She pushed her hair away from her forehead again. Had it gotten warmer?

Val glanced toward the patio door. "I think it might be cooler outside than inside now."

"Oh, dear." Tess stood. "So it's not just me?"

Val shook her head. "It's definitely warm in here."

Tess stepped out from behind the desk and placed her hand against the register in the wall. The forced air certainly wasn't cool. In fact, it felt downright warm. She turned the corner to the thermostat. Goodness, the temperature was up to seventy-nine. Warm air was worse than no air. She turned the system off and tried to think of a diversion for her guests.

"Winnie made delicious red, white, and blue tarts today. There's a pan left. Could your group take it off our hands?" Winnie's tarts had never failed them yet.

"Oh, that sounds wonderful," Val answered. "Can I help?"

"Sure. Follow me." Tess led the way into the kitchen and handed Val a stack of plates and a handful of forks and napkins. She retrieved the tarts from the refrigerator, and the two women headed out to the patio just as the first of the fireworks exploded over the river with a terrific boom. Tess jumped, and the whole building seemed to shake. The group squealed in delight. Sparkler-like stars in red, white, and blue filled the dark sky.

Val pointed to the tarts before another firework exploded. "Look, guys!"

Everyone oohed and aahed as Tess set the blueberry and raspberry tarts, dusted with powdered sugar, on the table. The group included Granny's daughters, Connie and Ellen, their husbands, Bob and Gary, and the twins, who were Connie and Bob's sons. Sadie and Collette, Ellen and Gary's teenage daughters, were off with Keeley and watching the display over the river. As another firework exploded, they all turned their attention back to the sky, and Tess quietly slipped back into the inn.

As she headed down the stairs to the basement, several more booms shook the building. She'd always loved the Fourth of July, and the town of Marietta did an exceptional job celebrating it.

Today wasn't turning out to be Tess's favorite Fourth though. She'd felt unsettled all day. She'd opened a financial investment statement that morning for an account managed by a man who'd been a friend of her late husband's. Frank Bryant owned an investment company that Jeffrey had invested in a decade ago. Tess had been ready to cash it out after Jeffrey died, but Frank assured her he'd keep earning her money. Now the account had taken a big dive.

She'd been trying not to worry about it, at least not until she could call Frank in the morning, but the situation kept nagging at her, so much so that she'd told Janice and LuAnn to go ahead and go watch the fireworks. She didn't mind seeing to their guests at the inn.

Last Fourth of July, LuAnn, Janice, and Tess had just purchased Wayfarers Inn and were knee-deep in renovations. The three of them had been eager to finish and open the inn. Now, after ten months of being in business, most of the kinks of running the inn had been worked out. She couldn't imagine that anything serious could be wrong with the AC system. It was brand-new.

She stood in front of it in the furnace room of the basement, on the opposite end of the underground tunnel that had truly put Wayfarers Inn on the map. Of course, the inn had been heated by coal during the 1800s. Now the furnace was natural gas, and the forced air was electric. She tried to remember the last time the filters had been changed. Thorn would know, but she wouldn't ask him to come over this late. Another boom caught Tess off guard. It sounded like a cannon.

The river would be packed with residents and tourists, their heads turned toward the bursts of red, white, and blue against the dark sky, celebrating the USA growing another year older. It truly was a wonderful day—even if she felt out of sorts.

She sighed as she stared at the air-conditioning unit. She pulled out a filter, but it didn't seem to be dirty. It was probably some electronic problem. Maybe it just needed to be reprogrammed. Not knowing what else to do, she typed out an SOS text to LuAnn and Janice. An inn with no AC in July was an emergency. It had been eighty-nine and muggy today. Tomorrow it was supposed to be over ninety. She hit Send, and another boom caught her off guard. She jumped again and then laughed at herself—until the crash of glass, followed by the sound of an alarm she didn't recognize, truly frightened her.

Tess bounded up the stairs, wondering what else could have possibly gone wrong. She stopped at the top of the stairs, ready to head to the kitchen. But as she hurried into the lobby, she saw that the curio cabinet had been broken into. The alarm continued to wail.

Tess stepped closer. Shards of glass covered the floor, and jagged pieces still hung in the cabinet. Tess had no idea how to turn the alarm off. She needed Maybelline. Or Keeley. ASAP.

CHAPTER TWO

Marietta, Ohio
July 4, 1863

The morning light danced with the breeze from the river and through the window of the Riverfront House as Prudence Willard stirred the pot of custard over the big cookstove. *Lord,* she prayed, *Thee knows what is going on in that village in Pennsylvania. Men are dying. Women are mourning. The residents have been overrun by the depravity of war. Please put an end to it soon.* She paused for a moment and then added, *Thy will be done.*

It was Independence Day, a time, in the past, to celebrate the birth of the United States of America. And freedom. Instead, all waited with bated breath to find out how the raging battle would end.

Word had come to the inn two days ago that the armies of the North and South had collided outside Gettysburg. Hopefully word would come soon that the battle had ended. She thought of their friends, Isaac and his daughter Ernestine, who'd settled on a farm outside Gettysburg a few years ago.

She'd heard of Southern soldiers rounding up free black people in Pennsylvania and forcing them over the Mason-Dixon Line into slavery. She prayed that wouldn't be the case for their friends. She prayed that by the next Fourth of July the war would be over and that the Emancipation Proclamation that President Lincoln signed last January would apply to every slave in the South. She prayed that, finally, all would be free.

For the last several months, she hadn't had any packages delivered for her to move along, but perhaps she would again. There hadn't been as much call to help in the last year, but one never knew what might be needed from those willing to do the Lord's work.

As a light-skinned Melungeon woman, the granddaughter of a man stolen from Africa and a woman from Portugal and the daughter of escaped slaves, Prudence knew from experience the dirty and diabolical business of slavery. Although she was born free, she was kidnapped along with her parents and forced into slavery for a time. Since that time, living with a Quaker woman, embracing that faith, and helping free God's people from slavery had helped her understand the redemption of the good Lord.

She shivered, even in the heat of the kitchen, as the filling began to bubble, then she pulled it off the stove, placing the pot on the oak table in the middle of the room. Eight parbaked crusts, along with boxes of blueberries and raspberries, covered the far half of the table.

The hotel was full of guests, most of whom were just finishing up their breakfast. She expected that some townspeople would gather for an Independence Day dinner later in the day.

As she ladled the custard into the crusts, a shout went up in the dining room. Prudence wiped her hands on her apron and stepped to the kitchen door to see what was going on.

Mr. Siloam, the caretaker of the hotel, stood in the middle of the room of patrons, holding up a telegram. "The North has won!" he exclaimed. "The battle ended last night. Lee is in retreat."

The room erupted in shouts of joy and relief. But Prudence noticed that Mr. Gidden stood off to the side with a sour look on his face. He was originally from Kentucky. Perhaps he'd been hoping the South would win. Mr. Bickerton, who owned the hotel, had left with his family for a trip to Chicago a few weeks earlier. Mr. Gidden was Mr. Bickerton's general business assistant. He had been spending more time than necessary at the inn, at least in Prudence's humble opinion. The man tended to give direction and advice when it wasn't needed or asked for.

Regardless of Mr. Gidden's glum response, Prudence was overcome with relief as she stepped back into the kitchen. Any time the fighting stopped was a good time. She finished ladling the custard into the crusts. As she put the last one in the oven, Mr. Siloam slipped into the kitchen with an annoyed expression on his face. "That man," he said. "I know he has other business to attend to for Mr. Bickerton, yet he spends all of his time here."

Prudence didn't respond. She couldn't risk having anything she might say overheard and misconstrued, but she understood Mr. Siloam's frustration with Mr. Gidden. She felt leery of the man and did all she could to stay out of his way.

"At least we've had good news today," she said.

Mr. Siloam agreed.

"Does thee think the Southern army is still stealing blacks away in Pennsylvania?" she asked quietly. "To take them south?"

"I can't say," he answered. "I imagine Lee and his soldiers are anxious to get back to Richmond, but who's to know what they'd do if someone was in their way."

Prudence nodded. She suspected he was right. Through the years Mr. Siloam had been one of the leaders in helping move "packages" once they reached the north shore of the Ohio River.

"Mr. Gidden wanted to know if you were making your berry custard for dessert. He expects the mayor, among others, to dine here."

She pointed to the oven. "They're baking right now. Once they've cooled, I'll put the berries on top." In past years, there would have been a town picnic in the park. Today, it seemed the dignitaries were coming to the hotel.

After Mr. Siloam left, Prudence turned her attention to preparing the pork roasts for dinner. She'd serve them with cooked cabbage and mashed potatoes and gravy.

Another cheer went up in the dining room. With the river being the Mason–Dixon Line, the town of Marietta had its fair share of citizens with southern sentiments, and there were plenty in town who had relatives on the Confederate side. But Mr. Bickerton embraced the ideology of the North, even providing his hotel as a stop along the Underground

Railroad. Prudence knew he wasn't the man of integrity he pretended to be, but she also knew, to one degree or another, that there wasn't a soul on God's good earth who was beyond reproach. And most people were a mix of good and bad.

She let out a sigh. Today she would be grateful. The battle had ended. As she breathed another prayer of gratitude, the back door opened, and Jason and Moses stepped inside the kitchen, hand in hand. "Has thee heard the news?" she asked.

Jason nodded. "We just did."

Moses held up a piece of paper. "Here, Mama."

"What is it?" She stepped toward him.

"It's a letter from Isaac, in Gettysburg," Jason explained. "He wrote that he wants to send Ernestine away from the fighting."

"Does thee think he still does? Now that the battle is over?"

Jason's brows knitted. "I imagine it will take some time for the people of the village to recover…"

Of course her husband was right. She couldn't imagine the damage that had taken place. She took the letter from Moses. It was dated June 30, before the battle even started. Isaac wrote: *I plan to send Ernestine to Marietta as soon as a Friend can accompany her. We know a few who have been kidnapped by the Confederates and shipped south. I can't bear that for my daughter. I will stay behind, see to my land, and then send for Ernestine when it is safe.*

She folded the letter and slipped it into her apron pocket. They hadn't heard anything about civilian casualties in Gettysburg.

"I have more news," Jason said.

"Oh?"

"There's word about a Confederate general headed north, with thousands of troops. I heard he's on the Green River."

That was a tributary of the Ohio River.

Jason continued. "Rumor has it he wants to wage more battles in the North so citizens of the Union can experience the horrors of war that the South has been experiencing for the last two years."

Prudence gripped the edge of the table. "Does thee believe he's headed to Marietta?"

A pained expression passed over Jason's face. "Hopefully not."

Perhaps Isaac should send Ernestine somewhere else. Prudence's eyes fell on her son. Was he at risk? They all passed as white. Locals viewed her as a farmer's wife who spent too much time in the sun—but, by Southern standards, they were colored. They were continually at risk, and would be until the North won. She couldn't bear to think of any other scenario.

She patted the letter in her pocket. She'd write to Isaac and suggest he send Ernestine somewhere else, if it wasn't too late. She wasn't sure they could protect the girl if a Confederate army was headed their way.

CHAPTER THREE

As Tess dialed Maybelline's number, the bell on the front door rang, and then LuAnn exclaimed, "Goodness, it's hot in here!" As she came around the corner with Brad beside her, she saw the cabinet and blurted out, "What in the world?"

Tess held up her index finger as the call went to voice mail. "Maybelline, this is Tess. We have an emergency here at the inn." She spoke loudly, above the wail of the alarm. "Please phone me back immediately."

As she ended the call, she turned to LuAnn. "I have no idea what happened. I heard the alarm and came up from the basement." She gestured to the cabinet. "This is what I found."

LuAnn and Brad turned their attention to the cabinet. "There's a keypad on the wall," LuAnn said.

"Do you know the code?" Brad asked.

LuAnn shook her head and looked at Tess as the booms from the fireworks continued.

Just then, Val hurried into the lobby to see what the noise was all about, and Tess explained what was going on. "Do you have Keeley's cell phone number? She might be able to help."

As Val rattled it off, Tess keyed the number into her phone. All she needed from Keeley was the code. But Keeley didn't answer either. After leaving a message, Tess turned her attention to the cabinet with the rest of them.

"I'll go get Nathan," Val said.

Tess wasn't sure what the boy could do.

"Call the alarm company," LuAnn said.

Tess didn't have the number. "Which one is it?"

LuAnn turned to Tess, wiping her forehead with the back of her hand. "Isn't it the same as ours?"

"I don't know," Tess wailed above the boom of another firework exploding. "Shouldn't the alarm company be contacting us by now?" Why hadn't they gotten more information from Maybelline? As she watched LuAnn and Brad punch more numbers into the keypad, she could hear voices coming down the staircase.

"But I was in the middle of a game…"

"I thought the internet was too slow."

"It is. I can't play with my guild. I ended up playing with people I don't know."

Val paused a moment and then said, "This will only take a minute."

"Can't someone else figure this—"

"Shh." Val popped down the stairs, followed by Nathan. The boy was lanky and wore his dark hair short against his head.

"Does he know the code?" Tess asked.

"I can probably guess it if Keeley set it up." He pulled some sort of tool from his front pocket. "Otherwise I'll just cut a wire…"

Tess's mouth dropped open. Who was this kid?

By now more of the Hines family, including Chad and Chet who were poking at each other, had come inside to see what all the racket was about.

LuAnn and Brad stepped away from the keypad, and Nathan, rubbing his hands together, took their place. He closed his eyes and then punched in a number. The alarm continued to wail. He tried a second number, this time with a flourish. It still wailed.

He pulled the keypad from the wall. "I don't think you should cut a wire," Tess said, holding up her phone. "Hopefully Keeley will call back..."

Nathan tried a third number. The alarm ceased, and the gathering of relatives that had gathered around began to clap. "Way to go, Nathan," his uncle Gary called out.

"So what was the code?" Ellen asked.

"7-1-7-5."

"How'd you guess it?"

Nathan started toward the stairs as he called out over his shoulder, "G-A-G-E. Our first dog. Keeley has no imagination."

Tess ran her hand through her hair. She called out a thank-you as Nathan bounded out of sight, and just as Maybelline hurried into the lobby. Marissa Endicott, from the *Marietta Times*, followed her.

The reporter wore a skirt, blouse, and a pair of flats. Most likely she'd been reporting on the Fourth of July festivities. "Maybelline," she said. "Why are we here?"

Maybelline, her gray eyes wide, stopped in front of the cabinet and gasped, "What was stolen?"

Marissa pulled her camera out of her bag and started snapping photos. "I was interviewing people down at the river, and I saw Maybelline headed this way. I knew something was up—she was practically running."

Maybelline frowned, pressing her hand against her reddish, dark hair. "There's no privacy in this town anymore."

"So someone just smashed the glass and took off with a historic artifact?" Marissa asked, ignoring Maybelline.

"Someone did smash the glass," Tess answered. "But we don't know yet what's missing." She couldn't recall everything that was in the cabinet.

"I'll call Keeley." Maybelline appeared exhausted. Her mouth turned down, extending her wrinkles. "She'll know where the inventory list is." She pulled out her phone.

"I already left her a message," Tess said, nodding toward Val as several fireworks exploded in a row. "This is Keeley's mother."

Val extended her hand and said, "I'll get our crew out of the way. Keeley probably can't hear her phone. She'll be here soon." Her sisters- and brothers-in-law followed her back to the patio. All of the adults seemed to be working together to shoo the twins along with them.

Maybelline went ahead and called Keeley, leaving her another message, and then stepped closer to the cabinet. "The first edition copy of *Uncle Tom's Cabin* is here. It's the most valuable item on display." She looked at Tess. "Have you called the police?"

"Not yet. I thought we should wait and see if something was stolen. It could have been an accident..."

LuAnn raised her eyebrows.

Tess sighed. One of her first thoughts had been that perhaps one of the twins had accidently broken it, but it didn't appear so. They were troublemakers, but they didn't look guilty. Nathan could have, but he'd have to be a pretty good actor to come down and crack the code if he'd just broken the glass. He seemed pretty honest.

"I'll call it in," LuAnn said.

Tess stepped closer to the cabinet.

Another boom shook the inn, followed by several more.

"It's probably the grand finale," Brad said, stepping to the front door. LuAnn and Marissa followed him out onto the sidewalk.

Maybelline peered into the cabinet and muttered, "I can't believe they didn't take the book. You'd think that would be the sole purpose of breaking in."

Tess rubbed her temples. She couldn't believe any of this was happening. The broken AC. The broken glass. Her broken finances. All she wanted to do was go to bed. Instead she still had a long night ahead of her.

⁂

Maybelline tried to call Keeley three more times. Finally, she sighed and held up her phone. "I wasn't crazy about getting an intern in the first place. Not that Keeley isn't a smart girl and a hard worker. But if I'd done this exhibit myself, I'd know exactly what was missing."

"She'll be here soon." Tess was thankful Val had gone back to the patio. And that Granny Hines was, hopefully, sound asleep in her room. Both would most likely be hurt by Maybelline's harsh words.

Maybelline folded her arms across her chest, her phone still in her hand. Just as Officer Randy Lewis came through the front door of the inn, the whistle of a bottle rocket, followed by two pops, exploded somewhere outside the inn.

Randy frowned. "As soon as the fireworks display ends, the main show begins," he muttered. But then he put a smile on his face and looked from Maybelline to Tess. "How can I help you ladies?"

Tess quickly explained what happened and that they had no idea—yet—what had been stolen. "If anything," she said, trying to remember what exactly was in the cabinet. She remembered the book, the old pair of boots, the knife. But there could definitely be something she wasn't remembering.

The officer stepped up to the cabinet, shining his flashlight around. "There doesn't seem to be any blood."

Tess hadn't even thought of that.

Randy leaned forward. "Most likely, the perpetrator used some sort of object to break the glass."

As they all peered into the cabinet, Keeley came through the front door with her cousins, Sadie and Colette, followed by LuAnn, Brad, and Marissa. And then Janice. It appeared that LuAnn had caught their third partner up on what was going on.

Keeley was out of breath. "I just listened to your voice mail," she said to Tess, brushing her long dark hair away from her face. She wore a blue skirt, a red top, and white sandals. Turning to Maybelline, she added, "And yours too. All five of them." She stepped to the cabinet, opened the bottom drawer, and took out a file folder. "The inventory list is in here." She riffled through the folder and pulled out a paper, peering at it through her retro black glasses.

A crowd gathered around, including Keeley's cousins. Her mother and aunts and uncles, along with the twins, came back in from the patio.

Keeley held the list up and turned to Maybelline. "How about if I read and you check?"

"Be careful of any glass." Tess stood to the side of the cabinet.

Maybelline pointed to the officer's flashlight. "Mind if I borrow that?"

He handed it over.

"I'll unlock the cabinet," Keeley said, taking an ornate key from her purse. "So you don't have to point the flashlight through the broken pane."

After she slipped the key back into her purse, taking care to secure it in an inside pocket, she cleared her throat. "The 1852 copy of *Uncle Tom's Cabin*."

"Check," Maybelline said.

"The 1857 hymnal."

"Check."

Keeley's voice lowered as she read, "A tin cup." Tess knew it had been found in the basement of a local home used on the Underground Railroad during an excavation.

"Check."

"A ledger written in code."

"Check."

"A wool blanket, dyed with indigo, that was used while transporting runaways."

Tess shivered as she looked where the flashlight was pointed. There was nothing like historical artifacts to bring the past to life.

Everyone remained quiet, even the twins, as Keeley and Maybelline continued down the list, going back and forth, ending with the abolitionist pamphlet.

"Check," Maybelline said.

Keeley glanced up, peering over her square-framed glasses.

Relieved, Tess said, "Then it must have been an accident, if nothing was stolen."

"No, there's one more item." Maybelline shone the light on a small item in front of the blanket.

"Impossible," Keeley said. "I put every item in myself."

Confused, Tess stepped forward. Keeley must have made a mistake in making the inventory list.

Maybelline reached inside the cabinet and pulled out the object. She turned toward the crowd and opened her hand, revealing a tarnished brooch with a hint of rose color to the gold— if it was gold. Perhaps it was simply a piece of costume jewelry.

Tess inhaled, sharply. It seemed the stones glittered red, white, and blue. Rubies, diamonds, and sapphires. Then again, maybe someone was playing a joke on them.

Marissa snapped a few photos.

"Maybe it was pinned to the blanket," Tess said. "And fell off when the glass was broken."

"Definitely not," Maybelline said. "That blanket has belonged to the museum since 1982. I'd remember this brooch. I've absolutely never seen it before. It's not part of our collection."

"Definitely not," Keeley echoed. "It's not part of the inventory. It wasn't in the cabinet when I put the collection inside." She held up her phone. "I took photos." She scrolled through her photos and then showed Tess each item.

Sure enough, in the photo of the blanket, there was nothing in front of it. Just a sliver of the bare shelf.

"It doesn't make any sense," LuAnn said. "Why would someone break into the cabinet to *leave* something?"

Tess agreed.

"And what do we do with it now?" Janice asked.

"Put it in the inn safe until we can get to the bottom of this," Randy said. "But check with all of your guests tonight to see if they know anything about it." Another bottle rocket whistled and then exploded. "I wish I could stay longer, but duty calls." Tess couldn't help but note the sarcasm in his voice.

She turned to Val and her sisters-in-law. "Do any of you recognize the brooch?" She made eye contact with Keeley too.

All the women shook their heads.

"I've never seen it before in my life," Keeley said.

"What about your grandmother?" Tess asked. "Could it be hers?"

"No," Keeley insisted. "I've been through her jewelry box plenty of times." She met Tess's gaze. "But don't ask her about it." She waved dismissively. "You'll only confuse her."

"All right." Tess glanced at Val for confirmation.

Val nodded.

"Granny's fine most of the time, but every once in a while she has a bout of confusion," Granny's oldest daughter, Ellen, said.

Tess tucked that piece of information away. Perhaps they were all hiding something. Or maybe they really were just trying to protect Granny Hines.

She turned her attention to Maybelline. "Are you okay with us putting the brooch in the safe for the night?"

"Certainly." She motioned to the items that were now on the front desk. "Do you have room for all of these things too?"

Tess assured her they could fit everything into the safe. "And we'll call the glass company in the morning to make the needed repairs."

Maybelline and Marissa left, and Janice began sweeping up the glass. Keeley held the dustpan for her while LuAnn and Brad worked together to remove the glass from the shelves. Then Tess removed all of the items from the case and carefully placed them, including the brooch, into a box. Finally, she headed to the office and placed everything in the safe.

When she returned to the lobby, Janice held the broom in one hand, brushing her platinum curls back from her face with the other. "My, it is hot in here, isn't it?"

Tess reached for her cell phone. "I was just going to call Thorn about the AC when I heard the crash." She looked at her screen. "But it's too late to call him now. It's after ten."

Janice waved at her. "Go ahead and leave a message. Thorn told me he turns his phone off at night. You won't disturb him."

Tess gave her an "Are you sure?" look but punched the speed-dial button for Thorn. She waited for the prompt, then said, "Hi, Thorn, it's Tess. Listen, our AC isn't running, so we wondered if you could look at it if you have some time tomorrow. We need to get it up and running as soon as we can. Thanks, and I hope to see you tomorrow."

She hung up. "What should we do in the meantime?"

"Tell everyone to open their windows—thank goodness they're screened. And find some fans."

"Everyone I know has central air," Tess said. "I'm not sure where I could find any fans."

"You'd be surprised who has one or two in their garage or attic." Janice sighed. "Even though it's late, I'll call Stacy and see if she has one. She won't be in bed yet."

Tess nodded. "I'll call Lizzie." Both women's daughters lived in town.

LuAnn must have heard their conversation from the couch in the lobby. "Brad and I would be happy to drive around and collect the fans."

"Great," Tess responded. "Just give us a second to make some calls."

A few minutes later Brad and LuAnn left on fan pick-up duty. Tess called Val, who was staying in Moonlight and Snowflakes with Granny Hines. "The best thing we can do right now is have everyone open the windows. We have some fans on the way. Is it all right if I call back when they arrive?"

"Of course," Val assured her. "Granny and the twins are asleep, but the rest of us will be up for a while."

Tess thanked her, and as she hung up the phone Janice said she was going to head upstairs to open all the windows on the fourth floor.

If only Tess could go with her. The lack of sleep, the long day, and the stress were all adding up.

"Call me when LuAnn and Brad get back with the fans," Janice added. "I'll help pass them around."

Tess thanked her friend and stifled a yawn. As Janice stepped into the elevator, Perry Cooper—the only guest not part of the family reunion—stepped into the lobby. He had a smile on his face.

"Those fireworks were amazing," he said. "Some of the best I've ever seen!" His sandy hair was cut short, and his dark eyes shone. "What a gift it is to be here. It's a dream come true to be in Marietta in July." Tess knew the man was a huge Civil War buff. He edited a historical journal and was in the area doing research. He'd said he was considering writing a book about Ohio and the Civil War. He'd booked almost two weeks at the inn, which seemed like an incredibly long time to Tess, but he said he was using it as a hub for all his research trips.

He stopped short when he saw the curio cabinet. "What happened?"

Tess quickly explained about the broken glass and that nothing was stolen. She didn't mention the brooch. If it hadn't mysteriously appeared, she'd bet that Chet and Chad had broken the glass. But now she had no idea. "At this point, it's a mystery who did this."

He let out a long whistle and said, "I hope you figure out who did it." Then he pointed to the baby grand piano in the reception area. "I know it's late, but do you mind if I play? It helps me wind down at the end of the day."

"Usually I'd say it's too late, but tonight I'll say yes." Granny's room and the twins' room were both on the third floor. The music wouldn't disturb them. Perry sat down, lifted the lid, and positioned his hands on the keys. First he played a couple of chords. And then he started playing a classical piece.

It was beautiful. Tess relaxed a little as Perry played, his fingers practically floating over the keys, filling the entire lobby with angelic music. For the first time all day, Tess felt a sense of harmony in her soul.

When Perry was done, he closed the lid, said good night, and then bounded up the stairs, whistling the music he'd just finished playing. As he disappeared, so did Tess's sense of harmony.

She wanted nothing more than to go to bed, but she needed to stay up until LuAnn and Brad returned. She hoped they'd come back with enough fans to keep most of the Hines family happy, but she knew she couldn't hope for any relief up on the fourth floor. It was going to be a hot, sticky night for the Inn Crowd.

⚜

Very early the next morning Tess peeled herself out of bed and took a cold shower to wake herself up. It was her turn to help Winnie get breakfast started for the guests and the café crowd, so she quietly left her apartment and made her way to the kitchen. Every step brought her closer to a cup of coffee and a muffin. Just as she reached the bottom of the stairs, she heard the door at the back of the inn slam. She halted in the darkness of the lobby. It was too early for Winnie to arrive, and besides, she'd come through the kitchen door. Was it the person who broke into the cabinet, come to actually steal something this time? She tiptoed through the reception area toward the back exit, reaching for the light switch, but before she could turn it on, someone stepped through the door. She gasped.

A man stood in the shadows.

"Bra-a-d?" Tess stuttered.

"Guess again," a gruff voice growled.

CHAPTER FOUR

Tess covered her mouth, but then she burst into laughter. It was Thorn, holding two box fans.

"What's so funny?" In the dim light Thorn looked tired, but when he took a step into the reception area, he appeared absolutely exhausted.

"You surprised me." Tess turned the light on. "I wasn't expecting you this early."

"Yeah, well, I woke up early and checked my messages." Thorn followed Tess into the lobby and ran his hand through his graying hair. "Sorry I didn't get the message last night."

"We wouldn't have let you come last night anyway—"

He waved his hand to stop her. "For you ladies, I would come." He put the fans down on the floor. "I brought these in case it takes me a little while to figure out the problem. I figured the rooms are warming up."

"Well, I can't thank you enough. You've gone above and beyond the call of duty to help us out."

Thorn grunted and headed to the basement.

A half hour later, after Janice and LuAnn had descended to the kitchen, Tess headed down to the basement to confer with Thorn.

He had a manual spread out on the floor and filters and tools sprawled around. He looked up at her. "I left a message for a repairman."

She gulped. "Okay."

"I think it's fixable."

"I'm sure it is," she answered. "If he's coming, you should go get started on your other calls. Be sure to get some coffee and muffins first, though. I'll let the repairman know what's going on."

"No," Thorn said. "I'll stay. I need to put this back together before he gets here." He rubbed his eye with the back of his hand and yawned. "Sorry, I probably shouldn't have taken it apart. I kept thinking it was an easy fix."

"I'll get you some coffee." Tess turned around to go back up to the kitchen. At least the AC was under warranty. Hopefully it still would be after Thorn's tinkering.

She took a cup of coffee down to Thorn and then took hers in a travel mug and headed out the front door for a quick walk down to the river with Huck, who did his best to keep up with her on his short little legs. As much as she usually loved the Fourth of July, she always enjoyed the morning after too. The evidence of the celebration from the night before hadn't been cleaned up—the remnants of sparklers and bottle rockets and snacks and drinks. But all was quiet as the partiers, and even the little children, were sleeping in after all the fun.

She hurried along the sidewalk and crossed the street with Huck managing to match her stride. A minute later she'd reached the path along the Ohio River, headed east into the morning sun. She paused for a moment and took a sip of her coffee, imagining what the Fourth of July might have been like back in the 1850s and '60s. She imagined orators in the park espousing the virtues of the young country. And children playing games, perhaps gunnysack and wheelbarrow races. It would have been too early in the year for watermelon back then, but late strawberries and raspberries and early peaches would have been ripe. She imagined picnics in the park and perhaps dancing too, as fiddlers played. Would they have had fireworks? She'd read one time that the first Independence Day fireworks in the United States were set off on July 4, 1777, in Philadelphia. She assumed that by the 1850s, Marietta would have had fireworks, although maybe not during the war.

A fish jumped in the middle of the river, and a green heron swooped over the water toward the shore, causing Huck to bark. Tess stopped for a moment and then urged the dog along. She wished she could linger along the river, but she knew she needed to get back to the inn. Winnie would be arriving any minute, and she needed to be there when the AC person came. She'd put an alert in her phone to call Frank Bryant, the investor whom she'd had the letter from. And then there was the brooch. Hopefully, Randy had discovered something about the case. She supposed they should at least find out the value of the piece, if the stones were genuine, any details that would help identify the period of time it was made, and anything else that would identify its origin.

She took another sip of coffee and then breathed a prayer. *Lord, I have a lot going on. Please help me to love You and others as I go through my day. Please give me clarity and grace. You know my worries, and I'm grateful for the guidance I know You'll provide.* She said, "Amen," out loud, took another sip of coffee, and then turned back toward the inn, with Huck trotting along beside her. She'd do her best to face the day.

When Tess stepped into the kitchen humming "How Great Thou Art," Winnie was bent over the counter, cutting up cantaloupe. "Goodness," she said, straightening her willowy figure. "Why is it so warm in here?"

Tess exchanged looks with Janice, who was folding napkins. "The AC quit last night."

Winnie pointed the knife to Big Red, the 1954 O'Keefe & Merritt Aristocrat stove that was the pride and joy of the kitchen and said, "I've got scones in the oven and some quiche I whipped up yesterday. It's getting hotter by the second."

Tess exhaled. "It can't be helped…" Winnie had high blood pressure and a bad knee. Tess hated the thought of her being even more uncomfortable than usual. She worked so hard as the inn's cook. Their business really depended on her. "Did I remember to tell you we have several young people as guests?"

"Yes, you certainly did." Winnie smiled and pointed at LuAnn, who was arranging muffins on a tray. "I baked chocolate muffins yesterday."

"Perfect." Tess cradled her mug in both hands. "Has anyone seen Thorn?"

Janice had finished with her napkins and was wiping the counters. "He came through here a couple of minutes ago. Is he all right?"

Tess held her cup tightly in her hands. "What happened?"

"He was muttering to himself. And when I dropped a cookie sheet, he jumped like he thought he was going to be attacked."

"Oh dear," Tess said. "I wonder if he's feeling all right. Did he leave?"

"I'm not sure." Janice put the disposable wipe in the trash. "Would you put the kettle on for tea?"

Tess nodded absentmindedly as she set her coffee mug down. Hopefully, Thorn was all right.

As she started the kettle, she heard a "Hello?" at the kitchen door. Tess stepped to open it and found a bleary-eyed Granny Hines.

"Oh, good morning," Tess said, wondering if Val or any of the others knew Granny was up. The woman wore lavender pajamas, a turquoise robe, and hot-pink slippers. Her snow-white hair was pushed up on one side.

"I'm looking for Cash," she said.

"Cash? As in money?" Tess asked.

"Oh, you!" The old woman swatted her hand toward Tess. "That's an old joke. Cash has heard it a million times."

"Granny!" Nathan came around the corner from the staircase. He wore the same clothes he'd worn last night, now rumpled. "You were supposed to wait for me."

She grinned and reached for his arm. "There you are."

Nathan rolled his eyes. "I'm not Gramps. I'm your grandson, remember? You need to get dressed before getting your coffee. Mom sent me to take you back upstairs."

Tess nodded to a table in the café. "She can have a cup here, if she likes. You can sit with her."

Nathan hesitated. Tess guessed he'd rather be up in his room instead of hanging out with a bunch of old women.

Granny Hines brushed past Tess into the kitchen. Tess immediately redirected her and led her out to the nearest table in the café area, helping her sit down. Nathan rolled his eyes again, and then sat down across from her.

Tess served Granny a cup of coffee and looked at Nathan. "Do you want a cup also?" At his nod, she poured him a cup and grabbed the sweetened creamer for him. Then she sat down at the table with them.

"How did you sleep?" Tess asked Granny.

"Great," she answered.

Tess turned to Nathan. "How about you?"

"I didn't," he muttered. "I'll get a nap later."

"But you're drinking coffee." Tess covered her mouth as she yawned.

Nathan shrugged. "It doesn't affect me." He stood. "Come on, Granny. I'll carry your coffee upstairs before Mom finds you down here in your pajamas. She'd be mortified."

Granny giggled. "I suppose she would." She pushed herself up, and Nathan led the way out of the café. Tess went back into the kitchen where Winnie was just pulling the scones out of the oven. The filled muffin tins were on the counter, ready to go in next.

Tess, Janice, and LuAnn set about getting the café ready for their guests, who were starting to trickle in. It was still an hour before the café opened to paying customers. Together they brought out plates, cups and saucers, and napkins, and then carried out the quiche and bowl of cantaloupe, followed by a large fruit bowl of apples, oranges, and bananas. Winnie carried out the basket of scones and muffins. And finally, Tess carried out an assortment of yogurts, placing them in a bowl of ice.

Robin and Taylor arrived while the guests were eating to ready the café for opening at eight. Tess was once again grateful for such dependable and cheerful employees. Robin Rogers, an absolute gem of a young woman, was handy at much more than serving tables and cleaning rooms. She was a jill-of-all-trades, and the Inn Crowd felt blessed to have her. Taylor was a college student working at the inn during his summer break. He was an enthusiastic and conscientious worker and kept the women on their toes to keep up with him.

Robin waved as she came through the café. "Good morning!" She held the *Marietta Times* up high. "You all are famous!" She flipped the paper open. "On page three, there's an article about a brooch."

Tess reached for the paper. "No way. How could Marissa have gotten the article in so soon?" She read the headline out loud. "'Mysterious Red, White, and Blue Brooch Appears at Wayfarers Inn on the Night of the Fourth of July.'" The article detailed what had happened the night before. Thankfully, the photo was black and white. She hoped a fortune seeker didn't read the article and think there was a true treasure to be had. It was probably just an old piece of costume jewelry. Then again, they wouldn't know until they got it appraised.

Tess handed the newspaper back to Robin. "I guess the word's out now."

Robin nodded. "And, be forewarned, Margaret Ashworth is headed this way. She was parking down the block when I got here."

"Oh, goody." It wasn't that Tess didn't like the woman, although Margaret wasn't always very likeable. If the brooch had any historical value, the curator of the local historical society would know. But if she didn't, hopefully she'd be honest about that and not speculate. Honestly, Tess would rather get the brooch appraised and then hear Margaret's thoughts on the matter.

The front door bell buzzed. "Yoo-hoo!" Margaret called out. "I've come for the brooch. I know exactly to whom it belongs. I can't believe, after all these years, it's been found!"

Margaret wore a pair of white crop pants and a navy blue top. Her gray hair was pulled back with a wide barrette at the nape of her neck, and her drawn-on eyebrows seemed a little thicker and darker than usual.

They shot up as she spoke. "The brooch belonged to the Bickerton family." Tess nearly gasped. They'd owned the inn way back in the mid-1800s, although it was called the Riverfront House back then. Margaret continued. "It was stolen at some point...Maybe during the Civil War, but I'll double-check."

"Are you sure the brooch was stolen?" Tess asked. "Maybe someone inherited it, thought it was costume jewelry, and sold it for a song."

"Oh, no," Margaret said. "It was gone years and years ago. I'm sure of that. In fact..." She tapped her finger against her temple. "Now I remember. It was stolen during Morgan's Raid."

LuAnn turned to them. "Morgan's Raid? Brigadier General John Hunt Morgan?"

"Yes!" Margaret's eyebrows shot up again. "The very same!"

LuAnn cuddled her coffee cup in both hands. "Wasn't that right after Gettysburg? In 1863?"

Margaret appeared to be thinking hard. "Correct..."

LuAnn sat down at a table. "Morgan's Raid started in Tennessee in June of that year. The Confederate General wanted to bring the war North so the Union soldiers could suffer too. He covered a thousand miles in about six weeks and raided towns all through the area and even threatened Marietta."

"Not only did he raid towns, but he pillaged too," Margaret said. "I'm certain the brooch was taken during that time. It's coming back to me..."

LuAnn smiled and then added, "He got away with it until he tried to re-cross the Ohio. He and some of the leaders were captured and put in the Ohio State Penitentiary—"

"—where they tunneled out and fled to Cincinnati." Perry Cooper had joined them in the middle of the café.

"And then they hopped on a train and crossed the Ohio River to safety."

"You're kidding, right?" Tess couldn't believe such a ridiculous story.

"No. He's not." LuAnn grinned at Perry. "That's exactly what happened."

"Oh, my." Tess had surely been sleeping during history class.

"I'm certain the Bickerton brooch was stolen during Morgan's Raid," Margaret said again. "Imagine that. It's been returned at last." Tess wasn't sure whether to believe her or not. After all, there must have been thousands of pieces of jewelry stolen during the Civil War. And they didn't even know if the brooch was real, let alone if it was an antique. It could be a costume piece from 1980 as far as they knew.

"What's this about a brooch?" Perry asked, a puzzled expression on his face.

"It was stolen last night," Margaret said.

Tess wondered if she needed to go check the safe.

Flustered, Margaret said, "I mean it was left. Left. Not stolen." She pointed to the display case and laughed nervously.

Tess's face grew warm as Perry turned to her. "Why would anyone leave an item like that?"

"We have no idea," she answered. "And we certainly don't know that it belonged to the Bickerton family."

"Have you had it appraised?" Perry asked.

"Not yet," LuAnn jumped in. "But it's definitely on our to-do list for the day."

Tess took out her phone. Seven thirty. She'd call Frank Bryant at nine o'clock. Then she'd take the brooch to the new jewelry store at ten, when it opened.

LuAnn and Margaret continued to talk while Perry filled a plate with a scone and fruit. Then the AC repairman arrived, and Tess showed him to the basement. When she came back upstairs, Granny—who was now dressed in a coral pantsuit— and Val sat at a table together. There was no sign of Keeley yet.

Tess filled her coffee mug and headed to the lobby desk. At least they didn't have any rooms to turn over, but all would need housekeeping services. She started a list for Robin and Taylor to start on after the café closed.

Perry approached her, his plate in one hand and his coffee cup in another. She smiled but did her best not to be too welcoming. She had a lot of work to do.

"I've heard about this brooch before," he said.

"We have no idea if this is the brooch in question," she clarified.

He frowned. "When will you take it to the jeweler to get it appraised?"

"I'm not sure…"

"I'd go with you if I didn't already have plans this morning and then an appointment to meet with a tour guide out at the Castle this afternoon. I want to know if it was raided by Morgan."

Tess had visited the Castle with her kids years ago. A gothic-revival-style mansion, it had been built in 1855. It was now a museum and one of the main historic attractions in Marietta.

Perry waved his coffee cup at her. "Each year I take two weeks and go to a different state to research the Civil War. I've been focusing on the border states the last couple of years. So far I've gone to eight states to do research. It's always the highlight of my summer."

"What a great experience." Tess pulled her cell phone from her pocket. "If you'll excuse me, I need to make a phone call and then tackle my to-do list. Have a wonderful time at the Castle."

Perry headed back to the café and sat down at the same table with Granny and Val. After he finished eating, he stepped to the piano. This time he played "The Entertainer." Granny began to sway to the music. Tess couldn't help but smile as she watched them both. She knew she better enjoy their guests' good moods now—if they didn't get that AC fixed, no one would be smiling.

CHAPTER FIVE

At nine o'clock, Tess stepped into the inn office and called Frank Bryant at the only number she had for him. The call went straight to voice mail. She tried two more times and then left a message. After stating her name and phone number, she said, "I need to speak with you about my dwindling investment as soon as possible." She surmised he was taking the day off—or coming in late. Next she called the glass repair company. They assured her someone would be out by the afternoon.

She stepped out of the office just as Keeley came through the front door asking Tess if there was any more information about the cabinet break-in or the mysterious brooch.

"Not a word," Tess answered. "But the glass should be replaced by this afternoon, and we can transfer the items back then."

"But without the brooch?"

"Of course," Tess said. "We'll have to see what the jeweler says before we know what to do about it."

"When will you take it by?"

"As soon as I can." Tess smiled, not wanting to say any more.

Keeley yawned, covering her mouth as she did. She wore shorts and a T-shirt that read, *I'd find you more interesting if you were in a history book.* The young woman really was an old soul. She'd told them a while ago that she belonged to all sorts of ancestry groups online and had even had her DNA tested.

"Do you work today?" Tess asked.

Keeley shook her head. "Maybelline gave me the day off." She nodded toward the stairs. "We're all going to go visit the Mound Cemetery." Her expression grew serious. "I've already been there a couple of times, but I'm looking forward to going back. I love Marietta so much. It's like generations of people are still here, walking around, telling us their stories."

Tess almost laughed. She guessed LuAnn felt the way Keeley did. But Tess couldn't really identify with them. It wasn't that she didn't appreciate history, but she lived more in the present instead of in the past, the way most people she knew did.

Perry Cooper certainly seemed to fall into the living in the past category.

"Have a wonderful time," Tess said to Keeley. Keeley waved down at her as she went up the stairs.

Robin and Taylor continued serving guests and customers as LuAnn headed upstairs to start the housekeeping, and Janice headed to the basement to start a load of laundry. When she came back upstairs, she whispered to Tess, who was at the front desk, "You should go check on the repairman. He seems befuddled. He has parts spread all over the floor."

Tess groaned. It sounded like he was doing exactly what Thorn had tried. "I'll go talk to him. Say a prayer we can get this fixed quickly."

Janice placed her hands together. "I am. This could be catastrophic. It's supposed to be in the mid-nineties by this afternoon."

Tess tugged on the collar of her shirt, not wanting to think about what the humidity would be, as she headed down the stairs.

The technician had his head in his hands, but when he heard Tess approach he quickly stood.

"How's it going?" Tess asked.

"Good." He smiled, but then his face fell, and he shook his head. "Actually, not so good. I can't figure it out. I'm going to have to call my supervisor." He looked her in the eyes. "But don't worry, we'll have this repaired as soon as we can."

"Great," Tess said. "That's what we like to hear."

He pulled out his cell phone.

Tess glanced at the tools and parts and filters on the floor again and then headed upstairs, glancing at her watch. Five minutes till ten. Time to go to the jewelry store. She stepped into the office, closed the door behind her, and moved the safe dial slowly, waiting for each click. On the final one she opened it. Tess pulled a little box from the bottom drawer of the desk and put the brooch in it. Then she pulled her purse from the closet and slipped the brooch inside. A few minutes later, she texted LuAnn to see if she wanted to go with her.

Yes! Just finishing the last room. I'll be right down.

They walked down the busy street. The tourists were out in droves, looking for breakfast, shopping, and heading to the museums, historical sites, the river, and every other spot of interest in the area.

They turned the corner. The sign was halfway down the block. *Uptown Jewelers.* It had only been open a few weeks. "Have you met the owners?" Tess asked LuAnn.

"No. Brad has though, and he said both seem really nice. How about you?"

Tess shook her head. "But I heard he's a gemologist and has a good reputation." The two increased their pace.

As Tess pushed the door open, a blast of cold air met her. Instantly she felt revived. LuAnn stepped inside first.

A middle-aged woman wearing bright-red lipstick stood at the counter, spraying cleaner on a glass cabinet filled with diamond necklaces. Tess wondered if there was a big market for such things in Marietta, but perhaps wealthy tourists liked to shop for fine jewelry when they were on vacation.

The woman smiled and asked, "May I help you?"

"We'd like to speak with the jeweler," Tess said.

The woman put the spray bottle down, and a tennis bracelet glittered on her wrist. "About?"

"A piece of jewelry... that was just found," LuAnn answered.

The woman's eyes lit up. "You're from the inn, aren't you?"

"That's right. How did you know?"

"Jim saw the article in the paper this morning." She stuck out her hand. Tess shook it as the woman said, "I'm Linda Walsh."

Tess introduced herself and then said, "This is my friend, LuAnn Sherrill. We own the inn, along with another friend."

"Pleased to meet you." Linda shook LuAnn's hand. "Jim and I were so excited when we read the article. We both love a good mystery—especially when it has to do with a historic piece of jewelry."

"Oh, this might just be a costume brooch."

"Well, I know Jim will want to take a look. Do you have the brooch with you?"

Tess nodded, and Linda grinned. She stepped away from the counter and walked on towering high heels toward a door at the back of the shop. She wore a fitted dress with a thin gold belt at her waist. Tess wondered whether she was an employee or the man's wife. She was certainly dressed for the part of working in a high-end jewelry store.

She opened the door, and after a few quiet words, a man appeared. He seemed to be in his late forties, maybe early fifties, with short gray hair and a trim physique. "Jim Walsh."

Tess introduced herself and then LuAnn, and he shook their hands.

"Linda told me that you're already aware of the brooch," Tess said.

He smiled. "News travels fast around here."

Tess laughed. "It certainly does."

Jim rubbed his hands together. "I was hoping I'd be able to get a look at this possible treasure."

Tess reached into her purse. "Like I said, it could be a piece of costume jewelry, but we thought we should get an expert opinion." She pulled out the box. Jim stepped behind the counter and pulled out a velvet-covered pad and an eye scope.

After he'd put on a pair of white gloves, he reached for the box. Tess thought how comical it would be, after all of the drama, if it turned out to be something made of plastic from the 1960s. Someone would have a sense of humor.

As he took a cloth and rubbed the stones and then looked at them through his loupe, Tess noticed the certificates on the wall. One was from the Zurich School of Gemology. Another was from a continuing education program in Chicago.

Jim cleared his throat and asked Tess and LuAnn if they would mind if he took a photo of the brooch.

The two exchanged a quick glance, and then LuAnn said, "That's fine." He pulled a camera out from behind the counter. As he shot photos, Tess took a couple of quick ones on her phone.

When he was done, Jim put the brooch back in the box, handed it to Tess, and motioned with his head for the two women to follow him down the counter, away from the front door.

When they reached the end of the counter, he said in a low voice, "The brooch is definitely an antique, circa late 1840s." If Margaret was right, and the brooch did originate with the Bickertons, that would mean Howard Bickerton brought it with him from England.

"May I?" Jim pointed at the box. Tess retrieved the brooch and handed it back to him. Jim continued, "The stones are diamonds, rubies, and sapphires. This symbol"—he turned the piece over and pointed to a tiny mark that Tess couldn't read— "is a hallmark, or a purity symbol. It means the brooch is 18-karat gold. A hallmark is an early form of consumer protection."

Tess nodded and thought of the 18K symbol on the inside of her wedding ring.

"The gold was most likely mixed with copper to give it the rose tint," Jim added. "The brooch needs to be cleaned up, is all."

LuAnn leaned against the counter. "Any idea how much it's worth?"

He shook his head. "I don't want to make a guesstimate. I'll let you know once I do the research."

"Any idea where it was made?" Tess asked.

"You're asking good questions, that's for sure." He smiled. "I may need to consult with an expert to determine that. In the meantime, where do you plan to store it?"

Tess nodded. "The safe back at the inn."

He shook his head. "Do you have a safety deposit box at the bank?"

"Yes."

"Take it straight there. And don't talk to anyone about this."

Tess was taken aback. Just how much did Jim think the brooch might be worth?

"Do you have any idea where the brooch may have come from?" he asked. "Is there anything more you can tell me?"

LuAnn quickly filled him in on the story of Morgan's Raid and that Margaret Ashworth, the director of the historical society, thought it had been stolen from the Bickerton family.

"That actually sounds plausible," Jim said. "You'd be surprised how much Civil War treasure is still out there, stashed away in attics, basements, and bureau drawers."

Tess gave Jim her phone number, and he promised to contact her as soon as he finished his research. Then he touched her elbow. "Like I said, go straight to the bank. Thank goodness it's a business day."

Tess nodded in agreement.

As they stepped out onto the sidewalk, LuAnn suggested Tess take the brooch to the bank. "I should get back and help Janice."

"Do you think it'll be safe?" Tess clutched her purse tightly to her body.

LuAnn dropped her voice to whisper. "No one knows you have it. You'll be fine."

Tess laughed. Of course LuAnn was right. She hurried up the two blocks in the heat, holding her purse tight against her body and keeping alert for anyone who might bump into her. A few minutes later, she hurried into the bank, her heart racing.

<hr />

Ten minutes later, her pulse back to normal, Tess left the bank, relieved that the brooch was safe. She started to walk back to the inn, praying that the AC would be fixed by the time she got there.

When her phone rang, she answered, hoping it was the technician calling with the good news. Instead, it was Frank Bryant, finally. "Frank." She stepped under the awning of the new ice-cream shop across the street from the jewelers. "Thank you for calling me back."

"Tess! How's it going?"

"Good." She didn't want to get chatty with him. "Except I'm worried about my investment."

"First of all, I need to apologize." His voice sounded carefree. The opposite of how she felt about the situation. "I may have overreacted in sending the letter. Things are looking much better than they were a few days ago."

"I see," she said, even though she had no idea what he was talking about.

"Can you give me a few days? And then I'll give you an update?"

She tried to make her voice match his breezy tone, but it didn't work. "Do I have any choice?" It came out more like a whine.

Frank laughed. "Don't worry. I'll be in touch by early next week. Hold tight!"

"Wait," she blurted out. "I need to think about this."

"Certainly," he said. "But I can give you more details to help you by Tuesday. I'll call back then."

Before she could think of what to say in response, Frank had told her to have a good day and goodbye, and hung up. She held the phone for a moment, a little stunned.

When Frank first pitched his investment company, Jeffrey invested a small amount of money but gained such a good return on it that he invested more. Frank seemed to have a knack for choosing just the right businesses—most of them became successful, and the returns were good.

Jeffrey trusted Frank, but Tess didn't feel as sure about him.

It wasn't that Jeffrey's insurance policy and Social Security benefits didn't meet her needs. They did. But the small-business investment was the money she planned to use to help either of her two children if they had an emergency, and help send her grandkids to college. And perhaps now, buy a new air-conditioning system for the inn. She shook her head. She was certain the problem wasn't going to come to that. However, she still needed the investment to be lucrative.

When Tess arrived back at the inn, Janice was sitting at the front desk. "Are all the guests out?" Tess asked her.

"Everyone except Nathan. Keeley said he was sleeping."

Tess wasn't surprised. "But the AC's not back on, I take it?"

"There are two repairmen down there now," Janice answered.

"That's good. Right?"

Janice chuckled. "It would be better if they could actually get it working. Oh, and the sink in the boys' room is backed up. We're going to have to call Thorn and see if he can work us into his schedule."

"Let's have Robin look at it first. Thorn was exhausted when he left." Tess put her purse back in the office and then returned to the desk. "Where's LuAnn?"

"In the kitchen heating up the soups for the café."

"Did she give you an update on the brooch?"

"Yes." Janice slipped some papers into a file. "She thought it would be a good idea if we all touch base about our newest mystery."

Tess agreed wholeheartedly.

"Winnie's knee was hurting, so I sent her to my room to lie down for a bit. She'll be back down soon."

"Come on," Tess said. "I'll tell both of you at once while we get things ready for lunch."

LuAnn stood at the stove, a wooden spoon in one hand and her notebook in the other. She was famous for her lists— to-do lists, shopping lists, goal lists, suspect lists. The list of her lists went on and on.

"Hey," Tess said as she put on her apron. She loved those rare moments when it was just the three of them, and they had time to discuss the latest conundrum.

Janice put her own apron on and got out baskets for rolls. "Do we have time for a meeting of the Inn Crowd?"

LuAnn laughed. "Sure, as long as it really is just us."

"Of course." Tess circled her hand around them. "Who else would it be?" They'd been the In Crowd in college. Now, in their sixties, they were the Inn Crowd, via their new careers.

LuAnn turned the heat down under the pots, sat at the table, and took her pen out of her apron pocket. "So, what do we have?"

"Do you trust this jeweler?" Janice asked.

"From what I saw, yes." Tess glanced at LuAnn.

"I agree," LuAnn said. "One of his walls was covered in certificates, and surely he has a license as a gemologist."

Tess nodded.

"But we should definitely google him." Janice pulled out her phone, and Tess took over with the rolls. "What's his last name?"

"Walsh. James Walsh."

As Janice keyed in his name, LuAnn leaned forward across the table and locked eyes with Tess. "This is our big question. Why in the world would anyone break into a cabinet to leave an expensive brooch?"

"I have no idea," Tess answered. "I don't even know how to investigate it. We're used to searching for missing items—not searching for the story behind a found item. It doesn't make any sense."

LuAnn turned the page in her notebook. "Let's brainstorm who might have left it. Tess, what do you think?"

Tess suppressed a laugh. "I have no idea," she repeated. She felt no closer to solving the mystery than she had the night before.

LuAnn wrote as she spoke. "Maybe Keeley planted the brooch after she took the photos of the display."

"But where would she have gotten the brooch? And why would she have planted it?"

LuAnn shrugged. "She's the only one who had access to the cabinet."

"But why would she have broken the glass?" Tess countered. "She has the key."

"Maybe one person planted it, and another person broke the glass," LuAnn said.

Tess sighed. "I'm baffled."

Janice looked up from her phone and held up a finger. "I'm interrupting this discussion with information about jeweler James Walsh."

Tess put the baskets of rolls on a tray. "What did you find?"

"Pretty much what you already said. Except there's also information that he graduated from Ohio State University and owned a shop in Manhattan before moving here."

"Manhattan." LuAnn's eyes lit up. "I wonder what brought him here."

"Well," Janice said. "This article in the Ohio State alumni magazine says that he recently married and wanted to return home."

Tess frowned. "Did we miss an article in the *Marietta Times*? Doesn't it seem like they'd do a new business profile?"

"Maybe it's in the works," Janice said. "Sometimes businesses want newspapers to wait a few weeks, until after all the kinks are worked out."

That was true. They'd certainly had kinks to work out even after they opened the inn. She thought of the AC unit in the basement, in pieces. They still did.

Janice glanced up from her phone. "That's it. He sounds aboveboard to me."

LuAnn sighed, closed her notebook, and got up to stir the soups again. "What are we going to do once he tells us how much it's worth?"

Tess shrugged. "Put a notice in the paper and hope the owner steps forward?"

"A whole multitude of people could claim it as theirs," LuAnn said.

"We can ask them to give us a description…" Janice's sheepish look turned into a laugh. "Except that Marissa already did that. In the paper."

"Exactly," Tess said. "Finding out if it's the brooch that belonged to the Bickertons that was stolen in 1863 would be a start. That might add some insight about who planted it."

"Why don't we go out and talk with Irene and Thelma?" LuAnn asked. "They might have heard about it through the years. Maybe there's a written description in their papers."

"Good idea."

"I'll ask Brad," LuAnn said. "He can call and see if they're up to a visit."

Tess hoped they would be, and having it come from their nephew really was a good idea. It was the only lead they had.

CHAPTER SIX

After the café closed at two, Tess sweltered at the office desk, crunching numbers when the lobby desk bell rang. She hurried out. The air-conditioning technician and his supervisor stood in front of the desk. "Bad news," the supervisor said. "The system needs a new condenser."

"Oh?" Tess glanced from the supervisor to the technician and back again and felt like crossing her fingers. "Do you have one at the shop?"

He shook his head. "We'll have to order one."

"When will it arrive?"

"We'll rush it," the supervisor said. "Hopefully by tomorrow."

Tess rubbed the back of her neck. They'd need to get more fans. And maybe some portable AC window units. She asked the supervisor if his company had any available. "That we could rent, perhaps?" she added.

He shook his head. "Sorry, no. The good news is, your unit's still under warranty."

Tess nodded. "So we'll see you tomorrow?"

"Hopefully," the man said.

Tess tried to smile but was certain it came across as more of a grimace.

She'd waited long enough to call Thorn. They needed his help. He answered on the second ring. She explained the situation. "I know you're busy," she said.

"I'm not, actually," he answered. "I had a construction project, an addition on a house, scheduled for next week, but the owner had an accident with a bottle rocket and ended up in the ER. He'll be out of commission for a while."

"Oh, how awful," said Tess. "I'm afraid people aren't as careful with fireworks as they should be."

"Ain't it the truth," he answered. "I'll be right over."

"I hope you got some rest."

He grunted and then said, "See you soon."

It wasn't like Thorn to be out of sorts, but that was exactly what it felt like to Tess. He didn't seem like himself at all.

After LuAnn and Tess discussed what was going on, they decided they needed to buy window units for the third-floor rooms and more fans for the second floor. "I'll call Brad and see if he's free to help me go get them," LuAnn said, taking off her apron.

Thorn arrived before LuAnn and Brad returned. Tess told him to sit in the café and offered him an iced coffee.

"Sounds good. Maybe that will perk me up." He yawned, and when she brought him the coffee asked, "Did you know the inn was on the local news?"

"What?"

"There was a piece on the radio on my way over. About that brooch."

"That makes sense," Tess said. "It's definitely local news."

A door slammed somewhere nearby, and Thorn jumped as if he'd been shot. It was Janice, coming out of the basement.

"Sorry about that," she called to them. "My hands are full, and I kicked it harder than I meant to."

Thorn's face was pale, and he was breathing hard, his eyes wild. "Are you all right?" Tess asked, touching him on the shoulder.

He jerked away. "I'm fine."

She put the coffee on the table. "This isn't about the AC, is it? It's not your fault you couldn't fix it. The technician and his supervisor couldn't either. They had to order a new part."

"Oh, that's too bad," Thorn said. "But that's not what has me out of sorts. Just give me a minute." His voice was low. "I'll pull myself together."

A few minutes later LuAnn and Brad came in carrying window fans. When LuAnn saw Thorn, she said, "I hate to ask, Thorn, but could you help us for a minute? I have six window air conditioners in my car."

All of them worked together to carry them inside. Just as they were loading them into the elevator, Nathan came shuffling down the stairs, still wearing the clothes he'd had on the night before.

"My room is burning up," he said.

"We'll put an air conditioner in there first," Tess said. "In fact, could you call your mom and see if it's okay if we put one in her room too? Or let me speak to her on your phone?"

He nodded and pulled out his phone. He touched the screen and thrust the phone into Tess's hand. She stepped out of the elevator as Nathan stepped on. As the door started to close, she held up his phone.

He shrugged and then disappeared behind the door. Val answered. "Val? It's Tess. I wanted to let you know we got some window air conditioners to tide us over till our central air is fixed. Would you mind if we installed one in your room this morning?"

"Mind?" Val said with a laugh. "You're kidding, right? Please go ahead. And I'm sure the others won't mind either. Just a second." Tess heard a short muffled conversation, then Val was back on the line. "They all say, yes, please. We're on our way back to the inn now."

Tess thanked her as she started up the stairs. When she reached the second floor, she found LuAnn leaving a window fan in front of each door that didn't already have one, with a note explaining to call down to the lobby desk if they needed any help or had any questions.

When Tess reached the third floor, the door to Nathan's room was open, and she could hear him talking with Thorn. She feared the boy was complaining about the Wi-Fi again, but when she approached she realized Nathan was helping Thorn install the air-conditioning unit. He was telling him about the game he'd been playing.

Thorn didn't seem to mind.

"What can I do to help?" Tess asked, returning Nathan's phone.

Thorn glanced up at her. "I think we've got this covered."

She handed him the master key to the rooms and then picked up the fan that Thorn had taken from the window. "I'll give this to LuAnn," she said. "And then I'm going out for a while. Call me if you need me."

"Will do," Thorn answered.

Nathan didn't look like he registered anything she'd said. Instead he picked up right where he'd left off, talking about the game again. Tess hoped the boy wouldn't add to whatever was already bothering Thorn.

Tess decided to drive rather than walk. She'd like to avoid sweating any more than she already was. She grabbed her purse and keys and headed out the back door to her Honda. Waiting had never been her strong suit—she might as well go to the Local History and Genealogy Archives now and see what she could find in the *Marietta Times* from July 1863. If the brooch had been stolen from the Bickertons, surely there would have been an article about it. And a description of the brooch.

Tess pulled into the parking lot of the archives, which was a satellite of the library. It took her a second to register that the lot was empty. She peered at the front door. A piece of white paper was taped to it.

Obviously the place was closed for the day, but she climbed out of the car to read the note anyway. *Closed July 4th and 5th for the holiday.*

She sighed. She'd have to wait until Monday. Pushing her hair away from her face, Tess headed back to her car as her phone began to ring. She dug in her purse and pulled it out to see an unfamiliar number on the display. *Please, Lord, don't let it be bad news about the air conditioner!*

"Hello," she answered.

"Tess. Jim Walsh here."

"Oh, hello." She expected him to tell her he'd appraised the brooch already. Instead he said he had a video call set up with an antique jewelry specialist in Manhattan. "Sorry about this," he said. "But could you bring the brooch back to the shop? So I could show it to him? The photos I took aren't that great."

She glanced at her watch. It was three fifteen. She'd have to get the brooch back to the safety deposit box before five.

"What time is the call?" she asked.

"As soon as possible."

"Then I'll go get the brooch right now. See you soon." She ended the call and climbed back into her car. Before she started it, she checked the temperature. Ninety-five degrees. She could just imagine the online reviews for the inn after two days without any AC. She hated the thought of buying all those units for the rooms, but they couldn't expect guests to suffer through the heat. She turned on the car and cranked the air, then called Janice to let her and LuAnn know what she was up to.

After stopping by the bank, Tess continued on to the jewelry store, feeling nervous again about the brooch in her purse. Thankfully, she found a parking place in front of Uptown Jewelers. She quickly climbed out of the car and hurried into the shop.

Linda greeted her and then motioned to Jim, who stood in the open doorway at the back of the room. "I don't want anyone to overhear the call," he said. "So I'll do it in here. You're welcome to join me."

Tess hesitated for a moment. She didn't know how long this was going to take, and she wanted to do a little research on her phone.

She glanced around the shop. It was completely empty except for Linda. "What if I sit out here, with the door cracked a little. That way I can hear what the man says, and if a customer comes in, I'll join you and shut the door."

"Sounds like a good plan," he said. "I already have the specialist online. I just need to show him the piece and talk things through."

Linda pulled a chair from behind the counter over by the door for Tess. Once she was settled, Tess took out her phone to research Morgan's Raid. What she found was exactly what LuAnn had already described, except Tess found more information about when Morgan was imprisoned in the Ohio State Penitentiary. A Captain Thomas Hines, also from Kentucky, had been captured and imprisoned with General Morgan. Tess thought of the Hines family and then Granny Hines, trying to remember where she was from. Somewhere in Illinois, she thought. Could they all be related? She kept reading. Captain Hines escaped with General Morgan and returned to the South. Hines survived the war, although Morgan didn't.

The bell to the jewelry store rang, and Tess stood, still looking at her phone. After the war, Hines studied law—

A scream unlocked Tess's eyes from her screen. Linda had her hands to her face. Tess followed her view to a man with a blue bandana tied over his nose and mouth. He rushed past her, shoving her as he did. Tess stumbled against the chair as the man pushed on into the back room.

"What's going on?" Jim yelled.

A crash followed as Tess struggled to right herself. Linda came running toward her, teetering on her heels. But as she tried to help Tess, she knocked her down between the chair and wall.

"Call 911!" Jim yelled. "He took the brooch!"

CHAPTER SEVEN

July 17, 1863

Mr. Gidden stood at the doorway of the kitchen and yelled. "Prudence!"

"Right here," she responded, turning toward him as she continued to stir the gravy on the stove.

"Someone's here to see you," he barked. As he stepped away, a white woman and a black girl came into view.

"Ernestine?" Prudence placed the spoon on a plate. "Is that thee?"

The girl nodded.

Prudence wiped her hands on her apron. "I thought perhaps thee wasn't coming after all."

Ernestine shook her head.

Prudence introduced herself to the woman.

"I'm Martha Dole," the woman said.

Prudence smiled at her. "Many thanks for bringing Ernestine."

Martha placed her hand on Ernestine's shoulder. "I was happy to have a reason to leave Gettysburg. I just wish we could have left earlier. We were delayed because the battle started and raged on and on before we could begin the journey." She shuddered. "Once the battle ended, it took a while before the trains began to run again. And then once the train tracks were repaired, the soldiers had priority, of course, and it took over a week to secure tickets."

It was evident she was shaken over the ordeal they'd been through. Ernestine stayed silent, but she appeared to be shaken too.

Alarmed, Prudence asked, "How is Isaac?"

"As well as can be expected," Martha answered.

Relieved, Prudence turned to Ernestine. "Thee was just a little girl last time you were here."

The girl nodded but still didn't speak.

Martha seemed to want to keep talking about the battle. "It was as if it was the end of the world. Soldiers from both sides swarmed all around, pillaging food and supplies. Then the shrapnel began to fly. A young woman in town was killed, and houses, barns, and sheds all through the area are now marred by cannonballs and bullets."

Prudence nodded to the table. "Sit," she said to them. "Thee must be exhausted. I'll make tea."

She worked quickly. Ernestine continued to remain silent while Martha prattled on. "One of the battles spilled over onto Isaac's property, and the Confederates moved into his barn for a day, but then the Union chased them out." Prudence shuddered. Martha continued on, describing the wounded who were left behind.

While the tea steeped, Prudence put biscuits on two plates and covered them with gravy. She set them in front of the women and poured the tea.

Martha finally stopped talking as she heartily ate her food, while Ernestine just picked at hers and took small sips of tea. The girl wore a covering over her head, a patched cotton dress with a brown apron over it, and a worn pair of boots. She had a small, scuffed satchel that she'd placed on the floor at her feet, along with a cloak.

Prudence's heart went out to the girl.

As soon as Martha finished eating, she stood. "I best be on my way. I have a sister here in town that I plan to stay with for a week or so."

Prudence collected her plate and cup. "Will thee be taking Ernestine back when thee returns to Gettysburg?"

Martha shook her head. "Isaac said for her to stay. He'll let thee know when she should return."

Prudence caught Ernestine's eye and smiled, but the girl ducked her head and took another sip of tea.

After Martha said goodbye, Prudence returned to the stove. She mashed the potatoes and took the roasted chickens out of the oven. Mr. Siloam stepped into the kitchen and nodded to Ernestine. "Who's that?"

Prudence answered, keeping her voice low. "The girl I told thee about."

"I see. Can she help you in the kitchen?"

"Not today," Prudence said. "But hopefully soon." The girl seemed too fragile to expect anything out of her so soon.

"All right," Mr. Siloam said, "but we need to get supper served and the kitchen cleaned and you on your way home. The rumor is that Morgan and his men are headed our way."

Prudence gasped. She knew the Confederate general and his men had crossed the river, but she didn't expect he'd come to Marietta. Prudence, Mr. Siloam, and one of the maids quickly served the food while Ernestine continued to sit at the table. But when Prudence came back into the kitchen, the girl had her sleeves rolled up and stood in front of the basin of pots and pans. It seemed she planned to help clean up.

Once all of the pots and pans were washed and then the plates, cups, and cutlery, Ernestine wiped down the kitchen table, then the dining room tables. Prudence packed biscuits for Jason and Moses in her basket, told Ernestine to grab her satchel and cloak, and started toward the back door.

"Hold on," Mr. Gidden called out. "I need your help."

Prudence exhaled, praying for patience. She whispered to Ernestine to step outside.

She turned to Mr. Gidden. "What can I do for thee?"

He held up a pouch. "I'm afraid Morgan might raid the bank, so I took this from the Bickertons' safety deposit box, but I don't want to take it back to the house. It will be a target too." The man was living in the mansion while the Bickertons were gone. "I'm certain Morgan won't raid your home—take the pouch and then give it back to me after they've left."

"Oh no," Prudence said. True, her modest home most likely wouldn't be raided, but she didn't want to be responsible for anything of value that belonged to the Bickertons. "Thee doesn't want to entrust anything of worth to me."

"Do it for your boss," Mr. Gidden said. "It's the least you can do to show your appreciation to him."

He continued to explain. "Mrs. Bickerton took her other jewelry with her, but she left this behind in the safety box. We don't want it to be stolen by marauders."

Mr. Bickerton was a complex man, but he had done good things, along with the bad. He'd been vital to helping with the Underground Railroad and doing that part of the Lord's work.

"Hurry," Mr. Gidden said. "They could be here any minute."

Prudence shook her head. "I have no business with anything of value."

He shoved the pouch into her basket. "I insist."

She hesitated for a moment, and he rushed out of the kitchen.

Prudence stepped out the back door. Slipping her arm through Ernestine's she started down the road to the farm. As they walked, Prudence told Ernestine about Moses. "He's only four," she said. "But he's a bright boy. He'll be happy to have you stay with us."

Ernestine smiled a little.

The sun fell lower behind them with each step, threatening dusk at any moment. As they rounded the curve in the road, where her house came into view, Prudence startled at the sight of a soldier coming toward them on the crossroad. She squinted. He wore gray.

She whispered to Ernestine, "Pull your cloak over your head." Prudence tugged the girl to the far edge of the road, in the brush before the ditch. Beyond the soldier she could see Jason and Moses on the porch, waiting for them. She held up her hand to Jason. The last thing she wanted was for him to intervene. Hopefully, if the soldier focused on her, he wouldn't see Jason and Moses at all.

"What do we have here?" the soldier called out, sliding off his horse and then leading it toward the women.

"We're on our way home," Prudence answered. "It is just a spell farther down the road."

"Is that right? Do you have any food in that basket?"

Prudence nodded. "Biscuits. I'm happy to share them with thee."

"Share?" He laughed and rubbed the stubble on his chin. "I'll take them all."

She took the biscuits out of the basket, careful to push the pouch to the bottom.

The soldier grinned. "What else do you have?"

Prudence raised her head, doing her best to keep a blank look on her face. Not wanting to lie, she remained silent. The man rammed the bottom of the basket with his fist, toppling it out of her hands. The pouch with the brooch, along with the cloth she had inside, flew to the ground, followed by the basket.

The man snatched up the pouch. "Well, well," he said. "Looks like I've found a treasure."

Prudence finally spoke, as calmly as she could. "It doesn't belong to thee. Nor to me. But I was attempting to keep it safe for the owner."

"Well," the man sneered. "You didn't do a very good job." He clutched the pouch and nodded to Ernestine. "If you make a fuss, I'll take her too. I know what's underneath that cloak. How would that suit you?"

The girl gasped and stumbled forward, as if ready to run.

Prudence grabbed her wrist and faced the man, breathing a silent prayer. That Ernestine wouldn't bolt. That Jason would stay put. And that the soldier would leave.

In the woods to the north, someone yelled. The soldier shoved the pouch into the bag strapped over his shoulder and jumped back on his horse, the cloth full of biscuits still in his hand. "Thank you, kindly," he yelled as he headed toward the woods.

Prudence whispered to Ernestine. "Keep thy cloak over thy head and stay put. We're not going to move until he's gone for sure." If he came back, he might take them all, Jason and Moses included.

CHAPTER EIGHT

Somehow, Tess managed to still have her phone in her hand as she struggled to her feet from the jewelry store floor. Once she was upright, she called 911 while Linda continued on into the back room.

"He's getting away!" Jim yelled, followed by a scuffle.

The 911 dispatcher answered and Tess quickly reported what was going on as she stepped into the back room. The back door was wide open, with Linda standing at it. Jim was gone.

"What's the address?" the dispatcher asked.

"Uptown Jewelers..." She called out to Linda, asking for the address. As the woman rattled it off, Tess relayed it to the dispatcher.

"I'll send someone right over."

Tess ended the call and then hurried past Linda, who seemed frozen. Out in the alley, Jim was on the ground, holding on to his right knee. His face was red, and maybe not just from the heat. It looked as if he'd been hit.

Tess continued on to him, catching sight of the perpetrator rounding the corner of the alley as she did. He was dressed completely in denim and wore a pair of running shoes.

Just like that, the burglar—and the brooch—were gone.

Fifteen minutes later, Tess stood in the alley with Officer Randy as EMTs loaded Jim into the ambulance. Linda had locked up the shop and was now marching toward her car on her high heels.

"Are you sure you don't want me to go with you?" Tess called out again.

Linda waved her handbag in the air. "No, but thank you! I'll be fine."

"I hope he didn't blow out his knee," Randy said to Tess. "But it could have been a lot worse." He sighed. "Common sense 101. Don't chase a robber." He turned to her. "I'll walk you back to the inn."

Tess almost agreed until she remembered she was parked out front. She said so to Randy. "I guess I'm feeling more shaken than I realized. But I'm fine," she said. "Especially compared to poor Jim." Of course the man felt worse about the brooch being stolen than his knee injury. Tess didn't blame him for going after the robber—it was instinctual to try to recover a valuable piece of jewelry like that. Especially for a jeweler.

"I'll walk you to your car," Randy said.

As they headed down the alley, breathing in the ripeness of the Dumpsters outside each business, he asked if she could recall anything else about the perpetrator.

She'd already told him he was dressed in denim, had a blue bandana tied around his face, and wore running shoes. She hadn't noticed what brand. She was actually impressed she remembered as much as she did. It was all such a blur.

Still he pressed her for more details. "Did the thief seem familiar to you in any way? His size? Demeanor? Aggressiveness?"

Tess rubbed her temples as she walked. "No."

"Any idea how old he was?"

She hesitated and then said, "He moved with ease, so he seemed younger, but I don't know that for sure."

"Did you get a look at his hands?"

She frowned, trying to remember. "I don't remember his hands in particular. I don't think he had gloves on—I think I'd remember that."

"Do you have any guests staying at the inn who overheard you talking about taking the brooch to the jewelers this afternoon?"

She thought back. "No. I was out doing errands earlier this afternoon when Jim called and asked me to bring the brooch by the shop. I didn't know I was coming until then."

"Are you sure the thief was a man?"

Tess massaged her temples. The person shoved her pretty hard. Surely she could tell the difference between a man and a woman. But the person was slight. "I guess I'm not absolutely positive, but probably ninety-nine percent certain."

"All right," he responded. "That's pretty sure."

When they reached the sidewalk, they joined the crowds of tourists. The Fourth had fallen on a Thursday, and that meant a long weekend, which was good for businesses all through town. They rounded the corner, and when they reached the middle of the block, Tess pointed to her car.

Randy's patrol car was parked right behind her. "I'll check in with you after I stop by the hospital," he said. "Jot down anything that comes to mind. And I'll touch base with Janice and LuAnn in the next couple of days too, just in case they heard anything around the inn."

Tess thanked him and climbed into her car. She turned the engine on and cranked the air to high. She waited for the officer to pull away first, gripping the steering wheel as she did. She felt hot and cold and shaky all at the same time. And guilty that the brooch had been stolen.

Jim hadn't given her an estimate of how much the brooch was worth, but it had to be a lot. And it had been stolen under her watch. Had she been foolish to trust Jim? Not that it was his fault. Who could have predicted that someone would steal it? If they only knew, Jim would have examined the brooch in the bank vault.

Ill at the thought of the brooch being stolen, Tess sat for a moment with her hands on the steering wheel. She'd have to tell LuAnn and Janice what happened, and the sooner the better.

After Randy pulled away from the curb, she did too. Slowly. Keeping an eye out for someone dressed in denim. She saw a couple of people, but both were large men who wore baseball caps. When she reached the inn, she still felt shaky, and then super hot when she stepped inside.

Nothing was going right.

Janice and LuAnn were in the library area, straightening the shelves and dusting chairs and tables. "So," Janice called out as Tess joined them, "are we all filthy rich?"

"Bad news," Tess answered.

Janice shook her head. "It's just a piece of costume jewelry after all?"

If only that were the case. That would make the entire ordeal much easier. "No." Tess's voice wavered. "It was stolen. A robber ran through the shop, grabbed the brooch, and sped out the back door."

LuAnn stepped to her side and put her hand on Tess's shoulder as she explained what happened to Jim. "Randy will come by sometime to talk to you both. In case you saw anything suspicious today."

"Oh, Tess." LuAnn tightened her grip. "How upsetting."

"I know." She fought back tears. "I'm so sorry I didn't protect it."

"That's not what I meant," LuAnn explained. "How upsetting for you to witness a robbery. This isn't your fault."

Tess couldn't stop the tears. It was so unlike her. She was always so upbeat and capable. But this had shaken her. She was responsible for the brooch being taken.

Janice came over and hugged her. "I'm just glad you're all right."

Tess wiped her eyes. "I really am sorry. Never in a million years did I think it would be stolen from Uptown Jewelers."

"I wouldn't have either," LuAnn said.

Tess didn't believe her. LuAnn was much more savvy about that sort of thing than she admitted.

"Neither would I," Janice stated. "Please don't beat yourself up about this. The brooch will be recovered. It's not as if it can be sold anywhere around here. As soon as someone tries, the police will nab the person. Easy as Winnie's peach pie, and we'll have it back."

Tess doubted it would be that easy, but they could hope. In the meantime, she'd never been more grateful for her friends and their love and grace.

———————

An hour later the glass repairman had come and gone, leaving the curio cabinet as good as new. Soon after, the Hines family tumbled into the inn, laughing and joking as Tess sat at the front desk, going through the file of registrations for the coming week.

"How was your day?" Tess asked the twins, mostly to get them to stop running through the lobby.

They skidded to a halt. "Great!" Chad said. "We went to the Earthworks and learned about the Native Americans. Then we went to the Mounds Cemetery, which was really creepy."

"Yeah," Chet said, elbowing his brother. "And then, because we were really good, we got to go to the arcade." The two fist-bumped each other and then Chet added, loudly, "Which was the best part of the day!"

They took off toward the stairs, making electronic noises and pretending to shoot at each other. Their mother didn't say anything, but Val called out, as she held on to Granny's arm, "Use inside voices."

They tore off up the stairs but stopped the noises.

Granny Hines appeared tired, but she grinned and said to Tess, "We've had quite the day."

"I'm so glad," Tess responded.

"Although I think I need a nap now."

Val nodded in agreement. "I think we all do." She asked Keeley to help Granny up to their room and then stepped to the counter. She lowered her voice. "Has Nathan been around?"

"As a matter of fact, yes." Tess closed the file. "He's been helping our handyman, Thorn, install the window air-conditioning units."

A puzzled expression passed over Val's face.

Tess exhaled. "Is that all right?" She knew Thorn was a good man, but Val hadn't even met him.

"No, that's fine," Val said. "I'm surprised, is all. Nathan doesn't really like that sort of thing. He's all about computers."

"Well, he was a big help. He's back in his room now." Thorn had finished installing the units and was now working on the clogged sink in the boys' room. Robin had gotten it temporarily working, but it needed some serious snaking.

"I'll go check in with Nathan." Val paused a moment and then said, "I know the AC problem has to be really stressful for all of you, but I want you to know we would have chosen to stay here regardless. This inn has such good vibes." She laughed. "I'm sounding like I'm from the West Coast, I know. Anyway, it's not just the atmosphere. It's you and LuAnn and Janice too. And Winnie. We couldn't ask for a more welcoming place to stay."

Tears welled in Tess's eyes, and she managed to say, "Thank you." She was grateful the Hines family had reserved nearly the entire inn. Other guests might not have been as understanding.

Just as Val turned toward the stairs, Nathan came out of the kitchen with a bucket in his hand.

"Oh, I thought you were upstairs," Tess said.

"No." Nathan jerked his head toward the stairs. "I was helping Thorn with the drain, and he needed another bucket." He smiled as Thorn came down the stairs, wiping his hands.

Tess introduced him to Val.

Thorn shook her hand and said, "You've got a fine boy here. He's been a big help this afternoon."

"I'm so happy to hear that." Val patted Nathan on the shoulder, but he seemed to be embarrassed and took a step to the side.

Just then a bottle rocket exploded, probably down by the river. Thorn jumped, Nathan got a concerned expression on his face, and Val said, "Those startle me every time too. Don't they know the Fourth is over?"

Thorn looked at Nathan and said, "We should get back to it."

"I'm right behind you," Nathan said with a grin. The two went up the stairs, discussing something about water flow and gallons per minute.

"He seems like a nice guy," Val said.

Tess nodded. "He is." But it wasn't like him to be so on edge. Then again, she was on edge too. She was trying to fake composure for everyone, except LuAnn and Janice. But she still felt as shaky as Thorn looked.

⸎

The next morning at six, Tess collected the folded newspaper from the stoop of the inn as Winnie stood in the doorway to the kitchen, fanning herself. When Tess turned back around, Winnie was shaking her head. "I think it might be cooler outside than in."

"Leave the back door open then." Thankfully, it was screened. "They'll have the air-conditioning system fixed today. Hopefully by noon. Hang in there." Tess knew she was speaking to herself as much as she was Winnie. *Hang in there.* Her side felt sore from her tumble over the chair the day before, and she still felt a little shaky.

After she fed Tom, took Huck for a walk, and then fed him too, Tess poured herself a cup of coffee, settled down at the kitchen table, and opened the paper. She gasped.

"What's wrong?" Winnie asked, turning from mixing up batter for waffles.

"Right here, on the front page—Marissa has another article about the brooch." The article was accompanied by a photo of Jim in the ER and a close-up photo of the brooch. *Marietta's Mysterious Brooch Stolen!* read the headline, followed by the lead: *It appeared, but now it's gone.* The article continued with an interview with Jim. He'd told Marissa that he'd dated the brooch to the 1840s, and when asked about how much the brooch was worth, he'd responded, *A lot.* Thankfully he didn't give a dollar amount, saying he hadn't come up with one yet.

Tess read the article to Winnie, unsettled that Marissa hadn't spoken with her. She wondered if Jim was still in the hospital or if he'd be back at the shop today.

Just as she finished reading the article, Granny Hines wandered into the kitchen in her pajamas and robe again. It must have been her regular wake-up time. Tess escorted her out to a café table and brought her a cup of coffee. "I'm waiting for Cash," she said. "He's the oldest of the Hines boys." Her faded blue eyes twinkled. "And the most handsome."

Tess decided to play along. "Where did you meet Cash?"

"Oh, way back home. He was five years older than me, and I thought he was the best thing since sliced bread. Of course, he didn't give me the time of day until I was twenty or so, while I'd been pining after him from the time I was fifteen."

Tess stifled a laugh just as Nathan hurried down the stairs. "There you are!"

Her face lit up. "Cash!"

"No, Granny. It's me. Nathan. Your grandson."

Her face fell. "That's right…"

"She's fine," Tess said. "Want to join us for a cup of coffee?"

"Sure." He appeared to be showered and dressed for the day—and well rested. After he poured a half-cup of creamer and then coffee, he settled down at the table and asked, "When does Thorn show up?"

"He's unexpectedly free this week," Tess said, "so I think we'll take advantage of that and have him come and take care of some repairs and maintenance we've put off. I'll give him a call." She was so thankful to have such a competent handyman in Marietta.

Nathan pursed his lips and said, "I hope he needs help again today."

"I'm sure he will."

Janice and LuAnn came downstairs, and the three of them helped Winnie prepare breakfast for their guests. LuAnn suggested to Janice and Tess that later they should take a few minutes to discuss what they knew about the brooch being stolen. They all agreed.

Keeley arrived at the inn, went upstairs, and escorted Granny, dressed this time, back down to the café. Tess was so impressed with how both of Val's children cared for their grandmother. In fact, it was Val and her family who seemed to look out for the elderly woman the most, far more than her own daughters. Granted, Connie was busy with the twins, who were a handful. And Ellen seemed a little oblivious to the needs of her mother. Tess knew what mattered most was that someone was caring for Granny.

LuAnn, Janice, and Tess had decided the day before not to say anything about the brooch being stolen, not even to Keeley, because they didn't want to interfere with Randy's investigation, or their own.

But Perry found the article in the paper. "What in the world?" He held the newspaper up high. "Someone must believe it's worth a lot of money."

Tess tried to downplay the theft as she shot LuAnn a desperate look. "We really don't know what it's worth."

Perry whistled. "Who would have taken it?"

"We don't know," LuAnn said, "but Officer Lewis is working hard to try to figure it out." She didn't mention that she, Tess, and Janice hoped to help too. "We'll know soon."

Tess nodded in agreement as she realized that Keeley had turned around in her chair. "What happened to the brooch?" she asked.

"It was stolen," Tess said. "In the jewelry shop. I was having it appraised."

Keeley's mouth hung open, reminding Tess of a cartoon character who needed her mouth closed by someone else. Finally, Keeley managed to say, "Who in the world would do that?"

"That's what we're trying to find out," Tess said.

Granny didn't seem to be tracking the conversation. "Cash Hines really was the most handsome of all of the brothers. And cousins. He was the most handsome man in all of Kentucky." She sighed.

Kentucky? Tess turned to Granny as she noted Perry leaving the café. "I didn't realize you grew up in Kentucky."

"Oh, yes," Granny said. "Born, raised, and married there." A confused look passed over her face.

"And then you moved to Chicago," Keeley said. "That's where your three children were born."

"That's right." Granny sighed again. She sounded so sad.

"I was just reading about a man by the name of Hines from Kentucky," Tess said. "A Thomas Hines. He was a captain in the Confederate army."

"His name sounds familiar," Keeley said. "There are quite a few famous Hines on our family tree, including Duncan Hines."

"Fascinating," Tess said.

"I'm not certain about Thomas though," Keeley said. "Granny might remember."

Granny smiled brightly at them. She wasn't even following the conversation.

And Keeley didn't seem to want to talk about it anymore.

CHAPTER NINE

Tess, Janice, and LuAnn took their cups of iced coffee out to the patio to escape the heat inside. After consulting with Winnie, they had put a notice on the inn door that the café was closed for lunch. They couldn't ask Winnie to work another day in a stifling kitchen.

They gathered at the far table, surrounded by pots of geraniums, impatiens, and fuchsias, all in shades of red and purple, with accents of white and enjoyed the cool of the morning. The space had turned out to be a whimsical garden that added an extra room, in good weather, to the inn. Tess breathed in the fresh air that in another hour would be growing hot and humid.

LuAnn opened her notebook and glanced down at it. "We have a very different scenario than we did before. We've gone from simply wanting to know who left the brooch to wanting to know who stole it." She glanced up. "It's much more complicated now. Tess, have you heard anything from Randy this morning?"

Tess shook her head and pulled out her phone. "I'll give him a call." She'd been meaning to call him since she saw the newspaper article, but it had been one thing after another. She'd call Jim Walsh too.

First she called Randy's number. When he didn't pick up, she left a voice mail. "Hi Randy, this is Tess Wallace. Please let me know if you have any updates concerning the robbery."

After she finished, she called Uptown Jewelers, but it went straight to voice mail too. She left the same message as she had with Randy. After she hung up, she brought her two friends up-to-date about finding out that there was a Captain Hines that had been part of Morgan's Raid.

LuAnn gripped her pen. "Is he related to our Hines family?"

"Keeley said that was possible, but she wasn't sure," Tess answered.

"How odd." Janice shrugged. "It could simply be a coincidence. It's not an uncommon name."

By the expression on her face, Tess guessed LuAnn wasn't as sure. "Maybe there's no connection, but we should definitely follow up on that." She made a note in her notebook.

"I'll do some research," Tess said. "And I also plan to go back to the jewelry shop today to at least talk to Linda—and hopefully to Jim too." She reiterated that the thief was slight of build. "Randy wanted to know if any of our current guests fit the description."

Janice's eyes grew wide. "Perry and Nathan are both thin."

Tess nodded. "But they both have alibis. Perry was at the Castle, and Nathan was helping Thorn. And besides, how would either one of them have known I was taking the brooch to Jim?"

"Well, I don't know," LuAnn said. "But it wouldn't take long to run through the shop like that. Nathan could have said he was going to play a computer game, only to slip out and hurry down the block. And maybe Perry just said he was going to the Castle."

Tess frowned. "You're right. We should double-check."

"I can call the Castle," Janice said. "And I'll ask Thorn about Nathan."

LuAnn made more notes and then asked, "Any fresh new ideas on who would have left the brooch in the cabinet? Or why?"

"I've been thinking about this." Janice tapped the side of her head and grinned, but then she grew serious. "Maybe it was someone who stole the brooch from someone else who didn't realize its history or value. Then the first someone planted it, hoping to steal it again and draw attention to it, so the person they stole it from wouldn't be suspicious."

Tess put her hand to her mouth but couldn't stifle the laugh.

"What?" Janice asked. "You don't like my theory?"

Tess couldn't stop her laughter. Perhaps it was the stress of the last few days—her investment going bad. The brooch showing up. Thorn being on edge. The AC going on the fritz. The brooch being stolen. Maybe the laughter was a way to release the stress.

Janice and LuAnn started laughing too, at her.

Finally, Tess was able to say, "None of this makes sense. Not that crazy theory. Not a brooch showing up in the curio cabinet. Not a robber stealing it."

Once their laughter stopped, LuAnn said, "This brings us back to what we decided yesterday. We need to focus on the history of the brooch. If it did originate with the Bickerton family. If it was stolen. Where it's been since. Hopefully that will explain how it ended up here."

"And why," Janice added.

Tess nodded in agreement. "And who would steal it."

"Yes." LuAnn closed her notebook. "Speaking of the Bickerton family, Brad said Thelma and Irene could talk to us at…" She paused and glanced at her watch. "Brad will pick us up in half an hour."

"You two go," Janice said. "Stacy is dropping Larry off after school for a playdate with Grandma."

"Are you sure?" Tess asked. "I could stay."

"Oh, no. I insist." Janice grinned. "I'll refine my theory about the brooch while I make cookies. Although, perhaps Thelma and Irene planted the brooch and then regretted it and stole it back."

Tess leaned back and crossed her arms. "I bet you're right. Mystery solved."

They all laughed again.

"I'll run over to the jewelry shop and see what I can learn," Tess said to LuAnn as they left the patio and headed back into the inn. "I'll text and let you know if you and Brad should pick me up there or if I'll come back here."

Tess grabbed her purse and hurried out the front door. On the sunny side of the street, the day was already hot. She walked as quickly as she could toward Uptown Jewelers. When she reached it, there was a crowd inside, which she hadn't expected. She'd never seen more than a couple of customers there at one time. On the window, someone had taped a matted copy of the newspaper article and a blown-up photo of the brooch. A sign read: *Come on in to find out the story of Marietta's STOLEN priceless brooch.*

Priceless? Had Jim come up with a value?

Tess frowned. It all seemed a little tacky. She pushed open the door. Jim sat behind the counter, talking with a customer, and Linda rang up a purchase. There were several sale signs around and baskets of rings and bracelets on the counter that hadn't been there before.

She made her way to Jim and waited until he was done talking. She jumped in before he moved on to the next customer. "How's your knee?" she asked him.

He held up a crutch that was propped next to the counter. "Hopefully, just sprained. I'll have an MRI on Monday though."

"Oh, I hope it's just sprained, although I know that's painful enough." She gestured toward the crowd. "Looks like business is doing well."

He agreed and then lowered his voice. "I should be home with my knee up, but we couldn't miss this opportunity. In fact, I ordered custom brooches to sell for ten dollars apiece. We put a rush order on them. Hopefully they'll be here by Monday. In the meantime, we have the bracelets and rings to sell."

"Fascinating," Tess said.

"I'll give you one for free. A memento to remember all of this by."

"Oh, I doubt I'll forget any of it." She tried to smile. "So, the brooch is 'priceless'? You came up with an amount?"

He shook his head and chuckled. "That's just a marketing term. Besides, historically speaking it *is* priceless, right? It's the Bickerton brooch. An important part of Marietta's history."

Tess balked at this newcomer exploiting Marietta's history—and then chastised herself. He had every right to. "When do you expect to have a dollar amount?"

"Why, does someone have it insured?"

She shook her head. "Not that I know of. But we'd like to know what it's worth."

"Right," he said. "The jeweler from New York City wasn't the expert I thought he was. I'll be speaking with one of my colleagues on Monday morning. I'll let you know then." He shifted his weight. "I have a doctor's appointment that I need to head out to. But call if you have any other questions."

Tess got the hint. Feeling unsettled, she made her way to the front of the store, but before she could exit, Linda slipped out from behind the counter and gave her a big hug. "Are you sore from falling yesterday?"

"I'm fine," Tess assured her.

"That was all so traumatic," Linda said, keeping her voice low. "And I know this doesn't look good." She gestured to the baskets of inexpensive jewelry. "But, you know, as a mom-and-pop shop we have to do what we can. You're a small-business owner. I hope you'll understand." She turned to the counter and picked up a brochure from a stack of what Tess recognized as Wayfarers Inn brochures. "And I'm putting a brochure for your inn inside every bag. I'm telling all of the customers that Wayfarers Inn is at the heart of the mystery and to stay at your place next time they visit Marietta."

"Thanks," Tess said. "That's really kind of you."

Linda gave her another hug, and when she stepped out of the shop, Jim called out a hearty goodbye. Tess waved in response as her feet landed on the sidewalk and the door swung shut behind her.

She texted LuAnn that she was on her way and walked slowly back to the inn, her thoughts returning to the jewelry store and the scene she'd just witnessed, dumbfounded by Jim and Linda's enthusiasm.

When she walked into the lobby, LuAnn was just hanging up the phone. She motioned for Tess to come close and then whispered, "That was the Castle. Perry was there yesterday afternoon, but the tour guide had to leave because of a family emergency."

"Oh?"

"It seems the tour guide left there around one. They don't know if Perry stayed much longer after that."

Tess's heart rate sped up. She checked her recent calls and saw that the time of her call to the 911 dispatcher was at 3:53. That meant Perry would have had time to leave the Castle and steal the brooch from Uptown Jewelers. "How about Nathan? Was he with Thorn all afternoon?"

Janice shrugged. "Thorn did say Nathan went back to his room to check on a game, but he can't remember what time that was." The phone rang, interrupting their conversation.

Tess headed on into the office and put her purse in the closet.

When she came back out, LuAnn was hanging up the phone with a pleased look on her face. "Linda Walsh just called."

"Oh?"

"She said she needs more of our brochures. She didn't realize she was running so low when you were just in."

Tess inhaled sharply. "I don't know how she got the brochures she has."

"I gave them to her," LuAnn replied. "She stopped by this morning."

"Oh."

"We can drop them off on our way to Thelma and Irene's. All publicity is good publicity, right? We might as well get our name out there any way we can."

In theory, Tess believed that to be true. So why did she feel so unsettled?

"Oh my. What a story." Thelma sat in the wingback chair in the parlor of the Bickerton mansion. "Didn't we go to bed early on the Fourth? That was night before last, right? We commented on all of the explosions going on. It was bang, boom, bang, all evening long. We finally decided to call it a night."

"Yes, I believe that's right." Irene folded her hands in her lap. "We couldn't have broken the glass to the curio cabinet."

Tess suppressed a smile.

LuAnn scooted forward on her chair. "We weren't accusing the two of you of breaking into the cabinet and leaving the brooch. We just wondered if you knew anything about the brooch."

"I don't," Irene said. "I've never heard of such a thing." As the younger of the two, she sometimes didn't remember things that Thelma did.

Tess shifted her gaze to the older sister.

"I do." Thelma looked at Irene as she spoke. "Our father mentioned it a time or two when I was little. Great-grandfather brought it from England. Well…"

This was where things got complicated. Tess, LuAnn, Brad, and the sisters all knew it. Just over a year ago, the sisters' ancestry had been turned upside down. Howard Bickerton, the man they thought was their great-grandfather, was actually Stuart Dawson. He'd killed the real Mr. Bickerton when they first arrived in Marietta and assumed the dead man's identity.

He was referred to as Mr. Bickerton in Prudence's diary. Although the Quaker woman knew the truth about him from the beginning, she seemed to have kept the secret for the rest of her life, even in the privacy of her writings. Mr. Bickerton, despite his obvious fatal flaw, supported the work of the Underground Railroad. Prudence lived in a time when a woman, especially one of color, even though she passed as white, had to make compromises to get the good work done and protect their families.

As it turned out, Thelma had known the big secret too. Her great-grandfather had confessed what he'd done on his deathbed when she was a young girl, but she was sworn to secrecy. It had been a relief when the truth was finally known by all.

A light bulb went off in Tess's head. "Oh…"

"What?" said LuAnn. "Did you figure something out?"

Tess looked at her, wide-eyed. "It just occurred to me. If the brooch came over from England on the boat with Howard Bickerton, it also came over with Stuart and Charisse Dawson. Who's to say who owned the brooch?" She shrugged. "How could we know? So whether the brooch was originally Stuart's or not, it would be known as the Bickerton brooch."

"Do you know what happened to the brooch?" Brad asked his aunts. "Is it still in the family?"

"Oh, no," Thelma said. "It was gone long before I was born. Father mentioned it whenever he needed an infusion of cash. He said it was very valuable but that it had disappeared during the Civil War. He still had hopes it would turn up someday, that someone would be convicted of the crime they'd committed, and it would be returned it to us."

Brad kept trying. "Do you have any photos of the brooch? Maybe one of your great-grandmother wearing it?"

"I don't recall any photos." Thelma turned to Irene. "Do you?"

The younger sister shook her head. "There are only a few photos of Stuart and Charisse Dawson."

Tess knew that. Photography wasn't common in the 1850s and '60s, but wealthy people usually had a few portraits done.

Brad motioned toward the far end of the parlor to a photo hanging on the wall. "That's them, right?"

Irene nodded.

Charisse wore a diamond necklace around her neck but not a brooch. Of course, both had what looked like sour expressions on their faces, but Tess knew they were simply staying as still as possible for the time it took for the shutter to stay open to capture the image.

Thelma pointed to the mantel. "There's another one over there."

Tess and LuAnn both rose from their chairs and stepped toward it. Stuart and Charisse Dawson stood with their two sons in a studio. The mother and father were seated with a boy on either side of them.

LuAnn stepped closer. "She has some sort of jewelry on the collar of her dress."

Tess squinted. "It's definitely a brooch, but it's not in focus enough to make out the jewels."

"Perhaps someone could try to enhance the photo," Brad said. "Isn't there a photographer on staff at the historical society?"

"That's a great idea." LuAnn turned to the sisters. "Would you be willing to let us borrow the photo? Just long enough to get a copy made? I'll be personally responsible for it."

The sisters exchanged a glance. Tess had no idea what passed between the two, but something obviously did because

Irene said, "We guess that would be all right. Just return it as soon as possible."

"So what happens once the brooch is recovered?" Thelma asked. "To whom does it belong?"

That was the sixty-four-thousand-dollar question. Brad and his brother Grant descended from Zephaniah Bickerton, the son of the real Howard Bickerton, making them the rightful heirs, while Irene and Thelma were the descendants of Romulus, the son of Stuart Dawson, who became the imposter Howard Bickerton.

The real Mr. Bickerton also had another son, Matthew, who'd stayed in England instead of immigrating to the US with his father. Charlotte Bickerton Lane, who also lived in Marietta, was a descendant of his. Her branch of the family had stayed in England until her parents moved to Marietta back in the 1950s.

Tess leaned forward. "Someone needs to tell Charlotte about the brooch."

"She's out of town," Brad said. "I don't think there's any reason to talk with her about it until she gets back."

They all agreed. It was all so confusing.

Then again, if possession was nine-tenths of the law, would the brooch go to Irene and Thelma since they had everything else? Or to Brad and Grant? Or to Charlotte? It was definitely a complicated situation.

Thelma asked again to whom the brooch would belong.

Tess, Brad, and LuAnn answered, "We don't know" in unison.

Irene laughed. "Well, at least there's one thing we can all agree on."

⚜

As Brad drove Tess back to the inn, before he and LuAnn would continue on to the historical society, he had the radio on low until a report that started with, "Mysterious brooch stolen..." caught their attention. Brad turned the volume up.

Tess knew the theft was definitely newsworthy, but it still made her feel unsettled to hear it discussed on the radio. At least the report was concise and short.

"The brooch was trending on social media this morning," Brad said as he turned the volume back down. "It probably still is."

Tess wrinkled her nose.

Brad stopped his car in front of the inn. "Next thing you know, you'll probably have the national media knocking on your door."

Tess hoped not. She thanked Brad and told LuAnn she'd see her soon. As she headed toward the inn, Brad continued on to take LuAnn to the historical society.

Janice waved from the front desk when Tess came through the door. "Good news," she said. "The part came in, and the repairmen are down in the basement installing it."

"That's fantastic." A wave of relief washed over Tess. "Did you and Larry have a good afternoon?"

Janice laughed and slumped her shoulders, feigning exhaustion. "We sure did. But Grandma's getting a little old for Larry's dinosaurs-ravaging-the-planet game."

Tess chuckled. "I'm sure you had some cookies and milk ready to appease the ferocious beast when you needed them. Are any of the guests back yet?"

Janice nodded. "Perry headed upstairs a few minutes ago." She dropped the volume of her voice. "I asked him how his tour of the Castle was yesterday, and he said it ended early, and he went on out to Buffington Island."

"Oh?"

Janice nodded. "Of course, I don't know how I'm possibly going to be able to confirm that." Buffington Island was located nearly an hour away.

"Interesting." Tess would have to think about that more. "What else is new around here?"

"Keeley put all of the artifacts back in the cabinet and reactivated the alarm."

Tess turned to the cabinet. Everything looked exactly as it had before. "Is Keeley still around?"

"She and Granny are out on the patio playing dominoes."

Tess loved how everyone was calling the elder Mrs. Hines "Granny" now. "Isn't it pretty hot out there?"

"It seems Granny likes it hot." Janice fanned herself with a piece of paper. "She said their room is too cold with the air conditioner on."

Tess laughed. "I'll get them some lemonade."

Janice increased the speed of her fanning. "Great idea."

Thankfully, they wouldn't have to wait much longer to have the air back on. Tess stepped into the kitchen, poured the lemonade, and then swung the patio door open with her foot.

Granny waved from the table in the far corner, under the most shade. She wore a wide-brimmed white hat and a white pantsuit and appeared to be enjoying herself, but Keeley, who wore shorts and a tank top, looked like a wilted rose. "How about some lemonade?" Tess called out as she walked toward them.

"What a splendid idea," Granny said.

Tess set the icy glasses in front of them. "How has your day been so far?"

"Wonderful." Granny wrapped both hands around her glass. "We took a boat ride on the river."

"Oh?"

"Down to Parksburg and back." Keeley took a long drink of the lemonade. "Granny got to ride with the captain in the wheelhouse, but the rest of us were on deck."

That explained why Keeley appeared to be overheated while Granny didn't.

"Sit down," Granny said to Tess.

"All right. Just for a minute."

"I've been thinking about what we were talking about this morning." Granny grinned.

Tess spread her hands, palms down, on the table. "Oh?"

Granny's eyes sparkled. "Do you remember?"

"Remind me," Tess answered.

"Thomas Hines, of course. The captain who rode with General Morgan."

"That's right." Tess definitely wanted to hear Granny's thoughts.

But when she didn't say anymore, Tess wondered if she'd forgotten what she was going to say already. "Go on," she said gently.

"Yes. Well, Thomas Hines was my Cash's great-great-grand-father. Thomas was born in 1838."

That was the date Tess had found online. Granny Hines seemed to have more clarity than she'd had during the last three days.

"He had quite an imagination. When he and Morgan were incarcerated in the Ohio State Penitentiary, Thomas got a hold of a copy of *Les Misérables*." She met Tess's eyes. "It was written by Victor Hugo and published in 1862."

Tess was impressed. She remembered that Hugo was the author but never would have remembered the year it was published.

"So, in 1863, it was just newly released." Granny tilted her head. "You know I have no idea if it had been translated into English yet. Perhaps he read it in French."

Keeley's eyes grew large.

Granny continued. "Anyway, he was reading the novel, and it gave him an idea about how to escape."

Keeley sat up straighter. "Are you sure, Granny? That sounds a little crazy."

"No, I'm certain, dear. You should do some research. See if you can find out when *Les Misérables* was translated into English, would you?"

Keeley pulled out her phone.

"Not now, dear," Granny said. "It's rude to use that thing at the table."

Keeley stuffed her phone back into the pocket of her shorts.

Tess smiled at the girl and then said to Granny, "Well, thank you for that information. It's fascinating." She stood. "I'm afraid I need to get back to work." As she stepped into the inn, she added more items to the mental list of things she needed to research. Was Thomas Hines inspired to escape from the penitentiary by reading *Les Misérables*? Even though that had nothing to do with the brooch it was fascinating. Thomas Hines was shaping up to be a very intriguing character.

⚜

After lunch Tess slipped into the office, closed the door, and logged on to the computer. She googled "Captain Thomas Hines" and "*Les Misérables* inspired escape from the Ohio State Pen." An article popped up on a government website. It was factual that Hines and Morgan escaped from the Ohio Penitentiary, on November 27, 1863. They'd bribed an inmate with privileges to get a train schedule for them and then caught a train from Columbus to Cincinnati. They jumped off before it reached the station, crossed the Ohio River, and arrived back in Kentucky. Although it couldn't be confirmed that Hines got the idea for the escape from *Les Misérables*, it couldn't be disproven either. He claimed that in reading the novel, he realized his own prison cell was dry and surmised there was an air chamber below their cells that they could tunnel into, which was exactly what they did.

The story of their escape became part of the Confederate lore of gallant Confederate officers outsmarting their Union jailers. Hines may have embellished the story through the years after the war, but the core points of their escape were accurate.

Tess jotted down a few notes for LuAnn to transfer into her notebook and then added, *Granny Hines knew her stuff on this one. The woman isn't as forgetful, at least not always, as everyone seems to think.* Tess would have to let Keeley know. She'd be tactful when she told her, but there was no reason for her to disbelieve her grandmother's stories.

Next, Tess searched Jim Walsh. She knew, from the certificate on his wall, that he'd graduated from the school in Switzerland, and she had the information from the online Ohio State alumni magazine Janice had found. She couldn't find anything criminal in his past—only rave reviews about his shop in Manhattan and his work as a gemologist. Everything seemed aboveboard. She decided to search for Linda Walsh. There were lots of entries, and she couldn't narrow down which one was Jim's wife without more information about her.

Then out of curiosity, she typed "Brooch stolen in Marietta, Ohio" into the search bar. Several entries appeared. The *Marietta Times* articles. The audio from the local radio station. A segment from the Columbus TV Station, including an interview with Linda and Jim. She squinted. A national network had picked up that segment. And on social media the hashtag

#stolenmariettabrooch was trending. Brad was right. They probably would have a reporter knocking on their door soon.

As Tess logged out of the computer, a blast of cold air shot out of the register in the office—followed by a shout in the lobby.

She hurried out of the office. Thorn stood on the other side of the counter, his hands in the air. Janice knelt down by the register on the wall of the café, a smile on her face.

Everyone looked happy, except for Nathan. He was slinking toward the elevator. Thorn didn't seem to notice, so Tess nodded to the boy.

"Hey!" Thorn called out. "Thank you for all your help. I'm here to change some lightbulbs on the second floor. Want to help?"

Nathan turned around and smiled.

After Thorn and Nathan headed upstairs, and the repairmen trudged up from the basement and out the front door, LuAnn arrived, carrying an envelope.

"What's in there?" Tess asked.

"Brad is returning the original photo to Thelma and Irene," LuAnn explained. "But I have the enhanced photo from the historical society. The photographer was working today, trying to finish a special project. He took a break to help us out. He scanned the old photo and then enlarged the brooch." She pulled out a print and placed it on the counter. "Do we have a photo to compare it to?"

Tess pulled out her phone, pulling up the best photo of the brooch. She placed her phone next to the enhanced copy.

All three women leaned over the counter, looking at each photo, comparing the pattern of the stones and the shape of the brooch.

"They look identical to me," Janice finally said.

LuAnn stood up straight. "Me too."

Tess's heart fluttered. "Me three." They weren't experts, but it seemed they'd identified the brooch. It had originated in England before 1856 and had been stolen in 1863. But where in the world had it been for the last one hundred fifty years?

CHAPTER TEN

July 17, 1863

As the thunder of hooves faded away and the soldier and horse disappeared into the woods, Prudence grabbed Ernestine's hand and lurched toward the house, but the frightened girl was now frozen to the ground, her cloak still pulled over her head.

"Now," Prudence whispered quietly. She feared drawing attention back to the two of them. Who knew how many soldiers were in the woods? "Walk beside me."

The girl shook like an autumn leaf hanging on until the last second, but she didn't move forward.

Prudence lifted her head toward the house. Moses was still on the porch, but Jason stood at the gate. He opened it.

She shook her head. The last thing they needed was for the Confederates to return and force Jason into protecting her and Ernestine. That could only end badly.

"Thee must move," Prudence whispered. "The Lord will walk with us. We must go."

Finally, small step by small step, Ernestine moved forward with Prudence. More shouts from the woods made the girl shake even more, but finally they reached Jason. He shut the gate behind them, wrapped his arms around their shoulders, and led them up to the porch.

"In the house, Son," Prudence said to Moses. Her son scampered ahead of them, opening the door and holding it until they'd all passed through.

Jason shut the door and bolted it behind him as Prudence directed Ernestine to the table, urging her to sit. After Prudence helped her remove her cloak and boots, Jason brought her a cup of warm milk.

Thankfully, Jason and Moses had already done the chores and had their own supper. Jason and Prudence hovered in the corner of the kitchen and spoke quietly.

"I heard farmers all over the county were chopping down trees across the roads to stop Morgan's men. I thought of doing it here—trees from the woods—but knew my leg wouldn't allow it. But if I could have, perhaps he wouldn't have harassed thee like that."

Prudence shook her head. "I doubt it would have stopped him."

"What did he take from the basket?"

Prudence's voice wavered as she explained that she didn't know exactly what it was. "But it belonged to the Bickertons, and it came from their bank."

"What a perilous situation. I regret not cutting down a tree to stop the marauders even more now."

"Don't say that," Prudence said. "As I said, it most likely wouldn't have stopped the thief anyway." They would never know. "I dread telling Mr. Gidden."

Jason put his hand on her shoulder. "I will go with thee."

She reached up and squeezed his hand. "I appreciate that. We will all go in together tomorrow. Ernestine can stay and help me in the kitchen." She wanted her charge close, where she could keep an eye on her.

Jason dropped the volume of his voice even more. "Is she all right?"

Prudence shook her head. "She was already unsteady at the hotel, but the soldier deeply frightened her."

"Did something happen to her in Gettysburg?"

"I do not know," Prudence said. "She is not speaking."

Jason's eyes grew concerned. "Is Isaac all right?"

"Yes." Prudence told him what Martha had told her, that one of the battles had spilled over onto Isaac's property and that the Confederates had moved into his barn for a day, but then the Union chased them out. "His farm is littered with the dead."

Jason shivered. "Those sights would be enough to frighten anyone half to death."

Prudence agreed.

Ernestine continued to sit, her eyes on the bolted door, until Prudence showed her Moses's bed. She shook her head.

Finally she spoke, saying, "I'll sit at the table."

"Not all night," Prudence said. "Thee needs to rest."

"I need to stay awake."

Jason spoke up and said he'd sleep with Moses. "Thee two take the big bed," he said.

Finally Ernestine agreed to crawl into the featherbed with Prudence, but her shaking didn't stop. Prudence quoted scripture to her, repeating the Lord's words from John 14, over and over. "Peace I leave with you, my peace I give unto you: not as the world giveth, give I unto you. Let not your heart be troubled, neither let it be afraid."

After a time Ernestine seemed to relax a little. Prudence struggled to stay awake, and Ernestine finally sighed and turned onto her side. Her breathing slowed.

Prudence, grateful for the blessing of sleep, drifted off too.

The next morning, Moses accompanied Jason as he did the chores while Prudence baked biscuits and boiled grits. As soon as they finished eating, they all headed into town. Ernestine had retreated into silence again.

When they reached the hotel, Mr. Gidden had yet to arrive.

Prudence began preparing breakfast for the guests while Jason and Moses loaded the woodbox, and Ernestine filled the reservoir in the back of the stove with water to heat. Finally, as the first of the guests wandered into the dining hall and Ernestine had started washing the pots and pans, Mr. Gidden arrived. He appeared as if he hadn't slept.

He launched into telling them how things had been in town last night. "There were a few skirmishes, and several houses and businesses were raided. But all in all, not as much damage was done as feared." He collapsed in a chair at the table. "How did your family fare?"

Prudence ducked her head as Jason came in the back door with more water.

"Jason," Mr. Gidden said. "What are you doing here?"

Prudence spoke, her voice weak. "We need to tell thee something."

"What is it?"

Prudence looked to her husband. He cleared his throat. "The pouch thee gave Prudence yesterday was stolen. By a Confederate soldier. I watched it happen from the porch."

Mr. Gidden's eyes narrowed, and he called Mr. Siloam into the kitchen, telling him that he'd given Prudence a valuable brooch that belonged to the Bickertons to keep safe, but now it was missing. "You are my witness," Mr. Gidden said to the manager of the hotel. "Remember what's happening here."

Mr. Siloam shot Prudence a look of pity as Gidden turned away from him.

Gidden faced Prudence and Jason again, spitting out his words. "Was the brooch stolen by a Confederate soldier? Or, more likely, did the two of you pocket it? It's worth more than you could ever dream of making in your entire lives."

Behind them Ernestine gasped. Prudence stood as tall as she could, and Jason stepped closer to her. "God is our witness," he said, his voice clear and strong. "We did not steal what was in the pouch. We didn't even know it was a brooch until thee said so right now."

Gidden's face grew red, and he turned to Mr. Siloam. "Go get the sheriff. I won't stand for thievery from those who work at the Riverfront House. From those with whom Mr. Bickerton has been so generous. I'll not stand for such betrayal."

CHAPTER ELEVEN

At breakfast the next morning, as Tess poured half-and-half into the pitcher, Val bemoaned the fact that it was their last full day in Marietta. "I'm tempted to move here," she said. "Except that Keeley will be going back to school next month, so it really wouldn't make any sense."

"What do you like most about our little town?" Tess asked, putting the pitcher back in place.

Val smiled. "I'll give you my top three. That everything is within walking distance, that there's so much history and culture, and how relaxed and easygoing my kids seem here."

"Interesting," Tess said. "What's it like back home?"

"Don't get me wrong. We love the Bay area, and even though this season of our life has its challenges, there are also lots of blessings in it too. But the downside of our situation right now is that any trip into the city takes a long time, especially during rush hour. My husband works long hours with his new start-up and travels all over the world. The high schools are super-competitive—the pressure on the students is intense. Of course Keeley is in college now, so she has a different kind of pressure, but she says it's not as bad as it was at her high school."

Tess couldn't imagine that.

"Anyway." Val held her coffee cup up as if making a toast. "We've had a wonderful time. Now we're going to enjoy our last day before we all leave tomorrow."

"Thank you so much for your kind words," Tess said. "It's been a delight to have all of you as guests." She wished she felt as settled as Val seemed to and as resigned to dealing with what life brought. Even though she still had the stolen brooch and her financial woes to deal with, she was blessed to live in Marietta.

After they'd cleaned up from breakfast and finished the housekeeping duties, Janice stayed behind to mind the inn while LuAnn and Tess headed to Christ Fellowship for the Sunday morning service, slipping into the last pew as Pastor Ben led the congregation in an opening prayer. "Lord," he prayed, "show us how to love You and each other in deeper and more meaningful ways. And above all, teach us how to trust You."

LuAnn echoed Pastor Ben's hearty "Amen." Tess nodded in affirmation.

As they sang "Savior like a Shepherd Lead Us," her mind wandered back to the inn. She didn't see Perry this morning. She couldn't imagine that he slept in. More likely he'd left before anyone was up. After the last note of the hymn, Pastor Ben started the sermon. Over and over Tess tried to focus only to find her mind wandering again and again. It wasn't until after the sermon, as they all recited the Lord's Prayer together, something that Pastor Ben had recently incorporated into the Sunday morning service, that her mind truly focused on the Lord. "Our Father...thy kingdom come, thy will be done on earth as it is in heaven..." *Thy will be done.*

As they finished the prayer together, she continued on silently, praying for the truth about the brooch and that it would be returned to the rightful owner. That would be justice. That was always what was best.

When she drove her car by Uptown Jewelers on the way back to the inn from church, there was a crowd milling around outside, and it appeared that the shop was packed.

"Wow." LuAnn craned her neck. "What in the world is going on there?"

"Marketing," Tess said. "There's a copy of the newspaper in the window. They've become the 'Famous Brooch Shop.' Either Linda or Jim or both of them know how to capitalize on a negative situation."

"Wow," LuAnn said. "I'd say what they're doing is working. We had a couple of reservations yesterday for the fall—when I asked how they found out about us, they answered 'from the jewelry store.'" LuAnn sighed. "We could still tie the brooch into the café. Create a brooch dessert. Red, white, and blue—"

"Tart?" Tess smiled. "I think we already have that."

"You're right. How about muffins with blueberries and raspberries? And brooch-shaped scones?"

"Yeah, well, we'd have to pull it off without being tacky." LuAnn pointed back to the shop as Tess sped up and then turned onto their street. "Unlike what they're doing."

As Tess parked her car at the back of the inn, Randy stepped out of his cruiser that was parked across the street. "How about if we go out to the patio, so we can speak in private," LuAnn suggested when he reached them.

"Sorry I didn't come by yesterday," he said as they all settled around the table still in the shade. "It turned out to be a crazy day."

"What happened?" Tess asked.

"A bad car accident out on the highway. An overdose." His eyes grew heavy.

"I'm so sorry," she said. "You have such a stressful job." They only had a glimpse of the tragedies he witnessed each day.

He gave her an appreciative smile. "I wish I had some sort of information to give you, but I don't." He glanced from LuAnn to Tess. "Do any of you have anything to share with me?"

LuAnn pulled her notebook out of her handbag. "We wonder where both Perry and Nathan were at the time the brooch was stolen. We can't verify Perry's claim that he was at Buffington Island nor Nathan's that he was playing a computer game."

"Do you have any probable cause that either is the thief?"

"No," LuAnn admitted.

"Well, keep an eye on both of them. Keep asking questions. Alert me if anything comes up."

Tess leaned forward. "Nathan and his family leave tomorrow." If he had the brooch, it could be gone for good. She went on to tell Randy about the Hines family connection. "Thomas Hines was definitely in this area when the brooch was originally stolen during the Civil War."

"And it seems it was the same brooch," LuAnn said.

Randy shook his head in confusion. "You think that the brooch is historically connected to the Hines family?"

"It's just a theory," LuAnn said. "We don't have any proof."

"Oh." Randy stood. "I'll keep working on this as time allows. Make sure and let me know, as soon as possible, if you come across anything new."

They assured him they would.

"Have you spoken with Jim and Linda Walsh today?" Tess wondered what he thought of the marketing plan they were running.

He shook his head. "I stopped by the hospital on Friday evening when Jim was being discharged. I'll stop by later this afternoon."

"Will you let me know what you think?"

He gave her a puzzled look.

"They're capitalizing on the theft. Marketing it to attract more business."

"There's nothing illegal about that," Randy answered.

"I realize that." Tess stood. "I'm just curious about what you think of it."

"I've interviewed both of them extensively in person, and I interviewed the expert he was consulting with over the phone. I can't rule any of them out for certain, but I didn't uncover any evidence that any of them are involved in the crime either." Randy shrugged. "But I'll continue to investigate them too."

After they told Randy goodbye, LuAnn headed upstairs, and Janice left to spend the afternoon with her grandson. Tess sat down at the front desk. A couple of tourists stopped by to take a look at the inn, holding brochures that they'd been given at Uptown Jewelers. Tess talked with them about the history of the inn and then directed them over to the curio cabinet. After they left, she ran down to the basement and started a load of towels. When she returned, Perry stood in front of the cabinet.

"Hello," she said.

He spun around. "You startled me."

"I didn't mean to." Tess apologized and then added, "You were off early this morning. Where did you go?"

"Buffington Island."

Tess hesitated a moment and then said, "Was that your first trip there?" She didn't want to let on that Janice had told her he said he went there on Friday.

She wasn't sure if it was her imagination or not, but it seemed his face reddened some. "No. I went day before yesterday too. But I had a few follow-up questions, so I went back."

Tess pressed him. "And what did you find out?"

"In general? Or specifically?"

"Either." Tess just wanted to hear him talk about his research and determine how sincere he seemed.

"Well," he said, "as you probably know, the Battle of Buffington Island was the largest Civil War battle to take place on Ohio soil. Over half of the Confederates were captured, but over seven hundred of them got away."

Tess chuckled. "Thank you for sharing that. I really should have listened better in history class." She stepped around to the other side of the desk. "What specifically were you checking on today?"

His face reddened even more. If he was the thief, he needed to learn to control his blushing better. "I knew General Morgan wasn't captured at Buffington Island. But I wasn't sure about some of the others."

"And what did you learn?"

Perry turned toward the stairs. "The information I wanted wasn't available." Before Tess could ask anything more, he said, "I've had a long day. I think I'll get some rest before the Hines family returns." He bounded up the steps, leaving Tess puzzled about what he might have been looking for.

A couple of hours later, the Hines family returned in a thunder of footsteps, conversations, and shouts. Tess was talking on the phone with her daughter, Lizzie, and had to get off, it was so loud.

Val and Keeley were hushing everyone, but it didn't seem to be working. The twins were laughing as they ran through the lobby. Sadie and Colette, who each had a bud in one ear, were giggling about a video they were watching on the same phone as they shuffled by. Nathan came in last and glanced around several times. When he saw Tess he asked if Thorn was around.

She shook her head. "He takes Sundays off, plus we don't have any jobs for him to do." Hopefully it would stay that way.

The boy's face fell. "I was hoping to tell him goodbye."

"What time do you leave in the morning?"

"Early, I think," Nathan answered.

Perhaps she should call Thorn in to look at the dripping sink in Lilac and Sage. "Maybe Thorn will be in before you go." Tess hoped so. Thorn had been a good friend—and vice versa—to Nathan.

After some members of the family ran up the stairs and then back down, they gathered out on the patio for a farewell barbecue. Val had purchased all of the food, plus paper plates and cups, and was coordinating the meal. Her brothers-in-law were manning the grill.

When they were nearly ready to eat, Keeley came into the lobby. "Do you have a couple of bowls and serving utensils we could borrow?"

"Of course," Tess answered. "I'll be right out with them."

When Tess returned with the items, Keeley echoed her mother's praise for the inn. "We've really enjoyed ourselves. Regardless of the AC problems and the curio cabinet break-in, and that weird stuff with the brooch... It's really been a fun reunion."

"How often do you have these events?" Tess asked as she handed Keeley two stainless steel bowls and two serving spoons.

"Oh, this is our first small one like this." She clutched the items. "We have bigger reunions every five years, always at a park or hall or something like that, moving around from location to location. I remember one in Philadelphia. Another in New Orleans. The reunions are really what got me interested in history. They're having one next year, but we didn't think Granny would be up for it. Once I was hired for the internship here, I sent information about Marietta to everyone, and they

115

all agreed this would be a great place for a mini reunion, one with just our family."

"I'm so glad you did," Tess said.

"Me too. It's the first time I had a part in planning anything like this. I created a private Facebook page to do the planning. That was weird. A cousin I'd never met requested to be added." She seemed to be enjoying reliving the planning of the reunion. "The guy seemed sort of odd, and when I explained it was only for our closest relatives, he backed off. It was really strange. I have no idea how he found us. I wonder if he hacked into one of our accounts."

"That is odd," Tess answered.

"Yeah." Keeley turned toward the patio. "I've been wondering if that guy could have something to do with stealing the brooch."

Tess tilted her head as she listened.

"Do you think I should tell Officer Lewis about it? Maybe he can figure out who infiltrated our group."

Tess crossed her arms. "But why do you think whoever that was might have something to do with the brooch?"

Keeley blushed. "It just seems suspicious, is all."

"You should tell Officer Lewis," Tess finally said. "Can you think of anyone else in your family who might be involved with the brooch in any way?"

"Like?"

"Maybe one of the boys did it as a joke. Either planting it or stealing it or both."

Keeley shook her head vehemently. "They would have needed access to it. We don't have things like that in our family. And the boys—the twins and Nathan—I can't see them setting something like that up, to be honest. Deceit and thievery really aren't in their toolboxes."

Tess had to agree with her. The twins were too young to be that clever, and Nathan didn't seem to be much of a joker.

By the time the Hines family was done with their barbecue, Perry came through the lobby. He told Tess he was going out for the evening. "Good night," she called after him. She hoped he was going out to listen to music or something like that— and not to arrange the sale of the stolen brooch.

LuAnn was working in the office and Janice hadn't returned yet, when a screech, followed by a thud, echoed up from the basement. LuAnn stepped out of the office. "Uh-oh."

Tess reached down to the register in the wall. No air was coming out at all. She sighed. "The repair shop is closed. I'll call Thorn to see if he has any ideas. Hopefully it's just a programming issue or something with the thermostat."

Thorn didn't have any ideas for Tess over the phone and insisted he'd come by, even though that wasn't her intention. By the time he arrived, even though it was four days past the Fourth of July, someone was setting off bottle rockets down by the river. Thorn took off his baseball cap and ran his hand through his hair. When another one exploded, he jumped.

Tess put her hand on his shoulder. "You okay?"

He shrugged. "I'll go check on the unit," he said.

As he turned toward the basement stairs, Nathan hopped down the last stair and landed in the lobby, followed by his twin cousins. "Thorn!" Nathan called out.

Tess thought the boy's enthusiasm might be too much for Thorn, but he seemed to welcome Nathan's greeting. "Want to help me take a look at the air-conditioning unit? Your cousins are welcome too."

"Sure," Nathan said, patting each of the boys on the shoulder. "Hey, I'll show you where the Underground Railroad tunnel is."

They didn't usually let guests in the basement, but Tess trusted Thorn to keep an eye on them. Still, she cautioned the twins by saying, "Make sure not to get in the way."

Nathan's face was as serious as Tess had ever seen it, which was saying a lot, as he said, "I promise I'll keep them in line."

It wasn't long until Thorn came up the stairs, followed by the boys. "I couldn't figure out what's wrong. It's not the programming. I left a message with the company," he said. "They should be out first thing in the morning to fix it again."

Another bottle rocket whistled and exploded, and Thorn jumped again. The twins ran to the window to see if they could see anything. Darkness had fallen, and as they stood there a fourth bottle rocket exploded.

"I'm going to go on home." Thorn's shoulders slumped. "At least the window units are still installed."

Tess nodded, though she and her friends on the fourth floor would have another hot night. She called Winnie and let her know the café would be closed again tomorrow, this time for both breakfast and lunch. She put a notice on the door saying they were closed until further notice and hoped word of mouth would help spread the news.

When Tess finally headed up to bed at eleven, she could hear a scuffle on the third floor. She hoped the twins weren't wrestling in the hallway, but if they were, at least Perry, who had come in around ten forty-five, was on the second floor.

When Tess reached the fourth floor, LuAnn sat in a chair in the common area while Janice stood, fanning herself with a piece of paper, with an overnight bag at her feet. LuAnn held a glass of ice water against her face.

"Déjà vu," Tess said.

"Yeah, it seems we've done this before." LuAnn moved the glass to the other side of her face.

Janice nodded to the bag. "I'm going to go stay at Stacy's. I can't take another night of this."

Tess smiled at her friend but couldn't help being a little jealous. Why hadn't she thought to escape for the night? But they couldn't all leave.

"I'll be back first thing in the morning," Janice said.

Tess put her hands on her hips. "You better be."

Janice grinned and headed for the elevator.

LuAnn took a drink of the ice water. "It's hotter tonight than it has been."

"I know, right?"

LuAnn yawned. "Well, I'm going to go get a head start on being hot and sticky and awake all night."

"I'm right behind you." But first Tess fixed a glass of ice water for herself. Then she shuffled into her room and stood at her window, looking out toward the river. In the inky darkness she could make out the light of a boat. Then a bottle rocket exploded. Even though she saw it, the sound startled her.

She thought of her prayer at church that morning and her willingness to trust. Now she felt cranky from the heat and worried about the AC, her investment woes, and the missing brooch again.

It wasn't like her to worry, but here she was. Worried. She pushed the window open all the way and breathed in the warm night air, saying a prayer as she did, trying to find some peace in the hot, sticky night.

But by the time she crawled into her bed, with just the sheet pulled over her, worry had crowded out her prayers once again.

CHAPTER TWELVE

Monday morning, at eight o'clock sharp, Tess stood at her window overlooking the river again. Two kayakers made their way out to the middle of the river, paddling around a brace of ducks. She held her cell phone in her hand, ready to call Frank Bryant, once again, about her investment, although she dreaded finding out exactly how much her losses might be.

She dialed, expecting it to go to voice mail, but thankfully, Frank answered on the second ring. "Hello, Frank. This is Tess Wallace." She took a deep breath and said, "I want to cash out what's left of my investment."

"Oh, that's a bad idea," he said. "The businesses I recently invested in have turned a corner. I was definitely premature in sending out the letter."

"Is that right? Please give me more of an explanation."

"You know that new ice cream shop downtown? The business doubled its revenue in the last two weeks. And that new boutique hotel—"

"What?" Tess knew her voice sounded shrill. She didn't care. "You invested my money in a competitor?" It was one thing to send Clint Lowery, the owner of Butterfly Farms and Bed and Breakfast, business. But it was a completely different issue to have her money financing his endeavor.

Frank paused. "What are you talking about?"

"Wayfarers Inn. I'm one of the owners."

"Oh..." His voice grew more serious. "I see your point. I'm happy to shift your money from that business to another, but I think you'll regret it if you bail out completely now. You know how much Jeff believed in local small businesses. I think he'd want you to stick with it."

Tess had had enough. "I'll think about it and get back to you," she said. She'd talk to Jeff Jr., who was a CPA, and see what advice he had for her.

She hung up and headed back downstairs. The Hines family had gathered in the café, talking and laughing. Except for Granny Hines and Nathan. Granny sat with her hand wrapped around her mug, staring into her coffee. Nathan dragged a forked bite of pancake through syrup, around and around his plate.

Val approached Tess. "Is it all right if Granny, Nathan, and I get a late checkout, around one? I'm going to drive halfway back to Chicago today, and I think she'll do better if we leave a little later. She had a rough night."

"No problem." Tess was actually happy to have the trio around as long as possible.

Val rejoined the rest of the group. Keeley, who was wearing a T-shirt with an oak tree on it that read, *A people without the knowledge of their past history is like a tree without roots,* was going around from table to table, hugging her aunts and uncles and cousins goodbye. Then she patted Granny Hines on her shoulder. "I'll come tell *you* goodbye over my lunch break."

Granny reached up and patted her granddaughter's hand, but didn't speak. Tess wondered if she was feeling sad at the thought of her family leaving.

The morning progressed quickly. Thorn checked in with the air-conditioning technician in the basement and then reported to Tess and LuAnn, who were both working at the front desk on the bills for the Hines family.

"He says the new part was defective, so he ordered another one."

Tess's heart fell. The new guests coming in might not be as understanding as the Hines family had been. "How long until the part arrives?" she managed to ask.

"A couple of days. They put a rush on it, and they're going to try to fix the part in the meantime."

"We need more window units," LuAnn said. "We have new guests coming in. Let's see what we can borrow—but we might need to buy a few more if we can't round any up." She pulled out her cell phone. "I'll call Brad. He might know of someone we can ask."

"I'll call Lizzie again," Tess said. Maybe her daughter had a neighbor or friend who had an extra unit.

After several phone calls they'd rounded up four more units, enough for the rooms on the second floor and one for the fourth. Thorn said to give him the addresses of the people who were willing to loan them out, and he'd go round them up. Val, Nathan, and Granny had told everyone else goodbye and seen them out the door and were now sitting in the café.

Val overheard and called out to Thorn, "You'll need help. Take Nathan with you."

The boy jumped up as Thorn said, "Great idea. I'll have him back by noon."

Tess smiled as the two traipsed out of the inn. She knew Thorn was on edge about something, but he'd still been so gracious and caring toward Nathan. And it seemed Nathan was blossoming under the extra attention.

Just when it seemed things had calmed down, a man in a suit strode into the inn with a cameraman behind him.

Tess almost said, *We've been expecting you.* Instead she poked her head into the office, thankful LuAnn was on the premises. "Hey, there's a reporter in the lobby. Would you talk to him?" She really was the best one to answer any questions, especially on camera.

LuAnn grinned. "I'd be happy to." She hurried out to the lobby, with Tess right behind her, and greeted the reporter.

He was from an affiliate of a cable news station located in Cincinnati. "I just came from Uptown Jewelers," he said, "and have some follow-up questions."

"And I'd love to answer them," LuAnn answered, "as long as you give me ten minutes to freshen up."

While they waited, Tess gave the reporter a quick history lesson of the inn and even took him down into the basement to see the entrance to the Underground Railroad tunnel. "As they headed back up the stairs, he said, "I'd love to come back someday to report on the history of the inn." He sighed. "But today I need to focus on the stolen brooch."

"Of course," Tess replied. "After all, the brooch is the *sujet du jour.*"

LuAnn returned, wearing a navy blue pantsuit and gold hoop earrings that gleamed against her silver hair. The reporter interviewed her in front of the curio cabinet. Tess was so impressed with how poised her friend was.

After asking about the history of the brooch, how it was found in the curio cabinet, and then where it was when it was stolen, the reporter asked LuAnn who she thought stole it.

"I have no idea," she answered. "But I'm confident we'll have that answer for you soon."

The interview was over in no time, and the reporter and cameraman left.

"Whew," Tess said as the door closed behind them. "It's nice to have that over with."

LuAnn laughed. "It was fun. I wouldn't mind if more reporters found their way to our inn. It really is great publicity."

"I hope so," Tess said. It would be nice if something good came from all of the stress around the stolen brooch.

A half hour later, Charlotte Bickerton strode into the inn. She was dressed to the nines, as usual. A fitted red dress, strappy sandals, a white designer bag, and complementary blue costume jewelry. Perhaps she was making up for being out of town on the Fourth of July. She grasped a newspaper in her hand, which she held up high. "Was anyone going to tell me about this?" She'd spent enough time in England to leave her with a slight British accent.

Thankfully, LuAnn stepped around the counter and said, "Yes! As soon as you returned. Brad and I were going to tell you together."

"Oh, so Cuz is in on this too?" Her voice sounded lighter than her words.

"He went with us to talk with Thelma and Irene. So yes. He definitely knows what's going on. He didn't want to bother you while you were gone."

Charlotte put the newspaper on the counter and spread it out. It was the Saturday edition, after the brooch had been stolen. "So this piece of jewelry, which once belonged to the Bickerton family, just appeared? And then it was stolen just as mysteriously?"

"That's right," LuAnn said. "We're all baffled by what happened." She went on to explain, in detail, everything they knew, including that the photo of the Dawsons from the Bickerton mansion proved that the brooch was most likely the one that had been missing since the Civil War. And was now missing again. "I promise you that we'll let you know whenever a new development occurs."

Charlotte folded the newspaper as she spoke. "And then who will the brooch belong to once it's re-recovered?"

"Your guess is as good as anyone's," LuAnn said. "I don't know if there's any way to prove who it really belonged to."

Tess speculated that it would be added to the Bickerton estate, to be settled after Irene and Thelma passed away. But she wasn't going to speak up about what she thought. It was up to the Bickerton/Dawson descendants to sort it all out.

"Well, thank you for the information," Charlotte said. "And I have to say, I don't mind that you didn't contact me while I was out of town. Paul and I went with my mother to Cleveland. We had a lovely time." She smiled at them, collected her newspaper and bag, and then strode out of the inn.

A few minutes later, after they'd finished up the paperwork, the phone rang. Tess answered to someone coughing on the other end. Finally, a woman managed to say, "I'm so sorry. Another spell just hit me as soon as you came on the line."

"I'm sorry," Tess said. "How can I help?"

"My sister and I have reservations for the next four nights. But I just got back from the doctor—I have the flu. Like the real deal. Influenza. Even though it's summer. We just got back from New Zealand, where it's not summer." She began coughing again.

"Do you need to cancel?" Tess asked. They certainly didn't want someone with the flu staying at the inn.

The coughing subsided. "Yes," the woman said. "Will we be charged for the first night?"

"Of course not," Tess said. "This can't be helped. I hope you feel better soon and come visit us as soon as you can."

"Thank you," the woman said. "We will."

After she hung up, Tess explained to LuAnn what the call was about.

"Well, I'm bummed to have a vacant room, but you're right—we don't want the flu to come visiting. Let's hope someone books at the last minute."

Tess agreed, but it wasn't likely someone would, not at this late date.

A few minutes later, Tess and LuAnn headed out to the Local History and Genealogy Archives. They decided to walk because it wasn't too hot yet. As they passed the jewelry store, two people were taking a selfie in front of the shop window with the newspaper article in the background.

Linda must have seen them, because she dashed out of the shop and gave Tess a hug and then LuAnn one too. "How are our friends today?" she asked.

"Good." Tess shielded her eyes. "How is Jim doing?"

"Better. He doesn't need surgery after all." Linda grinned. "He's been telling the story of the robbery over and over. We're so sorry about the brooch, but we're thankful for the increased business." She patted Tess's arm. "We're also counting on the police finding the thief and recovering the brooch."

Tess nodded in agreement.

"So who will the brooch belong to once it's found?" Linda asked.

"I'm not sure," Tess answered. She didn't want to discuss it.

"Someone named Margaret came in. She works for the historical society, and she said it would belong to the women who live in the Bickerton mansion. That they would be the rightful owners."

"That could be," LuAnn said. "But we don't know. That will be up to the law."

"Of course," Linda said. "It's all so fascinating." Then her brow creased. "Except for it being stolen and Jim's knee and you being shoved and all of that. I didn't mean to sound so flippant about all of it."

"Oh, we didn't take it that way," LuAnn assured Linda. "We'll see you soon."

Once they had passed the jewelry shop, Tess turned and glanced over her shoulder. Linda was ushering a couple inside, saying, "We're having a great sale!"

"My." LuAnn was looking over her shoulder too. "They really are marketing this whole incident to make every dollar they can off of it, aren't they?"

"Yep." Tess linked her arm through LuAnn's. "Different strokes for different folks when it comes to business, right?"

LuAnn agreed as they turned onto Washington Street.

A few minutes later they arrived at the archives.

Danny, the young man who worked at the archives, greeted them. "How's your Monday going?"

Tess stifled a yawn, grinned, and then said, "Great. How about yours?"

He laughed. "It's definitely a Monday. After a holiday weekend." He nodded to the counter. "I have a pot of coffee going. Of course, you'd have to drink it out here."

"Of course. We might take you up on it later." Tess grinned and then said, "We need to look at the newspaper from July 1863, during Morgan's Raid."

A couple of minutes later Danny got Tess and LuAnn set up with the microfiche. Tess began scrolling through it as LuAnn watched. The roll started in May of 1863. There were articles about a social in the park, a spelling bee at the grammar school, and a church picnic. And then there was the war news. There was Chancellorsville, in early May, where Stonewall Jackson was accidentally shot by his own men. On May 19, a battle was fought in Vicksburg, Mississippi. "Wow," LuAnn said. "I'd forgotten that there were over four thousand casualties for the Union Army and yet they gained no ground."

It was a horrible time in the divided states of America. Family against family. Cousin against cousin. Brother against brother.

Tess kept scrolling, reaching early July. She skimmed the articles about Gettysburg, and then an update about Vicksburg. General Grant had seized the city. She continued on. "Here we go." Tess pointed to the screen.

LuAnn read the headline out loud, "'General Morgan Transports His Troops Across the Ohio in Two Steamboats.'" The article had been published on July 9 and was about General Morgan arriving in Indiana.

There were a few more small articles about Morgan's travels through Indiana and then his arrival in Ohio.

"Here we go," LuAnn said. Tess stopped scrolling, and LuAnn summarized what was in front of them. "July 17, Morgan and his men raided Marietta the day before." The article explained that farmers had felled trees to slow the marauders, and about the homes that were raided. There was an attempted robbery at a bank, but it had been thwarted.

Tess commented, "The Bickerton mansion wasn't mentioned. Doesn't it seem if it had been raided, it would have been included?"

"You would think so." LuAnn pointed to the screen. "Maybe it will be soon."

Tess blinked a few times, trying to revive her tired eyes. Reading microfiche was a chore. She scrolled down and stopped on July 18 as Tess read, "'Bickerton Brooch Stolen.'"

"There we go," Tess said.

LuAnn inhaled sharply as they both read silently. The article stated that the brooch had been taken on July 17, but it didn't say where or by whom. There was also no description of the brooch and, not surprisingly, no photo.

"That wasn't very helpful," LuAnn said.

"I agree." Tess came to the end of the scroll. "I was hoping for something more straightforward."

"Me too," LuAnn said.

Tess rewound the scroll, pulled it from the machine, and secured it back in the box.

Both Tess and LuAnn returned to the desk. As Tess handed Danny the box, she said, "I'll take you up on that cup of coffee."

"So will I," LuAnn said.

As they sipped their coffee, Danny talked about his long weekend, starting with the fireworks. It turned out he'd stood with Keeley and her cousins, down by the river. "It was really crazy," he said. "In fact, I lost Keeley a couple of times in the crowd."

Tess held her cup in midair. "Oh?"

"Yeah. Her cousins kept taking off, running in and out of other groups. She kept trying to find them."

Tess smiled. At least the twins weren't with them.

"But then Keeley got separated from the rest of us. Thankfully, she found us later though, right before the grand finale."

"Interesting…" Tess took another sip of coffee. That meant Keeley could have returned to the inn during the fireworks, at the same time the brooch had been planted.

Danny went on to tell them about a hike he'd taken on Friday. "Boy, was it hot. And I went to a barbecue on Saturday at a coworker's." Danny really liked to talk. "Keeley was going to go, but she ended up hanging out with her family instead."

LuAnn smiled. "They all seem really close."

Danny nodded. "Like any family, there's some stuff that really bugs her."

Tess almost told him to stop talking. She didn't want him to tell them anything personal.

"Not anything bad. Stuff about her ancestors…"

Tess perked up. "Oh?" That wasn't gossiping, not exactly.

Before he could go into more detail, the front door swung open. Tess's face grew warm as Keeley appeared.

"Hi, there!" LuAnn said.

Keeley smiled, and Danny grinned. He didn't seem to feel self-conscious that they were just talking about her. "How's it going?" he asked.

"Great." Keeley plopped her backpack down on the counter. "I'm starting on a new project that I'm super excited about. Children on the Underground Railroad. What they brought with them. What challenges they faced. Who they usually traveled with. That sort of thing."

It sounded heartbreaking to Tess, but she didn't say so. Instead she finished her coffee.

Keeley asked for sources. Diaries. Ledgers. Articles. Anything Danny could think of.

"Do you mind pulling the next box of microfiche for us first?" Tess asked. "The second half of July 1863."

"Oh, sure." He grabbed the box Tess had left on the counter, smiled at Keeley, and said, "I'll be right back."

Tess wished she could ask about Keeley's feelings about her ancestors, but of course she couldn't. Before she could say anything at all though, Perry Cooper came through the front door.

"Fancy finding all of you here," Perry said with a twinkle in his eye.

"This is where all the cool people in Marietta hang out," LuAnn joked. "What brings you in?"

"Margaret over at the historical society pointed me this way. She said old copies of the *Marietta Times* are on microfiche."

LuAnn nodded and then introduced Perry to Danny, who had just stepped back up to the counter. "Here's the guy who can help you."

Before Perry could tell Danny what exactly he was looking for, the door dinged again. Marissa waltzed in, swinging a yellow legal pad in her hand.

"See?" Tess laughed. "All the cool people *do* hang out here." She turned to Marissa as she pointed to Perry. "Marissa, this is

Perry Cooper. Perry, Marissa Endicott from the *Marietta Times*." The two shook hands.

Danny turned to Tess. "I'll have to look some more for that roll you want. It isn't where it belongs. Let me help these two first though." He glanced behind Tess. "Who was next?"

"Go ahead," Perry said to Marissa, as he swept his arm toward her.

"I need the microfiche for the *Marietta Times*, all of July 1863."

Danny's face reddened. "I have the first half of the month but not the second. Tess is next up for that—as soon as I find it."

"All right," Marissa said. "I'll take what you have."

Perry spoke up. "I was looking for the second half of July 1863 also. I guess I'll wait my turn."

Danny retrieved the microfiche he'd just filed for Marissa. After that he disappeared into the back for a while and then finally came out empty-handed—and embarrassed. "I can't imagine what happened to it," he said. "But I'll find it. I promise."

Keeley pulled out her phone and glanced at the time. "You don't have to look for my stuff right now. I need to go tell my family goodbye." She smiled at Danny. "I'll come back this afternoon."

"I'll look while you're gone," Danny said. He turned to Tess and LuAnn. "And I'll keep looking for the missing microfiche. I'll let one of you know, before anyone else, when I find it." He seemed a little overwhelmed with all of them stopping by the archives at once.

Tess and Keeley thanked him, and then LuAnn turned to Keeley. "Are you walking back to the inn?"

"Yes."

"We'll walk with you," Tess said.

It grew warmer by the minute as they made their way back to the inn. The predicted high was for the mid-eighties, but it felt hotter than that already.

Keeley chattered on about her new exhibit. "I think a portion of it would be perfect for the inn," she said. "A sort of teaser to get your guests to want to find out what we have to offer."

"I'm glad you and Maybelline are willing to trust us with another exhibit," LuAnn said.

"Oh, we trust you," Keeley said. "In fact, the publicity from the stolen brooch has sent all sorts of people our way."

Tess exhaled. It appeared they could all take marketing lessons from Linda and Jim. A few minutes later, they passed the jewelry store. It was packed with customers, and more tourists were congregated around the window.

Keeley whistled under her breath. "They really seem to know what they're doing."

"It seems so," LuAnn said.

The three continued on down the street. As they turned the corner to the inn, a flashing light startled Tess. "What's going on?"

She grabbed LuAnn's arm and then Keeley's, dragging them along. An ambulance was parked in front of the entrance to the inn.

CHAPTER THIRTEEN

A s Tess, LuAnn, and Keeley stepped off the curb and into the street, Janice shoved the door of the inn wide open. And then paramedics started out, carrying a gurney.

Panic filled Tess as she prayed, "Dear Lord!" Who was it? Thorn? Winnie?

"Granny!" Keeley called out, letting go of Tess and hurrying across the street. Tess and LuAnn took off after her, as Val and Nathan appeared, rushing down the steps of the inn, chasing after the gurney.

"What happened?" Keeley yelled.

"We don't know," Val said. "I'm riding with Granny." She turned to Tess. "Could one of you drive the kids to the hospital?"

"Of course. I can," Tess said. She looked at the EMT. "Are you headed to Marietta Memorial?"

"Yes, ma'am."

"Come on," she said to Keeley and Nathan. "My car is parked out back." As she dug in her purse for her keys, she turned her attention to Janice.

Before she could speak, Janice said, "Stay as long as you need to. Keep us updated." LuAnn nodded in agreement.

Tess assured them she would.

The ambulance driver slammed the back door, and Val climbed in the front. The siren began to wail, the lights still flashing.

Tess led the way. When they reached her car and climbed inside, she asked Nathan what happened.

"We were sitting at a table in the café, playing dominoes, and Granny started talking funny."

"What do you mean?" Keeley asked.

"Her words were all jumbled and a little slurred. Mom asked her if she was okay, and she managed to say her head hurt. Then she kind of slumped over, and—" He paused. "The lady with the curls."

"Janice," Tess said.

"Yeah. She called 911."

"Did Granny fall?" Keeley had turned, as best she could, in her seat. "Did anyone do CPR?"

"No. Nothing like that. She was still breathing. It was like she fell asleep sitting up or something. Mom and I propped her up until the paramedics arrived because we were afraid to move her onto the floor."

"Sounds terrifying." Tess caught Nathan's gaze in the rear-view mirror.

He shrugged. "Not really. Mom and I think she had a stroke. It's not like she's dying or anything."

Keeley reached back and swatted his leg.

"Ouch!"

"Don't be so callous," she said. "You don't know she's not dying."

"She's breathing. Her heart is beating. Stick to the facts." Nathan's voice was as calm as could be.

"Now, now," Tess said as she turned onto Seventh Street. "We'll know more soon. In the meantime, we need to trust God."

"You sound just like Granny," Keeley said.

When they reached Matthew Street, the hospital came into view. As Tess drove up to the emergency room entrance, they could see the ambulance with the back doors wide open.

"Can you drop us off here?" Keeley asked.

"Of course. I'll park and then be right in."

After the kids climbed out, Tess prayed, "Dear Lord, please give Granny the best care possible and heal her, and hold Val, Keeley, and Nathan close as they love and support her." She said "Amen" as she drove into the parking garage. How hard to have a medical emergency when they were all so far from home.

For the next hour, Nathan played games on his phone while Keeley paced around the waiting room. She called Maybelline to tell her she was at the hospital, waiting for word about her grandmother.

Tess sat quietly, praying for Granny and the family and pretty much everything she could think of. The brooch. Her investment through Frank Roberts. Thorn. The AC. God's will for the inn. Lizzie and Michael and the triplets and Jeff Jr. and LuAnn and Janice. And then back to Granny again.

Finally, Val stepped into the waiting room.

She sat down between her children and put an arm around each of them. "Granny had a stroke, like we suspected.

Thankfully, we were with her when it happened, but she'll be in the hospital for at least a few days."

Nathan looked up from his phone. "So we're not going to Chicago today?"

"No," Val said softly. "And not tomorrow or the next day either."

"Where will we stay?" Nathan asked, looking past his mother at Keeley.

"Not with me," Keeley said. "I'm renting a room, remember? With a single bed."

"Of course we won't stay with you," Val said. "I'll see what I can find."

Tess remembered the cancellation from that morning. "We actually have a room open. With two twin beds. Nathan's room, in fact."

"Could we have it?" Val asked.

"Of course, unless someone else has already booked it. I'll call LuAnn."

Tess stepped to the side of the room and made the call. First she gave LuAnn the update about Granny and then asked, "Has the vacant room been booked?"

"No, it's still available."

"Oh, good. Val and Nathan need it."

"It's theirs," LuAnn said. "I'm so sorry about the circumstances but relieved they'll be with us."

As she said goodbye to LuAnn, Tess saw Val making a phone call and then heard her leave a message. "Call me back, honey," she said. "I need to speak with you ASAP."

Then she placed a second call. This time someone answered. "Yes, it's very important. An emergency, actually." She tugged on the heart necklace around her neck. "Would you please put me through to Robbie?"

There was a long pause. Then Val said, "All right. Please tell him to call me back as soon as possible."

She guessed Val was calling her husband. How hard for her to have him so far away at a time like this.

Tess returned to the inn with Keeley and Nathan at two thirty. LuAnn and Janice had already moved Val's things in with Nathan's and cleaned the room.

As they headed up in the elevator, Thorn came through the back entrance struggling to carry a window AC unit. "Let me help," Tess said, hurrying around and grabbing one end.

"Thanks," he said. "I'm taking it up to Maple and Mum. It's the last one to go in."

"Great." They'd reached the elevator, and Tess hit the up button. When the doors opened, she backed inside. "Nathan's still here," she explained. "And Val will be back."

A confused expression crossed Thorn's face as the elevator lurched upward.

She quickly realized he didn't know what had happened and filled him in.

"Poor Granny," he said, his eyes full of compassion. "And Val and Keeley and Nathan too. How are they all doing?"

"All right," Tess said. The doors opened again, and she followed Thorn onto the second floor, grasping the window unit as tightly as she could. "Nathan and Val were both relieved we had a cancellation today so they can stay at the inn."

"I'm relieved too," Thorn said. "I'd hate to think of them trying to find somewhere else—and then having to *go* somewhere else, if they could find a room." They stopped, and Thorn managed to unlock the door and swing it open with one hand as he balanced the unit with the other. Tess followed him into the room. It was immaculate. Perry had been forgoing housekeeping services except for a clean towel every other day, so Tess hadn't been in the room. The bed, with the green spread, was perfectly made. His closed suitcase sat atop the luggage rack in the closet. A row of shirts and then pants hung in the closet. And the door to the bathroom was closed.

"Let's just set the unit down," Thorn said. "Then you go back to the front desk. It's close to check-in time."

It was.

As they made their way to the window, the sound of footsteps thundered down the hall. Nathan. She called out his name. "We're in here!"

A moment later, as Tess and Thorn placed the unit on the floor, Nathan appeared in the doorway. "Hi, Thorn. Can I help?"

"Of course." Thorn stepped forward to shake Nathan's hand. "But first I want to tell you how sorry I am to hear about your grandmother's stroke."

Surprisingly, after he'd been so matter-of-fact in the car, Nathan teared up.

Thorn put his arm around the boy's shoulders. "It sounds as if she's getting good care."

Nathan nodded.

Tess couldn't help but think about Nathan's father not taking Val's call. Perhaps the man wasn't involved much in their lives. Maybe that was what drew the boy to Thorn. Tess stepped away from the window, bumping her hand on the desk. As she turned around, she noticed the stack of books on the desk.

She should have kept walking, but her curiosity got the best of her, and she couldn't pass by without reading the titles. She started at the top of the pile, reading the spine of each book as she moved down the stack. *Cry of Freedom. Of Brothers and Blood. Civil War Battles.* She blinked. *Morgan's Raid. Lost Treasures from the Civil War.*

What in the world? Was Perry really just working on an article about the Civil War—or was he searching for treasure? Including the Bickerton brooch?

In between checking guests in, Tess checked online to see which books in Perry's stack the Washington County Library carried. They had *Lost Treasures from the Civil War* and *Morgan's Raid*, the two she was most interested in.

She kept glancing at her watch as she waited for the last of the guests to check in, hoping she could get to the library before it closed at eight.

Janice was in the basement folding towels, and LuAnn was cleaning the kitchen. Thorn had left after he installed the unit in Perry's room. Keeley had gone back to the archives to see what Danny had found, and Tess assumed Nathan was playing games in his room.

Tess felt a little sad to have most of the Hines family gone. Usually old guests trickled out and new ones trickled in. Rarely did they have such a changeover, except for the few weddings they'd hosted.

However, she knew she'd most likely grow attached to the new guests too. Well, probably not all of them but at least some. She loved meeting new people, learning about their lives, and finding out what they thought of Marietta and the history of the town.

A family of four checked into the honeymoon suite for three days. Parents and their toddler and baby. LuAnn and Janice had set up a cot and crib when they cleaned the room.

One by one the new guests checked in, until seven thirty, when there were only two who hadn't. "Any chance you could cover check-in?" Tess asked LuAnn. "I want to slip out to the library before it closes."

"No problem. And take your time—things have calmed down," she said. "We'll be all right."

It had been quite the day.

Tess grabbed the list and her purse and hurried out the door just as Perry turned the corner of the inn.

He grinned at her. "Where's the fire?"

Tess did her best to smile back. "Things aren't that dire—but just about. I have a couple of books to pick up at the library before it closes."

"Go!" He motioned for her to hurry. "That could be a catastrophe."

She laughed and continued on down the sidewalk. Obviously he was a booklover. And he seemed like a really nice man, but if she'd learned one thing in life it was that people weren't always what they seemed.

She hurried to her car and then drove the seven blocks up Fifth Street. If she had more time, she would walk, but she didn't want to risk being too late.

Once she parked, she rushed up the front steps into the red brick building. She'd written down the call numbers and went straight to the stacks. She pulled *Morgan's Raid* first and then *Lost Treasures from the Civil War*.

After she checked them out, she sat down at a table to skim through them, but the librarian came around and said it was time to close. Tess headed out to her car, started it, turned on the air, and took the time to keep skimming. She looked through *Morgan's Raid* first. It provided more details than LuAnn and Margaret had given and what Tess had learned in her online research. She checked the index for entries about Captain Hines and read those. Granny's story about him getting the idea for the escape from the Ohio State Penitentiary was included, although the author said it couldn't be confirmed if it was true or a rumor that had become a folk legend.

There wasn't much information about Hines past that. Just that he'd survived the war, fled to Toronto, and then returned to Kentucky in 1866 and lived out the rest of his life in Frankfort with his family until his death in 1898. He wrote some about his espionage during the war, but mainly remained quiet. After he died, others told his stories.

Tess put the book on the passenger seat. She'd look through it more later. She picked up the second book and skimmed through it, page by page. It seemed lots of treasures went missing during the Civil War. Mainly in the South, but some in the North too. Gold. Silver. Pocket watches. Necklaces. Rings. Tess kept skimming through the book. But no brooches, at least none that were included in the book. She sighed and closed it.

As she drove back to the inn, she pondered why Perry would have the books in his room. Was he writing about Morgan's Raid? Of course. He was writing about the Civil War in Ohio—it sounded as if the raid was one of the big stories when it came to the state and the war. Perhaps he was tracking other items that disappeared during the raid. Apparently, gold was stolen from a railway station, although it didn't say to whom the gold belonged.

She parked her car behind the inn and climbed out, suddenly tired and dreading another sweltering night on the fourth floor.

When she entered the inn with the books, she was surprised to see Perry sitting at a table in the café talking with LuAnn. Why hadn't she slipped the books into her bag?

She said a quick hello and then turned toward the stairs.

"Looks like you got your books," Perry called out.

"Yes," Tess answered. "I got there just in time."

"Is the top one about the Civil War? I think I recognize it."

LuAnn stood. "What did you get?"

She kicked herself for trying to sneak books by history fanatics. "Actually," Tess said, "both are about the Civil War." She held them up. "I wanted to do some research and see if I could connect Morgan's Raid and the brooch."

"I have both of those books." Perry ran his hand through his thick hair. "I brought them with me. I've been researching the gold that disappeared, although I'm guessing that's long gone. It's not as identifiable as a piece of jewelry."

"Any luck?" LuAnn asked. "As far as tracking the brooch?"

Tess shook her head. "Not yet." And she wasn't any closer to knowing what in the world Perry Cooper was after either.

***

The next morning Tess fed Tom and took time to pet the cat for quite a while, feeling as if perhaps in all of their busyness, he'd been neglected. Then she took Huck on a quick walk. The shih tzu-terrier mix strutted along, enjoying the cool of the morning. When she returned, Val came down for coffee as Tess worked on her to-do list for the day. Val grabbed a to-go cup, filled it, and sat across from Tess. "Are you okay with me leaving Nathan here? I'll check in with him during the day, and Keeley will come by on her lunch break."

"That's fine," Tess said. She liked having Nathan around. "Is there anything I can do to help?"

"Encourage him to eat if he comes down for breakfast. I told Keeley to buy him lunch, so at least he'll eat then." She took a sip of her coffee. "I'll stop and buy snacks on the way back."

"How was your mother-in-law doing last night when you left?"

"She was comfortable and heavily sedated. But there's a lot to be thankful for. I'm so relieved we were with her when this happened."

Tess agreed fervently.

"And I can't let myself think too far ahead." She held her coffee cup with both hands. "There's no way, now, to know what she'll be capable of."

"Is she living on her own?"

"No," Val said. "We moved her into assisted living last year, so that's good. But I wonder, depending on what the prognosis is, if she should come home with us."

Tess felt a wave of empathy. Val had hard decisions ahead of her. "What about her daughters? Are they able to help?"

Val shook her head. "Not much. Connie works full-time, and she's so busy with the twins too. Ellen travels with her job, plus it's Sadie's senior year." She smiled, just a little. "Besides, selfishly, I'd rather have Granny stay with us. My mother passed away when I was twenty-three, from cancer, just after I met Robbie. Granny was always so good to me. She helped us plan our wedding and stayed with us after each of the kids was born.

She came out to California several times and watched the kids so Robbie and I could get away for a long weekend. And we'd visit her at least twice a year." Her eyes grew misty. "I can't imagine our lives without her."

Touched by Val's words, Tess swallowed the lump in her throat.

Val kept talking. "The doctor said she could recover, or mostly. But I don't want to leave her in Chicago. I run my marketing business out of my home office, and Robbie travels quite a bit, so my evenings are free. Nathan just goes to school and comes home. I can't convince him to be involved in extracurricular activities like Keeley was. And being around Granny is really good for him. And for me too."

Tess could see that. Even though having an aged parent move in could be stressful, she was certain Val would know what was best for her family when the time came. She wrote her cell phone number on a piece of paper. "Here's my number. Let me know what you and Granny need or what I can do for Keeley and Nathan."

She walked Val to the front door and collected the newspaper from the stoop. On the front page was another article about the Bickerton brooch. Tess settled back down at the table and kept reading. Apparently the imitation custom brooches had arrived at the jewelers the afternoon before. They were selling for ten dollars. *Buy a Piece of History,* read the headline. There was a photo of Jim and Linda, each holding a brooch.

Tess shook her head. Jim and Linda were marketing pros, there was no doubt about it.

She kept reading. The sidebar of the article was a reprint of the article from 1863 about the brooch being stolen. At the very end, Marissa added a paragraph, teasing readers to stay tuned. *Who will solve the mystery of the stolen brooch?* she wrote. *And when?*

At least Marissa hadn't managed to get a copy of the Bickerton photograph of Charisse wearing the brooch. But maybe after this article, the historical society would give it to her. Tess was surprised she hadn't interviewed Thelma and Irene yet. Or Brad. Or Charlotte.

Tess left the paper on the table and headed to the kitchen to help LuAnn and Janice finish setting out a continental breakfast for the guests.

An hour later, most of the guests had finished their breakfast when Nathan, showered and dressed, came down the stairs.

"Good morning," Tess said.

He grunted. It could have been a positive response, but she wasn't sure.

Once he'd filled his plate with muffins and poured himself a cup of coffee, he sat down at the table closest to the corner of the café. "What do you have planned for today?" Tess asked him as she cleared a table nearby.

He shrugged. "I've been researching what you all can do to boost your Wi-Fi speed. I think you must have an outdated router."

"Oh." She wasn't sure what to do about that, but it seemed they now had an IT expert on staff.

Nathan's eyes lit up as Thorn came around the corner of the office. Plus a handyman's assistant.

Tess's phone dinged as she headed back to the kitchen. Once she'd put the dishes in the sink and washed her hands, she checked it. A text from Val. *Granny's in the ICU with pneumonia. I hate to ask this of you, but could you give the kids a ride up to the hospital? I've called Keeley, and she's on the way over to the inn.*

Of course, Tess texted back. *We'll be right up. Do you want me to tell Nathan?*

I just texted him, Val wrote back. *He hates phone calls. Thank you!*

Nathan was waiting for her when she stepped out of the kitchen. He held up his phone. "I guess my plans for the day have changed."

Tess nodded. "I'll just grab my purse. Keeley should be here any minute."

"How bad do you think Granny is?"

Tears threatened to fill Tess's eyes. "I don't know. We'll have to see what information your mom has."

He nodded. "She's been old, like forever. But I guess I've taken it for granted that she'd always be around. It makes me feel funny."

Tess put her arm around him. "Life has a way of doing that."

CHAPTER FOURTEEN

July 18, 1863

Mr. Siloam squared his shoulders and turned to Mr. Gidden. "You know as well as everyone in this room that Prudence and Jason Willard did not steal that brooch. There aren't two more honest people in the whole state of Ohio, in the entire nation of the United States of America, North and South."

Mr. Gidden crossed his arms over his chest. "The evidence doesn't agree with you, Mr. Siloam." He glared for a moment and then said, "Now do as I told you to. Go get the sheriff. And then stop by the newspaper office and tell them to send a reporter. Make sure to explain I have a big story to share."

Mr. Siloam shook his head, and Mr. Gidden rolled back on his heels.

"It is all right," Jason whispered to Mr. Siloam. "Do as he says."

Mr. Siloam gave Prudence a pained look. She nodded. Finally, he headed out the back door.

Prudence turned to Ernestine. "Take Moses outside, and stay close to the hotel."

Ernestine took Moses's hand. Moses glanced at Prudence, but she simply nodded, and he followed along.

"Go along and finish cleaning up until the sheriff gets here," Mr. Gidden said, nodding at the stove.

Dumbfounded, Prudence stared at the man. "Haven't I already lost my job?"

"Not until you're arrested."

Prudence exhaled slowly. He wanted her to work right up until the moment she was arrested? Then again, if by some miracle she wasn't arrested, she'd still need a job. She pushed up her sleeves and returned to the stove.

Jason stepped to the door to check on Moses and Ernestine. When he came back he whispered that they were gathering wood chips.

Sheriff Jones arrived first. He was a white-haired man with a trimmed white beard. He seemed as puzzled as Mr. Siloam had been about Prudence being a suspect in a robbery. After Mr. Gidden explained the situation, Sheriff Jones said, "Tell me again, exactly, what you're accusing her of."

"Stealing Mrs. Bickerton's brooch. It's made of rubies, diamonds, and sapphires." As Mr. Gidden spoke, the newspaper editor arrived. He must have considered it an important story. That didn't bode well for Prudence.

The sheriff tugged on his beard and urged Mr. Gidden to continue. "And how did she steal it?"

"I'd given it to her for safekeeping. She stole it right out from under me."

"But how would she expect to get away with it?" the sheriff asked. "If you knew she had it."

Mr. Gidden's face reddened. "That's for her to explain."

The newspaper editor jotted down notes, writing furiously.

The sheriff turned to Prudence. "Tell me exactly what happened."

Prudence told him detail by detail everything that had transpired from Mr. Gidden giving her the pouch, to the soldier knocking her basket out of her hands and scooping up the pouch, to her and Jason telling Mr. Gidden what happened. "I did not know there was a brooch in the pouch until Mr. Gidden said so this morning."

"Arrest her," Gidden said. "And then go search her house. Hopefully they haven't buried it somewhere already."

Sheriff Jones shook his head. "I don't have enough evidence to arrest her." He looked at Mr. Gidden. "How will you explain entrusting the cook with the Bickerton brooch to your boss?"

The man's face reddened again. "It was the most prudent thing to do, considering the circumstances."

The sheriff sighed. "That, sir, is open to debate." He turned to Prudence. "I'll do some asking around. I know where to find you if I have more questions."

"Yes, sir. At home or here."

"Here? You haven't been fired?"

"No, sir."

The sheriff gave Mr. Gidden another long gaze.

When Gidden didn't respond, the sheriff bid them all farewell, and the newspaper editor, without asking anything, followed him out of the kitchen.

Gidden retreated to the dining room, and Prudence told Jason to take Moses and Ernestine on home.

"She'd be a help to thee," Jason said.

"I know, but I do not want to risk having her in town. There is too much uncertainty. If the sheriff comes back and arrests me, Gidden might implicate her too."

Jason agreed and left. Prudence heard voices outside, and then her family was gone.

She continued on with her work, finishing the cleanup and then starting the noon meal. Mr. Siloam came into the kitchen to ask what the verdict was.

"Undecided," she said.

"I've told the staff what Mr. Gidden has accused you of. Everyone is horrified. And the patrons who overheard are too."

"I appreciate your efforts," Prudence said, "but thee doesn't need to defend me. The Good Lord will see to it."

"Well," Mr. Siloam said, "everyone knows you'd never do such a thing."

Prudence thanked him and continued on with her work, silently repeating, "Be strong and of a good courage, fear not, nor be afraid of them: for the LORD thy God, he it is that doth go with thee; he will not fail thee, nor forsake thee."

She believed with all her heart that the Lord her God wouldn't fail her, nor forsake her. She kept repeating the verse as the noon meal was served, as she cleaned up, and then as she prepared supper. She kept repeating it after she'd finished for the day and stepped out the back door to head home.

The sheriff hadn't returned with more questions, nor had Gidden entered the kitchen for the rest of the day. If no news was good news, why did she still feel so unsettled?

Instead of going straight home, she detoured to the Quaker church. She went around to the back door, which was unlocked. "Hello," she called out as she entered.

No one responded. The interior was dim, but she was so familiar with the meeting room that she could have found her way around blindfolded. She settled onto the last wooden bench and rested her elbows on her knees and her chin in her hands. She stared down at the worn wooden floor. Life had a way of wearing people down, just like years of shoes shuffling over wood wore it down. But the Lord wanted her to remain strong in Him. To not give in to fear. He wanted to change the adversity in her life, even being falsely accused by a man like Gidden, into motivation to help others.

There were no packages to be transported, but that didn't mean there weren't people to help. There was Ernestine. And the sheriff. The reporter. And Mr. Siloam. And the staff who supported her.

There was Gidden too. He was horribly mistaken. Maybe he realized what a foolish decision he'd made to send the pouch with her and feared Mr. Bickerton's reaction.

Another verse came to mind. *"In every thing give thanks: for this is the will of God in Christ Jesus concerning you."*

She had so much to be thankful for. The brooch was taken and not Ernestine. The soldier didn't see Jason at the gate and pursue him. Moses hadn't run toward her. Yes, God had been faithful. The brooch was the least valuable thing at the scene of the crime. Thank the Lord that was all the soldier had taken.

Peace washed through her. The Lord would see to her needs.

She stood and walked across the worn wood to the door. As she stepped outside, someone called her name. "Prudence Willard!"

It wasn't Jason or anyone from the hotel. She stepped out of the shadow cast by the building and into the street. Sheriff Jones walked toward her, the reporter at his side.

"I am here," she replied, standing as tall as she could.

"You're under arrest," Sheriff Jones said. "For the theft of the Bickerton brooch." He said some other words that she couldn't comprehend. "I must take you to jail now," he said.

"May I go home and tell my family first?"

He shook his head. "You must come with me now."

"So be it," Prudence whispered, looking toward the heavens. She turned and marched with the sheriff down the road.

CHAPTER FIFTEEN

By Wednesday morning Granny's condition hadn't changed any, but Nathan stayed at the inn instead of going back to the hospital. Tess imagined it was tedious for him to hang out there all day and probably not a help to Val or Granny. Once Nathan had gone upstairs after breakfast, LuAnn brought out her notebook. Janice joined her and Tess at the counter. "Do we have any updates?" she asked.

Tess shook her head.

"Where did Perry go today?" LuAnn asked.

Tess didn't know and neither did Janice.

"How about if I go over to the jewelry store," Janice said. "I can find out what people are saying and maybe talk to Jim to see if he remembers anything more about the theft."

"How about the Hines family?" LuAnn asked. "Are there any more connections there?"

"Well," Tess said, "they are descendants of Thomas Hines."

Janice rubbed her forehead. "But there's no evidence Thomas stole the brooch or that it ended up in his family, right?"

Tess nodded. "That's right."

"I'll leave it as coincidental, at this point." LuAnn made a mark in her notebook.

"Let's talk more after you're back from talking to Jim. Talk to Linda too," Tess said. "She seems so innocent. But maybe she's just a good actress."

Janice grinned. "Oh, I will."

While Janice was gone, as LuAnn and Tess stood at the counter going over the to-do list for the day, Charlotte stopped back by the inn. This time with Brad.

Charlotte always looked like a million bucks. Today she wore a pencil skirt and a sleeveless silk blouse. She leaned against the counter and looked at Tess. "I didn't realize, until I did some digging, that it was under your watch that the brooch was stolen."

Brad looked uncomfortable.

LuAnn gasped. "None of us would have done anything differently than Tess did that day."

Charlotte bit her lower lip.

Tess tilted her head. She'd certainly felt the responsibility of that, but LuAnn and Janice had encouraged her not to feel guilty about it.

Charlotte's accent grew more pronounced. "Did you think about hiring security? Having it accessed in the bank vault instead of taking it to the jewelry store?" Her lip quivered. Cleary the topic was emotional for her, and she appeared surprisingly vulnerable.

"We had no idea what it was worth at that point," Tess said. "We still don't know what it's worth."

"Diamonds, sapphires, and rubies. I'd say it's worth quite a bit."

Tess agreed with her but didn't say so as she tried to calm the defensive feeling that was welling up inside of her.

"Officer Lewis is working on solving this. All of us want to find out where the brooch came from—and who stole it," LuAnn said, her voice low. "It's our main priority right now."

Grateful for her friend's words, Tess nodded in agreement, but she couldn't find her voice to say anything.

"Come on, Cuz, I'll buy you a cup of coffee," Brad said, tugging on Charlotte's arm.

"Here?"

"Anywhere you want."

"Then let's go to Jeremiah's." Charlotte turned back to Tess. "Hopefully the brooch will soon be found, and we can put this unpleasantness behind us."

Tess nodded. "That's what we all want, believe me."

After they said goodbye, as Brad escorted Charlotte to the door, he turned, and with his eyebrows raised, gave both Tess and LuAnn a shrug.

Tess knew he was trying to be reassuring, but her heart sank even more. She considered Charlotte a friend, not an adversary. She turned to LuAnn. "It is my fault the brooch was stolen," she said. "Of course there's more I could have done to prevent it."

"Don't go there," LuAnn answered. "And don't let Charlotte get to you. She's upset, is all. You've done nothing wrong."

Tess wasn't so sure.

After she and LuAnn cleaned the guest rooms and had some lunch, Janice finally returned—with a fake brooch pinned to her shirt. "They gave this to us." She laughed. "To share."

"How kind." LuAnn reached out and touched it and then said, sarcastically, "It feels so real."

Tess took a step backward from the brooch to get a better look at it. "What did you think about Jim and Linda?"

"Both are really nice," Janice said. "I got the same impression about Linda that you did. She was so worried about you and Jim as she told the story. She seemed traumatized by it, and still does. Jim seemed pretty matter-of-fact, but that could just be their different personalities."

"Was the shop busy?"

"Packed," Janice answered. "That's what took me so long—we kept getting interrupted. You're right about them being marketing geniuses. Everyone was really eating up the whole story." She shook her head. "Oh, and get this. They have a copy of the Bickerton photo showing the brooch. Linda went to the historical society, trying to find more information, and they sold her a copy."

Tess tried not to sound alarmed. "So is that image now part of their archives?"

"Apparently so."

LuAnn agreed. "Irene signed a comprehensive release for them to scan it, so technically the historical society does have the right to make copies and sell them."

"And Irene and Thelma probably don't care," Tess said.

"Well, it was fortunate for Jim and Linda. They've added the photo to their marketing display." Janice pushed her curls away from her forehead. "It's all pretty convincing."

Tess sighed. There was no doubt now that the brooch that had been in their possession for such a short time was the Bickerton brooch.

The next morning, after the breakfast rush, Jeff Jr. arrived at the inn to look at Tess's quarterly investment statements with her. It wasn't that she couldn't go through them herself. She had, over and over. She had experience with that sort of thing and managed her finances and the inn's just fine. But she wanted a second set of eyes in case she was missing anything. Plus she'd be crazy not to have her CPA son offer a second opinion.

They headed up to the fourth floor for some privacy, but when they arrived Thorn and Nathan were in the common area next to the window, by the comfy chairs. Their backs were to the door.

"What are you doing?" Tess asked.

Thorn glanced over his shoulder. "Oh, hello."

Now Tess could see what they were up to—installing an AC window unit. She wasn't sure whether to laugh or cry. Perhaps this meant it would be another week before the AC would be fixed.

"I know the three of you have been suffering up here," Thorn said. "I came across this unit at the secondhand store. Hopefully it will help up here."

Tess thanked him. "Any word on when the part will arrive?"

"Hopefully by this afternoon. Or tomorrow. I just put this in—"

A loud bang stopped him.

Tess stepped to the window. "What was that?"

Thorn barked, "Stay back." He put his arm in front of Nathan and scooted him away from the window too.

Jeff Jr. cleared his throat and said, "I think it was just a car backfiring."

Tess cringed.

Thorn exhaled. "I think you're right." He ran his hand through his hair. "Those fireworks have me on edge."

Just the night before, someone set more Roman candles off. It seemed like by now all the fireworks would be used up. Instead, they kept coming.

Jeff Jr. sat down at the table while Tess made a pot of coffee in the kitchen area.

A few minutes later, Thorn and Nathan secured the window unit and turned it on. "This will definitely help," Thorn said.

Tess thanked them, and then they left.

After she'd poured coffee for Jeff Jr. and herself, she retrieved the paperwork from her file cabinet and settled down at the table with him. They went through the documents together, one by one.

The losses had started a year ago. First they were so small that they weren't significant. But in the last quarter they'd dropped substantially.

"Did you notice when that happened?" Jeff Jr. asked.

"Of course," Tess answered. "But that has happened before, and the investment rallied. He's saying that it'll rally again."

"I wonder why he sent the letter that alarmed you. Why didn't he just wait it out?"

"I have no idea," Tess said. "When I asked him, he said he'd overreacted."

"That sounds unlikely." Jeff Jr. stared at the document. "I wonder if he was considering getting out of the business at one point."

Tess pressed her palms down on the tabletop. "Why would he do that?"

"Maybe he'd made a really bad investment and hoped people would cash out before it was evident."

While Jeff Jr. read through the statements again, Tess googled Frank Bryant on her phone. It seemed he'd been in the Marietta area since he graduated from Ohio State's School of Business in 1988. He'd been a member of the Chamber of Commerce for years and the president a few years back. She clicked on the next article, one that had run in the *Marietta Times* when he was interviewed during the financial crisis of 2008. He was quoted as asking people to hang on to their investments until the economy rebounded. *"I have confidence that if people can sit tight, they'll make their investment back and more. It's important to rely on financial professionals who won't panic."*

Tess thought of all the professionals who made unwise decisions during the financial crisis that only made it worse. Had Frank Bryant held on to his investments during that time? Or had he only expected his clients to? Jeffrey had held on to theirs, and it had paid off. But that didn't mean she needed to do the same thing now.

"What's up?" Jeff Jr. asked.

She read the quote to him.

Jeff Jr. chuckled. "That's the standard line, right? Investment 101."

"I suppose you're right," Tess said.

"How about if I go with you to talk to Mr. Bryant?" Jeff Jr. slipped the documents back into the file. "In person. Maybe we can get more information out of him than what he's given you so far."

"That's a great idea. Thank you." Tess picked up the file. "I'll give Frank a call and set up a time."

They took the stairs instead of the elevator. As they reached the lobby, a little boy yelled, "Where is Mimi?"

"Liam!" Tess called as she turned the corner.

Lizzie and the triplets sat in the parlor. Lizzie held her phone to her ear, and Tess's began to buzz.

She laughed, pulled it from her pocket, and held it up. "It's you."

The triplets were running toward her. Liam wrapped his arms around Jeff Jr.'s legs as Harper and Henry nearly tackled Tess.

"Sorry to stop by unannounced." Lizzie put her phone back in her pocket and stood. "We were out running errands and decided to stop by. We haven't seen much of you in the last couple of weeks."

Tess scooted to her daughter, pulling the kids along in exaggerated moves, laughing as she did.

"Hey, let go of Mimi." Lizzie grabbed Harper by the arm. "You could topple her over and hurt her."

Tess feared they nearly could. In another year or two, they could without a doubt. Henry let go, but Harper hung on. Liam was already on Jeff Jr.'s shoulders. "What a great surprise," Jeff Jr. said. "I'm glad I was here."

"Speaking of, what exactly *are* you doing here?" Lizzie patted her big brother on the back. "It's not like you to be out and about in the middle of the day."

Jeff Jr. glanced at Tess.

"He was giving me his opinion about an investment."

"From Dad's life insurance policy?"

Tess shook her head. "It's a small-business investment your father made years ago. It took a dive. Jeff is trying to help me sort it out."

Tess turned her face away from Harper and toward Lizzie and whispered, "Do you have time for a snack? Winnie made chocolate chip cookies."

Lizzie nodded and smiled, and they all herded the kids into the café. There was nothing Tess loved more than to be with her children and grandchildren. For a moment she had a respite from all her worries.

Friday afternoon, as Tess went over the accounts, her phone buzzed again. This time it was Val. Each time the woman called, Tess feared something horrible had happened.

But this time it was good news. "The antibiotics did the trick, and Granny has been moved out of ICU," Val said. "I called Nathan's phone, but he didn't answer. Have you seen him?"

"He's helping Thorn fix a stuck window." Tess wondered if they should put the kid on the payroll.

"He must be absorbed with the task," Val said. "But I'm just so glad he's out of his room and doing something helpful. Would you tell him to check his phone when you see him, please?"

"Of course," Tess answered. "And I'm so happy to hear the good news about your mother-in-law." Tess knew that didn't mean they'd all be going home anytime soon, but hopefully it wouldn't be too long. They only had a few days until they'd have to give up their room at the inn for another reservation.

When Nathan followed Thorn off the elevator, Tess relayed the information to Nathan.

He grinned. "That's great news." But then his face fell. "Does that mean we'll be leaving soon?"

Tess wanted to give him a hug. "Your mom didn't say."

"It's not that I don't want Granny to get well and be able to go home. It's just that..." His voice trailed off.

"What?"

He shook his head.

She took a teasing approach. "You like it here? You like us?"

He smiled as he hurried to follow Thorn down to the basement. "Don't let it go to your head," he called over his shoulder.

A few minutes later, Jeff Jr. stopped by to take Tess to meet with Frank Bryant. He worked out of an office on the edge of town. Tess had been there one other time, a couple of months after her husband had died.

As she led the way out of the inn, her face lit up at the sight of the vintage red 1953 Chevrolet pickup truck that had belonged to Jeffrey and that Jeff Jr. had helped his father restore.

Jeff Jr. hurried ahead to open the passenger door. "I thought we'd go in style."

"How thoughtful of you." She climbed up onto the black bench seat. After Jeff Jr. closed her door, he hurried around to the driver's door. He drove slowly through town, drawing stares and waves. Everyone appreciated the old truck. It brought back memories for some—and struck awe in others.

As they passed Uptown Jewelers, several tourists walked out, carrying large cloth bags. Tess craned her neck. The brooch was printed on the outside of the bags. She shook her head. Jim and Linda were now giving away swag connected to the brooch. Or, more likely, they were charging for the bags.

She rolled down her window, which was a necessity because the pickup didn't have AC. The wind blew through her hair — and also made it hard for her to understand what Jeff Jr. was saying. She listened harder and realized he was talking about the accounting firm he worked with. They'd recently added several new clients, and his workload had increased.

Tess nodded as he talked. Jeff Jr. took after his dad as far as his work ethic and dependability.

Once they reached Frank Bryant's office, Jeff Jr. parked the pickup and quickly hurried to open Tess's door. He was like his father in so many ways. Tess led the way into the waiting room of the office. The furniture had been updated in the last few years with a couch and matching chair that were sleek leather, and a stainless steel coffee table and end tables. An abstract black and brown painting hung on the wall, and the window coverings were a modern, accordion style.

The receptionist greeted them and said Frank would be with them in just a minute.

Twenty minutes later, Frank still hadn't appeared.

"I'll go check on him," the receptionist said.

When she returned, she said that he was on an important call. "Can you come back in an hour?"

"An hour?" Tess couldn't imagine why his call would last that long.

The woman seemed embarrassed by the request. "Or he could give you a call as soon as this one ends."

Tess glanced at Jeff Jr.

He shrugged.

Tess turned back to the receptionist. "I really wanted Jeff to be in on a meeting with Frank."

"That's understandable," she said. "But I don't know what to tell you. You can stick around—or Frank can call."

"All right," Tess said. "If Frank can't call soon, I'll set up a new appointment with him."

When they reached the inn, Tess suggested Jeff Jr. come in for an iced coffee. "Just for a few minutes," she said.

Jeff Jr. agreed, but then, just as they entered the inn, her phone rang. It was Frank. "Let's go into the office," Tess said to Jeff Jr. and then answered the phone, putting it on Speaker.

"Tess! So sorry to have kept you waiting," he said. "I was double-checking with one of the companies I've invested in to give you the latest information—but I was put on hold. Finally they picked up, and I got the information I needed."

Tess thought it odd that he kept her waiting for that when he could have had his receptionist take the call, but she didn't address that. Instead she said, "My son is here with me. He's a CPA." She sat down at the desk. "I had him go over the statements from the last year."

"Great!" Frank's voice sounded cheery. "I apologize again for sending that letter. Thankfully, I only sent it to my most vulnerable clients, ones whose investments are pretty thin."

Frank had tried to get her to invest Jeffrey's life insurance money with him, but she'd declined. She didn't want the bulk of her resources in risky investments. Again she regretted not closing the account earlier.

Frank continued. "Like I said before, I have an investment that's really turning around. I wasn't sure the owners had the savvy to pull it off, but, one day at a time, they are."

"What's the business?" Jeff Jr. asked as he leaned against the wall.

"The new ice cream shop, Fundae, located on Front Street. Now that the tourist season is in full swing, they're doing much better."

Tess knew exactly where the business was—across the street from Uptown Jewelers. Nathan and Keeley had gone there a couple of days ago and had to wait thirty minutes for a table. "That's wonderful," she said, placing her phone in the middle of the desk. "I'm very happy for them. And you. But I need to know, what procedure do I follow if I want to close the account?"

"I strongly advise against it."

"Of course you do," Tess answered. "But what's the procedure?"

Frank paused and then said, "Jeff wouldn't want you to cash out. He believed in investing in small businesses."

Tess leaned back in her chair. "Yes, he did. But my circumstances are very different now than ours were back then. I think he would want me to be prudent with my investments."

Frank didn't answer.

"What is the procedure?" Jeff Jr. asked. The volume of his voice startled Tess. "What document does my mom need to fill out? How long from when she makes the request until it's processed?"

The man cleared his throat. "I'm only looking out for your mother's best interests."

"My mother is perfectly capable of doing that herself."

Frank guffawed. "Then why did you come with her to my office today?"

Jeff Jr. crossed his arms and didn't answer.

Frank cleared his throat. "Look, I've been stressed out with all of this. I'm sorry. Could we start over?"

Jeff Jr. continued to stay quiet, and Tess said, "Go ahead."

"Look, I know you're capable of sorting all this out and making your own decision," Frank said. "And I really apologize for being condescending. I don't know what got into me. I just ask that you give me another week. That's all."

"I'll need to give this more time before I make my decision." Tess stared at her phone. "I'll let you know what I decide."

"Thank you." Frank's voice grew louder. "You won't regret thinking it over. Or sticking with me."

Tess, wanting to end the call, said, "Thank you for your time" and added a quick "Goodbye."

Frank grunted and then said, "Jeff Jr., I'm truly sorry I didn't get to meet you in person."

"Goodbye," Jeff Jr. said.

After she ended the call, Tess said, "That was weird. I don't remember him being on edge or manipulative like that."

"Yeah." Jeff Jr. stood up straight. "He was definitely over the top. I wonder what's really going on."

Tess did too. Her gut told her to recoup her money, even at a loss. She'd sleep on it until Monday morning and then decide.

After Jeff Jr. left, Tess went to the front desk, staring at the reservations ledger as if it might give her the answer of what to do concerning her investment.

It didn't. But someone yelling brought her back from her conundrum. Tess stepped out into the lobby.

The shouting continued. "You followed us here to Marietta and the inn, right? You were the 'cousin' who showed up on the Facebook page. Who tried to get included in our family reunion." It was Keeley, yelling at Perry, who sat at the piano, his hands suspended just above the keys. "Was it your intention to steal the brooch all along?"

Tess stopped in the middle of the parlor area, dumbfounded. What was Keeley saying?

Perry's hands fell to the keys with a clunk and a cacophony of sound. Then he stood and faced Keeley. "You're right. I've always been fascinated with Thomas Hines—both with his gumption and his genius. I wanted to hang out with his descendants. I thought maybe I could learn more about him from all of you."

"But how did you find us?"

"I friended a third cousin of yours who lives in Pennsylvania. She told me about the Facebook page. That's how I found you."

Keeley crossed her arms. "Keep talking. About the brooch."

"I'd read, in the research I'd done, that one historian suspected the Bickerton brooch ended up in the possession of Thomas Hines. But I didn't think for one minute the brooch would be here. Why would it be? Who would bring something that valuable along on a family reunion trip?" He shook his head. "And regardless of your suspicions, I certainly didn't steal it."

Keeley's face was red and not just from the heat. "Why would we believe you? You've been stalking us."

"Look." Perry held his hands up, as if surrendering. "It was a stupid thing to do. I don't expect you to forgive me, but I really am sorry. I needed to come to Marietta anyway, so I thought I might as well stay in the same hotel as Thomas Hines's descendants."

Keeley stomped away to where Tess was standing while Perry sat back down at the piano. This time he started playing the blues.

"I actually heard from that third cousin who told Perry about our reunion page." Keeley shook her head. "She sent me a message and asked if Perry had shown up. He'd friended her online on another family page a couple of years ago." Keeley sighed. "When he asked about joining the group, he implied he was related. He knew a lot about the family. Now I know why. He used the name Walter though—apparently it's his middle name. It just really freaks me out."

Tess agreed. She could see why. Tess was seeing Perry in a whole new light.

The music grew a little louder.

"Have you told your mom?" Tess asked.

"No, she has too much to worry about."

"She'd probably want to know." Tess hoped Nathan was really safe staying at the inn all day. Perry hadn't interacted with him, that she knew of, but come to think of it, the man had seemed intrigued with the Hines family, usually staying around at breakfast time until they'd left before he went off on his day trips.

Keeley slipped her backpack over her shoulder. "I came to check on Nathan. Mom's been calling him, but he hasn't been picking up."

"I'm not sure where he is..." Tess looked around. "Janice and LuAnn should be around here somewhere though. Maybe they've seen him."

"Here I am!" Janice came up from the basement, carrying a basket of towels and doing a little dance to Perry's music as she reached the lobby. "My, he's good, isn't he? We could start a piano bar while he's here."

"I agree." Tess was aware of the lack of enthusiasm in her voice. What in the world was Perry up to? She changed the subject. "Have you seen Nathan?"

"Last I saw him, he was helping Thorn power wash the patio."

Keeley shook her head. "I don't know what's happened to my brother. We can barely get him to leave his room back home. Here it seems as if he hasn't been on his computer all week."

Tess doubted that was true, but it was good to hear he was doing more interacting than usual. Keeley headed out to the patio, and Janice carried the basket to the elevator.

Perry finished his song and came to the front desk. "That was beautiful," Tess said. "Where'd you learn to play like that?"

Perry smiled. "My mother was a pianist. She had high hopes when she was young, but the most she ended up doing was playing the organ at our church. However, she dedicated herself to teaching me everything she knew."

"I'd say it paid off." Tess nodded to the baby grand. "Do you play professionally? For weddings? In clubs? Anything like that?"

"Some," he answered. "I've also done some musical theater. But the thing I like best about music, besides being a conduit for emotion, is the history behind it. For example, if I'm playing B.B. King, I'm thinking about him growing up on a cotton plantation and then going on to become the 'King of the Blues' and all the things he witnessed in between."

Tess could see how that would be the perspective of someone who loved history so much—if that was in fact what he loved. Perhaps that was a front, and what he really loved was lost treasure.

She did enjoy his music, but she was also alarmed by his deception. "Is there anything else you need to tell me about choosing to stay here at the inn while the Hines family was here?"

He winced. "I know it makes me look creepy, but please believe me. My intentions were only to observe Thomas Hines's descendants. The man fascinates me—not exactly in a good way. But still, he fascinates me."

Tess nodded. "But I need to know our guests are safe—all of them."

"Absolutely," he said. "In fact, I'll speak with Val and explain everything to her. I don't want anyone to think worse of me than they already do."

Tess wasn't sure whether to believe him or not. Either he was sincere or a very good actor.

Perry yawned. "I'm going to head upstairs and rest for a while."

He headed off, and Tess concentrated on the reservations for the day. Two new sets of guests were coming in.

A few minutes later, when LuAnn arrived from running errands, Tess motioned her toward the office. When they'd entered and closed the door, Tess told her about the interaction between Keeley and Perry. "Don't you think that's odd that he followed them here? And that he knew about the brooch and speculated that Thomas Hines might have ended up with it after the war?"

LuAnn pulled out her notebook. "All of that is definitely worth writing down. I'd say Perry Cooper is our number one suspect at this point."

CHAPTER SIXTEEN

On Saturday morning, after breakfast was served, the original AC repairman arrived. As he walked into the inn, he held up a part. "This better do it," he said. "If it doesn't, we'll need to put in a whole new unit for you. This has gone on too long."

Tess agreed. The window unit on the fourth floor helped, but she woke up several times during the night from the heat. She hadn't gotten a good night's sleep in over a week.

The repairman headed down to the basement, and Tess joined Janice in cleaning up after breakfast.

Janice wiped her forehead with the back of her hand. "What do you think the chances are the repair will work this time?"

Tess shrugged. "It's either this latest fix works or else they need to put in a whole new unit. It's one thing to try to keep the rooms cool, but it's impossible to keep the entire inn cool." Thankfully, the guests had been understanding.

"It wasn't that long ago that we managed to live without AC," Janice said. "Remember?"

"I do." Tess chuckled.

"What are you thinking of?" Janice asked.

"The hotel my parents ran. There were ceiling fans in some rooms. Box window fans in others. Screens on all the windows."

Janice nodded. "Sounds like the house I grew up in. We'd open the windows at night and then close everything up during the day."

"Exactly," Tess said. "And when there was thunder and lightning and then rain, the whole house smelled wonderful."

Janice sighed. "You know I kind of miss those days. I remember my mama in the morning going through the house, shutting the windows. Trying to keep the cool air in as long as possible." Her eyes lit up. "Now we don't think we'll survive a day without AC, without every little luxury."

Tess laughed. "And we're right. We're so much more comfortable now. Believe me, I wouldn't have it any other way. And, if you're being honest, you wouldn't either."

Janice laughed too. "You're right. Still, it's good to remember how things used to be. How we all got by."

Tess agreed. By the time they had everything cleaned up, there was a whirring noise and then a *thunk* in the basement as if the repairman had just slammed his toolbox shut. Tess hurried to the nearest register. Cold air was flowing through it.

She turned to Janice with a huge smile on her face.

"Yeah, well, that's happened before." Janice had her hands on her hips. "Remember? And it didn't last."

"It's going to this time," Tess said. "I'm sure of it."

She stepped out of the kitchen as the repairman reached the lobby, followed by Thorn. "How about some of Winnie's berry tart to celebrate?" Tess asked.

The repairman declined the invitation and said he needed to hurry along to his next assignment, but Thorn took her up on the offer. Considering that the AC was fixed—hopefully for good—he seemed a little down.

"Are you doing okay?" Tess put a cup of black coffee and a piece of tart in front of him.

He didn't answer, but his eyes grew a little cloudy. Finally he said, "I think so."

She sat down beside him. "What's up?"

"First of all, I'm sorry I've been on edge this last week or so."

"Well," she said, "we've had a lot going on."

He nodded. "To be honest, the Fourth of July always puts me on edge."

"Oh?"

"The fireworks. The explosions. The Roman candles."

She tilted her head as she listened.

Thorn took a bite of tart and then said, "You're not getting it, are you?"

Tess thought harder. What was she missing?

"Desert Storm," he said. "I started on the Saudi border but ended up going into Iraq. Scud missiles were coming in at us. Some days nothing would happen, and all we'd do was hurry up and wait. But other days we were targets without any rhyme or reason."

"Oh." Tess exhaled slowly. "How obtuse of me."

He shook his head. "People rarely think a Desert Storm veteran has any reason to be affected. It was barely a war.

Everything was over in a month, practically. Not that many people died..." His voice trailed off.

"But?"

"It was still traumatic."

Tess reached over and put her hand on his arm. "What happened?"

"It seems like ancient history if I think about how long ago February 1991 was." He paused for a moment and rubbed the side of his face. "But in my mind, it's as if it were yesterday. Especially when all of those fireworks are going off."

He took a deep breath. "I was part of a special operations force on a 'scud hunt.' We were trying to find the camouflaged Iraqi trucks that were launching the scud missiles at coalition troops. One hit a barracks in Saudi Arabia and killed twenty-eight and injured a hundred more."

Tess nodded. She remembered. It had been a horrible time.

"I had a young kid working with me, only nineteen years old. Just out of boot camp. He was a little awkward and took everything literally. I was forever having to correct him and keep him in check. The sun was just setting as we found one of the camouflaged trucks. We'd started approaching it when we came under fire. I motioned for everyone to fall back." Thorn paused a moment and took a sip of coffee. Then he continued with his story. "Everyone did but the kid. Probably because he had the initial instructions stuck in his head. Anyway, this kid got hit by a sniper and fell to the ground."

Thorn took another sip of coffee, and for a moment Tess feared he was done with the story. But then he said, "I knelt beside him. His eyes were wide with that deer-in-the-headlights look. I scooped him up to get him out of there. His helmet fell off, and I could see he'd been hit in the forehead. For a moment I thought we could save him, but he gasped a few times and then died in my arms without saying a word." Thorn's gaze met Tess's. "Just like that, he was gone."

Tess squeezed his arm.

"His name was Kevin Randolph, and he was from New Mexico. I always intended to write his parents a letter, but I couldn't seem to come up with the courage to do it." His gazed shifted to the window. "We hunkered down in the sand and radioed for backup. They didn't come until dawn, and we waited in the dark with the stars shining down on us as gunfire and rockets ricocheted through the night. I held on to Randolph as the back-up troops blew up the truck and until the chopper landed to take him home."

"Thorn, I'm so sorry," Tess said.

He clenched his jaw. "So am I. If I'd yelled 'fall back, Randolph,' he wouldn't have been killed. If I'd made it clear he needed to follow the new instructions."

"It wasn't your fault."

"I know that," he said. "Intellectually. But I'll never believe it."

Tess wanted to cry, but pressed her lips together to keep from it.

"It's ridiculous that I'm still haunted by that event, from nearly thirty years ago. But I can't seem to shake it."

"And the sounds from the Fourth of July bring it all back?"

He nodded. "But this time it's been more than that. This isn't a bad thing, but Nathan reminds me of Private Randolph. A little geeky." Thorn smiled. "But wanting to always do the right thing. Following orders. Taking things literally. Not stopping—retreating—until told."

Tess's heart sank at the thought of a young man like Nathan dying at such a young age and in such a horrible way. No wonder Thorn had been so affected.

Tess stood at the counter in the lobby, going over the reservations for the next couple of days, as Val stood across the counter from her. They'd juggled the room assignments to make room for Val and Nathan for the last two nights. The big question now was if they could continue to. Although Granny Hines was out of ICU, she wasn't ready to be released from the hospital.

There was no way around it. "We're booked for tonight and tomorrow night," Tess said. "But sometimes we have a late cancellation." Not usually on a Saturday though. "Let's put your things on the fourth floor, in the common area that LuAnn, Janice, and I share."

"That would be great," Val said. "I'm on the waiting list for a couple of hotels tonight. Hopefully something will work out."

Tess doubted it would but didn't say anything. They didn't have a room available until Monday, the day after tomorrow. As Val went to pack her things, Tess sent a group text to LuAnn and Janice about the situation. *If nothing opens up, could we accommodate them in our common area? Val could sleep on the couch and Nathan on a cot.*

LuAnn immediately texted back *of course*. A couple of minutes later Janice texted, *Sounds like a plan.*

Val texted when she and Nathan had everything packed, and then Tess met them on the third floor and took them on up to the fourth. As they walked down the hall, Tess told Val that if they wanted to, they should just plan to spend the night in the common area.

"Oh, Tess," Val said. "Could we?"

"Of course. We'll put a cot in here. One of you can sleep on the couch. You can use my bathroom." Tess smiled. "I cleaned it this morning."

"You are angels. All of you," Val said. "Add it to my bill."

"Oh no," Tess said. "This is on us. We can move you back into a room by Monday afternoon. And we'll start the bill again then."

"I can't thank you enough." Val reached for Tess's hand and squeezed it. "I don't know what we would have done without all of you. Without this inn."

Nathan placed his laptop on the table. Tess smiled, realizing he hadn't complained about the Wi-Fi for the last few days.

Soon they were all back in the lobby. Keeley was waiting at the curio cabinet, ready to go out to lunch with her mother and brother. She turned as they came down the stairs, and greeted each one. Then she looked at Tess and said, "I have that new exhibit ready to go."

"Oh?"

"The one I mentioned. About children on the Underground Railroad. Danny came up with some amazing stuff."

"Great." Tess rubbed the bridge of her nose. "Did he ever find that microfiche?"

Keeley shrugged. "He hasn't mentioned it. I'll ask next time I'm in. Or you should give him a call. He may have forgotten all about it."

Tess doubted he had. Not when she, Perry, and Marissa all wanted it.

Saturday evening, when Tess stepped off the elevator onto the fourth floor, the first thing she noted was the cool air. Oh, what sweet relief. Finally, she'd get a good night's sleep. Then she noticed the smell of fresh popcorn.

Laughter erupted from down the hall—Janice's distinct high-pitched laugh, followed by a deep chuckle that she guessed was Nathan. And then Val saying, "I haven't had this much fun in ages."

Tess quickened her pace, wondering what she was missing. As she stepped into the common area, Val threw a piece of popcorn at LuAnn's open mouth, and she caught it with a flourish. Then Val lobbed a piece high at Nathan. He jumped off the couch, caught it in his mouth, and threw his fist up in the air in triumph.

"Tess!" Val called out. "Here's one for you."

Tess froze as the piece of popcorn came toward her, but instinctively her mouth flew open. The popcorn bumped off her chin, but she managed to scoop it up in her hand and pop it in her mouth. They all clapped, and Tess took a bow.

"I think we're all a little loopy," LuAnn said. "It's been quite a week with Granny Hines, the brooch, the AC..."

Val clutched the bowl of popcorn with both hands. "At least the AC has been fixed. And Granny truly is on the mend. That leaves the brooch... Any word on that?"

Tess shook her head. "I haven't heard from Randy for the last few days—" She glanced from LuAnn to Janice, and they both shook their heads.

"I'll touch base with him in the morning," Tess said, "but I'm guessing he hasn't come up with anything. The brooch seems to have disappeared into thin air."

Nathan turned to Val. "Hey, did Keeley tell you one of the other guests followed our family here?"

Val sat up straight. "What?" Obviously Perry hadn't spoken to Val like he said he would. But maybe he hadn't found a time. She'd been at the hospital most of the day, after all.

"He posed as a cousin on that Facebook page Keeley set up," Nathan said, "and then booked a room here."

Val put the bowl on the coffee table. "Why would he do that?"

Nathan shrugged.

Val made eye contact with Tess.

Because Nathan had brought it up, Tess decided it was all right to add what she knew. "He edits a historical publication and has a specific interest in Thomas Hines."

"Perry," Val said. "Right?"

LuAnn nodded.

Nathan added, "Keeley confronted him about it."

"She hasn't said a word to me," Val said. "She actually hasn't said much of anything for the last few days, but I thought it was because she's worried about Granny."

"No. She's been acting weird again," Nathan said.

"Keeley's working on a new exhibit." Tess sat down beside Janice. "Maybe that has her distracted."

"Maybe," Val said. "I invited her to dinner tonight and then to hang out after, up here. I didn't think any of you would mind."

"Of course not," Tess said.

"But she said she was busy. We're in town, and she's busy." Val sighed.

"She's busy fixating on our family tree again," Nathan said. "That's all she could talk about the other day. That it was because of people like our ancestors that the Underground Railroad was necessary. I think she hoped interning at the museum would be some sort of penance—but it's not working."

Val frowned. "Nathan—"

"You know it's true, Mom. Ever since she figured out what plantation life was like before the Civil War, when she was like eight, she's been this way."

"I can't say that I blame her," Val said. "Growing up in Chicago, your dad didn't think about it much. But Keeley's really educated all of us, which is good. I'm really grateful for that."

Tess wasn't sure what to say. Keeley *was* educating all sorts of people about the horrors of slavery and the need for the

Underground Railroad. She hoped Keeley felt good about
that.

"Keeley did say she'd spend the day up at the hospital
tomorrow." Val reached over and patted her son on the
shoulder. "You too, bud?"

"Yep," Nathan said. "I'm in."

Tess looked at Val. "Speaking of your family, Perry seems
to think the Bickerton brooch may have ended up in Thomas
Hines's possession after the Civil War and has been passed
down through the generations. Are there any family stories
that your husband has ever told that include a valuable
brooch?"

Val shook her head. "No, like I said before. But I suppose it
could have gone to another branch of the family. Do you know
why Perry thinks it might have belonged to Robbie's family,
besides the fact that it turned up here—at basically the same
time we did?"

"I'm not sure," Tess confessed.

"Maybe because he found us on Facebook and hoped some
twig on our branch still owned it," Nathan said. "Would he need
any more of a reason than that to stalk us?"

Tess shrugged. "I have no idea." She believed Val, but she
understood Perry's thinking. It still seemed like too much of a
coincidence that the brooch would turn up at the inn while
Thomas Hines's relatives were staying at the place. Perhaps one
of Val's sisters-in-law had inherited the brooch. There was still
the possibility the twins could have broken the glass. Perhaps
they took the brooch from their mother's or one of their aunt's

things—but why would Connie or Ellen have brought it along? And not been alarmed by what happened to it?

Nothing made sense when it came to the missing brooch.

"Do you think Perry stole the brooch from the jewelry store?" Val asked.

LuAnn grabbed the bowl of popcorn off the coffee table and scooped up a handful. "One can't help but wonder," she said. "But there's no evidence."

Tess hoped they hadn't said too much. She reiterated that there was no evidence against Perry.

"He seems like a nice guy," Nathan added. "I've been listening to B.B. King all day." He patted his back jeans pocket, where his phone was. "I'd never heard of B.B. King until Perry told me what he was playing the other day. Perry's an amazing piano player."

Tess agreed. But she knew that being an amazing piano player didn't mean you weren't also an amazing thief.

CHAPTER SEVENTEEN

July 18, 1863

Sheriff Jones took Prudence around to the back door of the jail and then into the office. Mr. Gidden was waiting inside for them.

"Are you sure you want to press charges?" the sheriff asked.

Gidden nodded. "But wait to read Prudence her rights until the reporter arrives."

None of it made sense to Prudence.

As they waited, Mr. Siloam arrived. He slipped through the door into the office.

Mr. Gidden's face reddened. "What are you doing here? Who's in charge of the hotel?"

"No one," Mr. Siloam answered. "Everyone's outside the door. We're all here to testify about Prudence's character. You know she didn't steal anything—and so do all of us."

As he spoke the reporter came through the door, asking, "What's going on? Why is the staff from the hotel waiting in the alley?"

Mr. Gidden stepped out of the door and shouted, "Get back to the hotel! That's an order." There was a pause, and then he said, "Get back to the hotel right now, or all of you are fired."

Prudence inhaled and held her breath in anticipation. What was going on?

Mr. Gidden turned to the sheriff. "Hasn't she been arrested? Shouldn't she be in a cell?"

Sheriff Jones held his hat in his hands. "Perhaps you're rushing to conclusions."

"She was the last person to have the brooch, and now it's gone. What conclusion am I rushing to other than that she's responsible for its theft? Perhaps it's hidden in the floorboards of her home. Or maybe she sold it to a soldier for a pittance." He was shouting now. "The brooch is gone, and I want her held responsible for it." Mr. Gidden wiped the spittle away from his mouth and then glared at the sheriff. "Mr. Bickerton will be home soon, and he'll have both of our heads if you don't deal with this now."

"I believe," Sheriff Jones replied, "that I'll put Prudence in a cell for her own safety." As he spoke, Mr. Siloam opened the door, and the staff from the hotel started to file into the office.

"What are you doing?" Mr. Gidden yelled.

"They'll be staying here until Prudence is released," Mr. Siloam replied. "While I go tell Jason what is going on."

The sheriff unlocked the cell, and Prudence entered the small, stark room. He then asked Prudence to describe again the soldier who she claimed took the brooch. She did, giving a description of his scraggly beard and long mustache. She guessed a thousand Confederate soldiers fit the description—nearly. She reminded the sheriff that this one had a scar along his jawbone where his beard didn't grow.

"I had someone else describe the same soldier," the sheriff said, closing the cell door. "He robbed the Groat farm, not too far from your place."

"We know them," Prudence said.

"They had their life savings stolen. Somehow, the soldier went right to the spot where they kept it."

Prudence found that odd, but as she thought about the soldier upsetting her basket, it seemed that he may have known where to look for the brooch too.

Mr. Gidden was yelling at the employees, again telling them they were all fired. Prudence would never understand why Mr. Bickerton left the man in charge. She could see, from the corner of the cell through the bars, that her coworkers had lined the wall of the office. She couldn't help but be aware of the irony that she had been arrested for stealing a brooch on the north side of the Ohio River—something she didn't do—when so many times she could have been arrested for helping slaves escape on the south side of the river. Something she had done. Over and over. God's ways were so much better than man's. She had much to be thankful for in her life.

Mr. Gidden told the sheriff he had to return to the hotel, under the circumstances. "For all I know the place has been ransacked by now."

The sheriff met Mr. Gidden's gaze and said, "'For what shall it profit a man, if he shall gain the whole world, and lose his own soul?'"

"What are you talking about?"

Sheriff Jones shrugged. "I think you know."

Prudence saw something pass between the two men before Gidden turned his eyes to the floor.

"I'll walk with you," the sheriff said to Mr. Gidden. "I have a few more questions to ask."

The reporter's eyes lit up, and he followed the two out the door.

Prudence grasped the bars and thanked her friends for supporting her. "But I do not want thee to be without work," she said. She didn't want herself to be either. With Jason's injuries, they needed the money she earned.

Her coworkers sang hymns as they waited for the sheriff to return. Prudence joined in, thankful for their encouragement and reminder of God's care.

It wasn't more than a half hour until the sheriff, Mr. Gidden, and the reporter returned.

The sheriff cleared his throat and said to Prudence, "Mr. Gidden seems to have had a change of memory. He doesn't think the brooch was in the pouch he gave you after all. He says that contained money, and the brooch was at the Bickerton home."

"Oh?" Prudence's eyebrows shot up. "Is it still there?"

"Mr. Gidden says no." Sheriff Jones nodded at the man. "He seems to think the home was raided after all, and the brooch was stolen."

Prudence shook her head in disbelief but didn't say anything. Gidden seemed to be saying crazy things, all the way around.

The sheriff approached the cell and unlocked it. "And an explanation will be written up in the *Marietta Times*." The reporter nodded in agreement. "At the moment, Mr. Gidden is headed out to send a telegraph to Mr. Bickerton."

Mr. Gidden, whose face was red, turned to Prudence and then the people who lined the wall. "Will you go back to work now? All of you?"

There was a murmur, and the employees began to file out of the building.

The sheriff opened the door for Prudence, and she stepped out.

The reporter asked if he should use the description of the perpetrator that Prudence gave.

The sheriff tugged on his white beard and finally said, "Not yet. Just say he could be a possible suspect. I don't think we can know at this point. I'll take a look at the Bickerton house and see what I can find. In the meantime, perhaps Mr. Gidden will remember more details. Let's wait to give a description until we get a name to go with it."

Prudence and the staff started walking to the hotel. On the way, they met Jason and Mr. Siloam. Relief washed over Jason's face, and he wrapped his arms around Prudence.

"All is well," she whispered to him.

He kissed the top of her head covering and then the two walked side by side while the others explained to him and Mr. Siloam what had transpired.

After Prudence fixed a quick pudding for dinner and served it with cold ham at the hotel, she cleaned up, with Jason's help. He'd stayed to walk Prudence home. "I am not taking any chances," he said.

Mr. Gidden still hadn't returned, and Mr. Siloam finished the work at the hotel for the night. As Prudence and Jason walked home, he put his arm around her and held her close without saying a word. When they reached the porch of their house, Moses and Ernestine both came rushing through the door.

"Blessed be," Ernestine said. "The good Lord took care of thee."

Suddenly, as Prudence hugged the children, weariness overcame her. God had given her the strength she needed. Now it was time to rest.

CHAPTER EIGHTEEN

Sunday morning, as Tess put the quiches in the oven, Janice waltzed into the kitchen, wearing the brooch Jim and Linda had given her. With a laugh, she said, "Why shouldn't I wear it to church? It's bound to start a few conversations."

Tess smiled in appreciation. She loved Janice's sense of humor. She could use it about now. She'd tossed and turned last night, even though her bedroom was finally cool. Several times as she lay staring at the ceiling, she prayed. She'd feel peace for a moment, but soon her thoughts shifted back to her worries. The brooch. Her investment. Charlotte accusing her of being negligent. Then she'd think of what she was grateful for. That the AC was finally fixed. That Thorn had shared his grief. That Val and Nathan were at the inn. That Granny was out of ICU. There were so many things to be thankful for.

"Isn't it amazing that a mystery from 1863 could repeat today?" Janice tied an apron around her waist as LuAnn stepped into the kitchen. Janice added, "If only we could crack the case."

Tess hit her forehead with the heel of her hand. "Of course. *1863.* Why haven't we thought to check Prudence's diary?"

LuAnn's eyebrows shot up. "Because we'd remember if she'd written anything about a stolen brooch. Or anything about any brooch at all."

"But maybe she mentions something else that could help us." Tess headed into the office, pulled the copy of Prudence's diary from the desk drawer, and brought it back to the kitchen. She quickly leafed through the pages to find July 1863. On July 1, Prudence wrote about the beginning of the Battle of Gettysburg. Then on July 4 she wrote that word arrived that the battle had ended, and the North had won but at a horrible cost for both sides.

On July 18 she wrote about a girl, Ernestine, coming from Gettysburg to stay with the Willards. *While we were walking home, something of value, in my safekeeping, was stolen by a Confederate soldier.* She feared she'd be accused of the crime. She wrote: *God knows my heart, He knows what is true. I'm praying and giving it all to Him. If the authorities won't believe me, so be it. I'll go wherever God leads, even if it is to prison. The most important thing is that Ernestine is safe. And that Jason and Moses are too.*

"Oh dear," Janice said. "This doesn't sound good at all. Do you think it has to do with the brooch?"

"Either that or the timing is as amazing a coincidence as Thomas Hines's family staying in our inn the day the brooch appeared," Tess said, flipping to the next page.

The next entry, written on July 19, was nearly as vague: *God certainly works in mysterious ways. That is a certainty. In a turn of unexpected events, the accusation against me was retracted. I doubt I'll ever know the truth of what transpired, but I will stay true to what God has called me to. As of now, I'm praying I'm clear of the trouble I thought might land me in jail for the rest of my life. Whatever the outcome, so be it.*

"She was certainly closemouthed about what happened," LuAnn said.

Tess was frustrated that the entries were so guarded, but Prudence did write that a Confederate soldier stole something of value. How could it be a coincidence that Prudence would be accused of a crime the day after a brooch owned by her employer was stolen?

She read the last entry again. There had to be more to the story. Tess was touched by Prudence's words: *So be it.*

LuAnn said, "Again, Prudence showed such incredible grace no matter the circumstances."

"I agree." Janice cradled her cup of coffee. "I think we all have events from our pasts that we need to let go of, on some level."

"And the present too," Tess added. "We all need to be willing to say 'So be it.'" Which, of course, was easier said than done. Could she say "So be it" in response to Charlotte's accusations? Could Tess show the same grace to others that Prudence did, over and over throughout her life?

⸎

Once breakfast was finished, Tess, LuAnn, and Janice cleaned up. When they were done, Janice asked Tess if she was ready to go to church.

"Why don't you go on ahead," she said. "I have some think-ing to do."

It was LuAnn's turn to stay at the inn, and Tess volunteered to take her turn.

"Absolutely not," LuAnn said. "You go have some time to yourself. You deserve it."

It only took Tess a couple of minutes to realize it wasn't that she had thinking to do. It was more that she needed to try to understand something. The Society of Friends might offer her a clue. She wanted to discover more of what Prudence meant by, *So be it.*

Tess quickly checked the time of the service on her phone. *Ten thirty.* If she hurried, she'd make it. She found a place to park, then slipped into the building and into the last row of the meeting room.

A white-haired woman up front was explaining the order of the day's service in a quiet voice. "We're having a silent service today," she explained. "For those of you Friends who are visiting, we are following the unprogrammed Quaker tradition of expectant waiting. Meditate on Psalm 46:10, 'Be still, and know that I am God.' If you are led to share a word from the Lord with all of us or to lead out in prayer, please do. In the mean-time, experience the Lord and pray silently where you are."

Tess couldn't imagine remaining silent for the next hour without singing out loud or listening to a sermon or a Bible reading. But she'd have to give it a try. She closed her eyes, taking a deep breath and exhaling it slowly, silently repeating Prudence's words, *So be it.*

She began to pray. For Jeff Jr., Lizzie and her family, LuAnn and Janice, Thorn and Bev. The inn, as a whole, and the work she and her friends were doing there. Her investments. And then she found herself praying for Frank Bryant. Then about the brooch, and again, for Jim and Linda. And Charlotte too. Next she started thanking God for everything she could think of, going as far as thanking Him for the Ohio River, the town of Marietta, the brave slaves who'd escaped through the area, the people of the Underground Railroad all those years ago...

About twenty minutes into the silence, a man cleared his throat, and Tess peeked. He stood to her right and held an open Bible in his hands. He read, "'Come unto me, all ye that labour and are heavy laden, and I will give you rest. Take my yoke upon you, and learn of me; for I am meek and lowly in heart: and ye shall find rest unto your souls. For my yoke is easy, and my burden is light.'"

Praying for twenty minutes straight had certainly lightened Tess's burden, which was nothing compared to what Prudence's burden had been. Tess was concerned about a brooch, a material object, and her finances. Prudence had been concerned about the survival of those fleeing slavery and about the well-being of her own family. What did Tess know about suffering? Aside from her grief over her husband's passing.

Tess continued to pray, going over her list again. Then she began to silently sing the lyrics to her favorite hymns. Then she silently recited scripture. At the end of the service the white-haired woman from the beginning stood and said, "What has happened has happened. What hasn't, hasn't. So be it."

Tears stung Tess's eyes. The woman echoed Prudence's exact words. Tess thought of Thorn, of the money she most likely had lost, of Granny Hines, of the stolen brooch. *So be it.* She felt a peace that wasn't fleeting.

Yes, God wanted her to take action and do what was right. But when there was nothing that could be done to fix things, then saying "So be it" was the next step.

Over one hundred fifty years ago, Prudence acknowledged that God worked in mysterious ways. Tess knew she must trust Him to work just as mysteriously now, in the present.

After the service ended, Tess slipped out of the meeting hall, enveloped in a sense of peace. When she reached the inn, Randy stood outside the front door. Tess smiled broadly. "Do you have good news for us?"

He shook his head. "I'm not here with a report. I'm here to question you."

CHAPTER NINETEEN

July 19, 1863

The morning after she'd been freed from jail, Prudence returned to the hotel and began preparing breakfast for the guests. As she slid a tray of biscuits into the oven, a knock fell on the back door. She opened it to find Sheriff Jones, with his hat in his hand.

"Good mornin'," he said. "I'm looking for Mr. Gidden. Have you seen him?"

Prudence shook her head and invited the sheriff into the kitchen. "Please sit down," she said as she poured him a cup of coffee. "I'll fetch Mr. Siloam."

She found him in the lobby and led him back into the kitchen, where he greeted the sheriff. "I haven't seen Gidden this morning," he said. "Which isn't like him. He usually checks up on me first thing."

"All right," the sheriff said. "After I finish my coffee, I'll see if he's at the Bickerton mansion." He seemed deep in thought as he sipped his coffee.

Prudence went on with her work, and a few minutes later, the sheriff thanked her and slipped out the back door.

A couple of hours later, he returned, this time entering the kitchen through the lobby door, with Mr. Siloam. "I need to speak with the two of you," he said.

All three sat down at the kitchen table.

The sheriff spoke softly. "Gidden wasn't at the mansion when I arrived. Finally, I tracked down the groundskeeper, who said he hadn't seen the man since yesterday, and that Gidden's horse was missing." He went on to say that the groundskeeper let him into the house, and together they checked the downstairs back bedroom where Gidden stayed. "The room looked as if it had been ransacked, and at first I suspected there had been a robbery. But it was the only room in disorder, and it seemed that all of Gidden's personal items were missing."

The sheriff rubbed the side of his face. "The housekeeper soon arrived and went through the house. She said none of the Bickertons' belongings are gone."

As the sheriff finished the story, he placed a telegram on the table. "This came from Chicago, from Mr. Bickerton. He says he brought the brooch with him from England, and he's offering a reward of a thousand dollars for its return."

Prudence felt lightheaded. She couldn't imagine how much the piece of jewelry was worth.

She looked at the sheriff. "I am sure that brooch was in the pouch."

He nodded. "I am too."

"But you seemed to believe Gidden when he said it had been taken from the house."

The sheriff shook his head. "I was only going along with what he was saying. I think he was involved somehow—that he planted the brooch in your basket intending it to be stolen. Now he's gone to reclaim it."

Mr. Siloam gasped.

The sheriff nodded. "Gidden came here from Kentucky. That's where Morgan and most of his men are from, including Private Xavier Hines, who fits the description of the soldier who took the brooch from you." He shrugged. "But who knows." He paused a moment and then added, "Private Hines is a cousin of Captain Thomas Hines, one of General Morgan's right-hand men."

Prudence stared at the sheriff, not sure who the two Hines men were. She'd never heard of them. "Does thee think the brooch will be recovered?"

Sheriff Jones folded his big hands together on top of the table. "I have no idea. Someone might have retreated back to Kentucky with it. But if it's still in the area, I wouldn't be surprised if Mr. Bickerton's reward entices someone to come forward with it."

"Will you pursue Mr. Gidden?" Mr. Siloam asked.

"I have a warrant out for his arrest," the sheriff said. "But I'm guessing he's far away from here. The question is whether he has the brooch or not. And, of course, if he's south of the river, I doubt I'll ever see him or it again."

Prudence guessed he was right.

"What now?" Mr. Siloam asked.

"I'll notify Mr. Bickerton that he needs to hire a new general business assistant." The sheriff picked up the telegram. "In the meantime, you two should carry on as you always do."

They did, for the next week, until the Bickertons returned long enough to hire a new man to fill the position. The reporter interviewed Mr. Bickerton about the brooch and wrote an article for the *Marietta Times*. That evening, Prudence took a copy out to the farm, and she read the article to Jason, Ernestine, and Moses on the porch. The heat of the day lingered and hung heavy all around them.

Dusk had fallen, and lightning bugs flitted along the edge of the woods. Footsteps fell on the road coming toward them.

Jason stood. "Hello!"

A deep voice called out, "It is me. Isaac!"

"Papa!" Ernestine flew down the steps, down the path to the gate, and into her father's arms.

Prudence cried from joy for her friends and then prepared a meal for Isaac. Later, after the children had gone to bed, he described what had happened around Gettysburg. "They're still burying the dead," he said, "and more die every day. Our land is soaked in blood and pocked with cannonballs. I lost my entire crop. I'm afraid to plow come fall, not knowing what I'll dig up." He shuddered.

"What does thee plan to do?" Jason asked.

"I could not stay in Gettysburg. It is all death and loss. I sold my farm to a neighbor." He glanced up toward the loft. "We are going to head to Oklahoma," he said. "There is a group going. Ernestine and I will meet up with them."

Prudence folded her hands. *So be it.*

CHAPTER TWENTY

"Y ou want to question me?" Tess shaded her eyes to see Randy better. "About what happened at Uptown Jewelers? The day the brooch was stolen."

He cleared his throat and glanced toward the front door. "Could we speak somewhere? In private?"

"Sure," Tess answered. "Let's see if anyone's in the café." She led the way into the inn. Janice wasn't back from church yet, LuAnn was nowhere to be seen, and it was Winnie's day off.

The café was empty. "Would you like a cup of coffee?"

"No thank you," Randy answered.

As they sat, he folded his hands together and then unfolded them.

Tess stared at him. He seemed nervous. "What's going on?" she asked.

"I had a call this morning…from someone who didn't want to give their name."

Tess waited while he folded and unfolded his hands again.

"This person said I should ask you if you have the brooch. He said it was pretty suspicious that you saw the thief in broad daylight and couldn't describe him, and that Jim was the one who was hurt, not you. He said if I didn't say I'd question you, he'd go to the papers."

Tess leaned back in her chair. "Are you really asking me if I had something to do with the theft of the brooch?"

He managed to nod, but it appeared to be a struggle.

"I absolutely did not."

Randy didn't respond. Obviously, all of this was making him very uncomfortable.

"Do you think I'm responsible for not preventing the theft? Or do you suspect that I might be responsible *for* the theft? I mean, I guess I can't prove I didn't hire someone else to take it, but then neither can anyone else in town."

"Look," he said. "I had to ask because it had been brought to my attention." He met her gaze and muttered, "And I sure didn't want your name in the paper."

Tess understood. But still, she was miffed. "I hope I don't sound defensive, and like 'but what-about-so-and-so,' but have you followed up on Jim and Linda Walsh? At this point, they're the ones profiting off the stolen brooch."

He nodded. "That's a valid question. I can't find any evidence linking them to the crime, and there's nothing to indicate they preplanned benefitting off the theft, such as ordering the brooch merchandise beforehand or anything like that. They seem to be opportunists is all." He stood. "I'll be in touch," he said.

⚜

Monday morning, Tess stood at the desk, checking out the couple who'd stayed in Val and Nathan's room for two nights. Thankfully, their long-term guests would be able to move back in as soon as the sheets were changed, the floor vacuumed, and the bathroom cleaned.

After she finished the transaction and the couple left, Perry stepped off the elevator with a backpack, a duffel bag, and a book bag. He had another day left on his reservation.

"What's going on?" Tess asked.

"I'm headed out early," he said. "Just this morning, I decided to spend one more day at Buffington Island. I'll stay close to there tonight and then head west. I'm going to fly out of Columbus on the day after tomorrow."

Tess reached for Perry's information card. It would be harder to determine if he stole the brooch with him gone, but she wouldn't let on to that.

"I'll pay for tonight though," he said. "I didn't give you twenty-four hours notice."

"No, that's fine," Tess said. He'd stayed for eleven days. "Just come back again sometime." She smiled. "You've been a delightful guest."

He grinned. "I'd love to return." After he settled his bill, he nodded to the grand piano. "Mind if I play one more song before I go?"

"Be my guest," she said.

He grinned, and she half expected him to play the song from *Beauty and the Beast*, but instead he played "Amazing Grace."

She glanced at him a couple of times as the lyrics played in her head. *'Twas grace that taught my heart to fear, And grace my fears relieved; How precious did that grace appear, The hour I first believed.*

When he finished the last note, Tess clapped. He took a bow and then grabbed his bags.

"I have a question for you," Tess said. "Considering you were staying at the inn when the brooch appeared, do you mind if I contact you if anything comes up? If I have a follow-up question?"

"No problem," he said. "I know LuAnn is a great resource for history, as are Maybelline and Margaret, but if you have any general questions about Morgan's Raid and all of that, feel free to ask."

Tess stepped out from around the front desk and shook his hand, trying to imagine him pushing her over in the jewelry store. She couldn't. "I hope you'll come and visit us again someday."

"I'd like that," he said.

She smiled as an additional question came to mind. "Out of all the research you did and the places you visited, what was your favorite location?"

He took out his phone. "Definitely Buffington Island." He held up his phone. "Would you like to see some photos?"

"Sure," Tess answered.

Perry opened his phone, tapped on his photos app, and scrolled backward. "These are from my second trip." He handed her the phone.

The date was July 7. The photos didn't mean much to her. There was a rock memorial. A mound. An old stone building. Perry gave a detailed description of each one. Then he took the phone back and scrolled up to July 5. That was the date the brooch was stolen. Too bad there wasn't a time on the photos, but she remembered he'd said he left for Buffington Island after visiting the Castle. The photos confirmed he'd actually gone there. But, then again, maybe he returned early, and he was showing her the photos to give himself an alibi. This time there were several photos of interpretative signs. "I always take photos of those," Perry said, "so I can read them again once I start writing." As the pictures progressed, the light changed until there were long shadows. He'd stayed late in the day, that was obvious.

Tess looked at each one and then said, "I'll have to go visit someday. It looks fascinating."

"It is," Perry said. "As is Marietta. And this inn too. It was a privilege to stay in a place that played a role in the Underground Railroad. I'll definitely come back."

"And I'll give you a call if I have any questions before then."

"It's a deal," he said, shaking her hand again. "Thank you for everything."

As he walked out the door, Tess had to admit that it was very unlikely Perry was the thief.

When Tess went to the office door, LuAnn held up the morning paper with a concerned expression on her face. She'd been down first and had snatched it off the stoop before Tess had a chance. The main headline read, *Who Stole the Brooch? Both in 1863 and on July 5th of this Year?* The subtitle read, *And Could the Two Thefts Be Related?*

***

First Tess read about how Uptown Jewelers' business grew busier every day. Besides selling the costume brooches, they were now selling matching bracelets and necklaces. *"The Bickerton brooch is famous now," Linda Walsh says. "We're praying every day that the real one is found—but in the meantime we're helping to promote the history of Marietta and the Underground Railroad. We're fortunate to have the museum here and the Wayfarers Inn. We have so much history to celebrate—we just hope the brooch will be found and join its rightful place with the other treasures of Marietta."*

Again Tess noted the marketing genius of Jim and Linda. But it wasn't as if they were only promoting the shop. They were promoting all of Marietta. There was a coupon right under the article good for two Fundae Sundaes for the price of one if the customer had a receipt from Uptown Jewelers. Now she knew why the lines were so long at the ice cream shop.

Tess finished that article and then jumped to the sidebar, which was an article dated July 25, 1863. As she read, she realized that Marissa must have accessed the missing microfiche, although she didn't run the entire article this time. But Mr. Bickerton had offered a reward for the brooch and returned home for a short time before leaving again for New York.

Tess put the paper down.

"Danny certainly didn't contact me when he found the roll of microfiche. Did he contact you?" LuAnn asked.

Tess rubbed the back of her neck, fighting the sense of betrayal welling up inside of her. "I can't believe he gave it to Marissa. He assured us he'd contact us first."

LuAnn stood. "I'll give him a call."

Tess gestured for her to sit back down. "First, I have an update for you. Grab your notebook."

LuAnn pulled it out of the desk drawer, and Tess proceeded to tell her what Perry had said, and then she described the photos he showed her.

"Very interesting," LuAnn said. "It seems we can pretty much rule him out unless he somehow tricked you with the pictures."

Tess shrugged. "I don't see how he could have."

LuAnn put her pen down. "You never know. But it appears we no longer have a prime suspect." She closed the notebook.

"Hopefully the old newspaper articles will give us a clue."

"Maybe about the original theft, but I don't see how it could shed any light on the most recent one."

Tess could see LuAnn's point but said, "Let's see what I can find out."

"Why don't you go ahead and leave for the archives," Luann said. "Maybe Janice would want to go with you. Robin and Taylor and I can handle the café. People are just now realizing we're open again."

"Great idea," Tess said.

She found Janice straightening up the common room on the fourth floor and quickly explained the situation.

"I'd love to go," Janice said. "I hope we find something that can help us crack the case."

They decided to walk through the historic district on their way to the archives. Of course, as soon as they finally got the

AC fixed, the days had cooled down some. Tess took a deep breath. A cool breeze was blowing in off the river, and the sky was a baby blue without a cloud in sight.

"Do you think of Prudence walking these same streets all those years ago?" she asked Janice.

"Yep. All the time." Janice pointed to the Washington County courthouse. "Of course, this was built after Prudence had passed, but so many of these buildings were here, including the Ohio Company Land Office."

Tess knew, as the oldest building in Ohio, that the land office dated back to 1788, long before Prudence was born. Thank goodness for the National Register of Historic Places and for all it preserved.

They turned down Washington Street and soon arrived at the archives building.

Danny looked up from his desk. "Hi, Tess. Hi, Janice. How are the two of you on this fine Monday morning?"

After Janice greeted Danny, Tess smiled, hoping to soften her words. "You might not want to know how I am," she teased.

"What's going on?"

"Obviously you found the missing microfiche. I saw Marissa's article in this morning's paper."

His face fell. "I meant to call you, honest. It was crazy in here on Friday. Perry was here and Marissa. And then Keeley came in."

"Where did you find the microfiche?"

"I didn't. Perry did."

Tess gulped. He hadn't said a word to her. Was that why he'd decided to leave early? "Where did he find it?"

Danny closed one eye as if he was trying to remember. "It was definitely out of place." He pointed to a bookshelf by the far window. "I think it was over there."

"How odd."

He nodded. "I have no idea how it ended up on the shelf, but I know where it is now. Would you like to look at it?"

"Yes, please," Tess answered.

Danny disappeared into the back room. He was gone way longer than he should have been, and Janice began tapping her fingernails on the countertop. Tess felt like doing the same but restrained herself.

When Danny finally returned his hands were empty.

"Again?" Tess sputtered.

He nodded, blushing as he did. "I don't know how this happened a second time. I feel so incompetent." He sighed. "The archives were open Saturday morning for a tour. I'm hoping something happened then—that's it not me again."

"Maybe it ended up back over on the shelf." Janice headed that way, and Tess and Danny followed her.

He looked on the bottom shelf. "It's not here."

Tess scanned the other shelves. She only saw books.

Stepping to the side, Janice stopped in front of a small cupboard. "What's in that?" she asked.

"Supplies," Danny answered. "Pencils and gloves and paper. That sort of thing."

After asking his permission, Janice opened the doors of the cupboard, and Tess stepped closer. The light was dim in the corner, making it hard to see. Janice bent down and reached inside.

"What's in there?" Tess asked.

"A box of pens, archival gloves, and reams of paper." She reached in farther. "And a box."

Janice stood, holding a microfiche box. "Is this it?"

He read the label on the box and then looked up at the ceiling. "What is going on?"

Tess wondered what his system was for checking microfiche out and back in. "Do you have a logbook?" she asked.

"I do," he said. "I checked it. I logged this back in on Friday."

"So maybe something did happen to it on Saturday."

He nodded. "Let's hope." He handed the box to Tess. "Have at it."

Tess sat down at the microfiche reader with Janice settling into the chair beside her, opened the box, and took out the reel. An odd rattle surprised her. She lifted the box. There was something else inside.

"What is it?" Janice asked.

"A key." Tess stood and turned to the counter. "One I've seen before. Danny," she said, holding up an ornate key, "do you recognize this?"

He shook his head. "We don't have any keys like that around here."

She walked over to the counter and handed it to him. "You do now."

Tess and Janice began with an article from July 19, 1863, the first issue of the *Marietta Times* on the scroll. A local suspect had been identified, but the sheriff requested that the name not be released until further notice.

"Do you think that could be Prudence?" Janice said.

Tess continued scrolling. A description of the brooch had been provided by a Mr. Albert Gidden, who was listed as Mr. Bickerton's general business assistant. Rubies, diamonds, and sapphires. Red, white, and blue. He also said that Howard Bickerton brought the brooch with him when he moved from England to Ohio.

Tess continued reading. The reporter included that the Bickerton family was visiting Chicago at the time of the theft.

"That's a five-hundred mile trip," Janice said. "And a fair distance away from the relentless stress of the war."

The next day, July 20, there was another article. This one identified the suspect, a confederate soldier. A description was given—shoulder-length hair and a beard. The distinguishing mark was a scar across the man's cheek. The article said that there was speculation that the suspect could be a Private Xavier Hines, cousin of Captain Thomas Hines.

Tess reread that sentence out loud and then said, "Perhaps our original suspicions were correct. Maybe someone in the Hines family did have the brooch—and planted it in the curio cabinet at the inn."

Janice leaned forward, peering at the article. "We never ruled out Keeley."

Tess nodded. "Nathan and Val said she was embarrassed by the past of the Hines family. That they'd defended the Confederacy. That some had owned slaves. Maybe Keeley didn't want anyone to find out."

Janice spoke rapidly. "Perhaps Granny Hines had the brooch, and Keeley figured out what it was. She planted it in the curio cabinet. But why would she steal it back? Maybe for Granny. Or for the worth of the brooch." Janice wrinkled her nose. "Maybe she decided the money could help her father's start-up and figured she should keep the brooch in the family after all. Or keep it for herself."

Tess had a moment of horror at the thought that Keeley could do such a thing. She was sweet and idealistic. She loved history, her grandmother, and all of her family. She loved the town of Marietta and working at the museum.

But neither could Tess ignore Janice's speculation. "Obviously Keeley didn't plant it herself," Tess said. "She had the key to the cabinet, after all. Who would she have convinced to do it for her?"

Janice shrugged. "I have no idea."

Neither did Tess. She glanced at Danny, who seemed focused on a document on the counter. He wore archival gloves and held a magnifying glass in his hand. He was slight of build, and it seemed that he and Keeley had become good friends. Would he have planted the brooch and then stolen it back for her?

But she had no proof that Keeley had read the articles in the paper. Were there any other sources that would identify Private Xavier Hines as the possible thief?

Tess focused back on the microfiche, and so did Janice. On July 21 there was an article that Mr. Bickerton's assistant, Mr. Gidden, had left town and that he was wanted in connection with the missing brooch. Tess rubbed her forehead. So, had Xavier Hines stolen it? Or Thomas Hines? Or Mr. Gidden?

She kept scrolling. She found the article that Marissa had put in the *Marietta Times,* dated July 25. Sure enough, the Bickertons had returned to town and had offered a $1,000 reward for the return of the brooch. "That was a lot of money back then," Janice said.

Tess stopped scrolling. "Didn't the Castle cost $10,000 in 1855 to build?"

"I believe so," Janice answered. "And, if I remember right, the Bickerton mansion cost nearly as much."

The next article that had anything to do with the case was from July 26. It stated that General Morgan and Captain Hines had been captured. There was no mention of an Xavier Hines or a Mr. Gidden.

Tess kept scrolling, forcing her eyes wide.

Janice rubbed hers. "I can't imagine doing this all day."

Tess kept turning the knob. "We're almost through this scroll."

Janice gasped. "Oh no." On October 18 there was an article that Sheriff Jones had died after being thrown and then dragged by his horse.

"He would have known more than anyone about the investigation into the missing brooch and Mr. Gidden's disappearance." Tess continued scrolling, surprised at the grief she felt for a man who died so many years ago.

Next Tess stopped for an article from November 1863 about General Morgan and Captain Hines escaping from the Ohio State Penitentiary.

After they finished reading the article, Janice said, "There was no mention of Hines getting the idea from *Les Misérables,* but it was probably too early for that story to have made the rounds."

"Good observation." Tess kept scrolling and skimming but there was nothing more about the brooch. There was an article that the Bickertons had left on a trip farther west right before she came to the end of the scroll.

"Fascinating," Janice said.

"It really is." Tess felt as if they'd traveled back in time. "Thomas and Xavier Hines. General Morgan. Sheriff Jones. Mr. Gidden. The Bickertons. What a cast of characters."

After she rewound the microfiche, she returned it to Danny just as the phone rang. He answered it.

As Danny listened, he glanced at Tess.

After a long pause, he said, "As a matter of fact a key did show up."

Then he said, "Tess found it."

After a pause, he added, "In the microfiche box."

CHAPTER TWENTY-ONE

After Danny hung up, he said, "Keeley is up at the hospital—she said she'll stop by and get the key later, when she has a chance. I'd take it up to her if I could..."

Tess hoped she didn't sound too eager as she said, "We'd be happy to take it up to her."

Danny handed the key to her. "That would be great. Thank you."

When she and Janice reached the sidewalk, Tess said, "I'm not sure what I'll say to her when I give her the key."

"You'll figure it out," Janice said. "Why don't you take LuAnn with you? Her perspective might be helpful in talking to Keeley."

"Great idea," Tess said.

Fifteen minutes later, as Tess drove up to the hospital, she filled LuAnn in on what she and Janice had read at the archives.

When they arrived at the hospital, they stopped at the front desk. "We're here to visit Mrs. Hines," Tess told the receptionist.

"Oh, Granny Hines?" The woman smiled.

Tess wasn't surprised that the staff at the hospital was calling her "Granny" too.

"She's in Room 25B."

Tess led the way, with LuAnn at her side. When they reached the room, Tess knocked, and Val opened the door.

Tess was ready to launch into why they were there, but LuAnn blurted out, "How is Granny doing?"

"So much better." An expression of relief passed over Val's face. "You can imagine how grateful I am. How grateful we all are."

Tess certainly could. She remembered her own mother's waning years and how every day with her was a blessing.

Val smiled. "What brings you two here?"

Tess held up the key. "I have something for Keeley."

"Oh dear. Is that to the cabinet in the inn? Keeley's been looking all over for that."

Tess nodded. "I found it at the archives and told Danny I'd make sure Keeley got it right away."

Val tugged on her heart necklace. "Yikes."

"She'll learn," Tess said.

Val's eyebrows shot up. "I hope so." She nodded to the door. "Both kids are down in the cafeteria, grabbing a bite to eat."

Tess nodded. "We'll find them and come up again before we leave."

When Tess and LuAnn arrived in the cafeteria, they found the siblings sitting in the back. Keeley had her back to them, and Nathan didn't see them approaching until Tess and LuAnn were nearly at the table. He grinned and waved. Keeley glanced over her shoulder but immediately turned away.

LuAnn sat down at the table beside Keeley, and Tess sat beside Nathan as they all said hello. Then Tess took the key out of her purse. "I brought your key."

Keeley took it from her. "Thanks."

"Don't you want to know where I found it?"

"At the archives. On the floor, probably."

"No. In the box for the microfiche, for the last half of July 1863 through November of that year."

Keeley's face grew red. "That's really weird."

Nathan crossed his arms. "No. It's not. What's up, Sis?"

"Mind your own business."

He leaned forward. "I probably am, if this has to do with the Hines family. As in Nathan Hines. And Keeley Hines. It's as much my business as it yours."

"No, it's not. You've never cared about family history."

He shrugged. "But I'm still part of the family." He stared his sister down. "There's no way it was a coincidence that the key was in the box. What's going on?"

Keeley put her hands over her eyes.

"All you have to do is tell the truth," Nathan said.

LuAnn nodded, even though Keeley couldn't see her. Tess leaned forward, waiting for Keeley to confess.

She splayed her fingers. "Okay, okay." Her eyes were wide between her fingers. "I admit it. I hid the microfiche."

It wasn't the confession Tess expected.

Nathan put his elbows on the table and leaned forward. "But why?"

"Why do you think?"

"Are you still embarrassed about something you had nothing to do with? Something you had no control over? Something that happened over a hundred and thirty years before you were born?"

"You make me sound so stupid."

"No, I'm pointing out that you're feeling guilty for something you didn't do."

Tess wanted to jump into the conversation, but she couldn't do it without confronting Keeley. It would be better for her to admit to what she did.

Keeley put her hands down. "You're absolutely right."

Tess inhaled. Here it came.

"I did steal—"

Tess exhaled.

"—the box of microfiche and hide it."

Tess's eyebrows shot up.

Nathan cocked his head.

Keeley put her hands up to her face again, which muffled her voice. "Twice. I did it twice."

Tess reached out across the table and touched Keeley's arm.

Keeley lowered her hand and grasped Tess's. "Do you think Maybelline will fire me? Do you think my internship is over?"

Tess said, "You'll have to talk with her." But she doubted the infraction was serious enough for that. Then again, breaking into the curio cabinet might be. But that didn't make sense—not when Keeley had the key.

LuAnn touched Keeley's shoulder and said, "Could you tell us how the key ended up in the box?"

Keeley cringed. "Absentmindedness, I guess. The question you really want to ask is why I hid the microfiche. Right?"

Tess nodded. That, and if she planted the brooch and then had a part in stealing it. But Tess didn't say any of that.

"Once the brooch appeared, and the talk of Morgan's Raid started, I was sure attention would turn to the Hines family. To our family. And that no one would believe it was a coincidence that it turned up while we were all in Marietta." She exhaled. "It was stupid, I know. But I thought if I hid the microfiche no one would suspect that our long-lost cousin was a suspect at one time."

"So you're saying"—LuAnn looked from Keeley to Nathan—"that neither one of you had anything to do with the brooch. Not in its appearance. And not in its disappearance."

Both of the young people nodded in agreement. Tess definitely believed Nathan. She wasn't sure about Keeley.

"You know Nathan is innocent. And I'm absolutely innocent too," Keeley said. "I know it doesn't look good that I'd hide evidence. But I would never steal—'cause, you know, I really didn't 'steal' the microfiche. And as far as planting the brooch, I'd have to have it in the first place. I know there's been speculation that Thomas Hines had it. But there's never been a trace of it on our branch of the family tree. I'd never even heard of it before."

"Are you sure?" LuAnn asked. "Could your grandmother have ended up with it but with her memory problems forgot she had it? Perhaps she brought it with her for some reason. And someone took it from her?"

Keeley seemed to consider that for a moment. "I guess I can't say for one hundred percent sure that's not the case. But

I've never seen any evidence or even heard a rumor that would support that. I can't tell you how many times she let me look through her jewelry box when I was a kid. I never saw anything like it."

Hopefully, if she'd owned the brooch, it would have been in a safety-deposit box, not her jewelry box, but Tess didn't say that.

"We should go ask Granny," Keeley said. "I mean, we already did back when the brooch appeared, and she said she'd never seen it. But her long-term memory is pretty good. Maybe our great-grandfather said something about it. Maybe there's some bit of information from the past."

"Good idea," Tess said. "But we'll wait. I don't want to stress her out now."

Nathan stood and picked up his tray. "It's fine. She's getting pretty bored. A couple of questions won't hurt her."

Keeley nodded. "Come on up. She'd like to see you."

LuAnn gave Tess a questioning look. Tess shrugged. "We can go up, say hello, and see how she seems."

Granny was laughing with the nurse when Tess and LuAnn followed Nathan and Keeley into the room.

"You have visitors," Keeley announced. "The nice ladies from the inn."

Granny grinned. "Come on in." She looked good. There was no physical sign of the stroke. Thankfully the EMTs had gotten her to the hospital immediately.

LuAnn and Tess stopped at the end of the bed.

Keeley continued on to her grandmother's side. "We have some questions about the Bickerton brooch. Did you ever hear anything from Gramps's family about the brooch? Did anyone in the Hines family ever have it?"

Granny's pale blue eyes sparkled under her wave of white hair. "Well, I've been thinking about all of that, and some memories have surfaced. Isn't it funny how that works?" She smiled again. "There was talk that someone in the family way back when might have had it. In fact, there was some tension, it seems, after Thomas Hines died. Some were sure he had the brooch, and different branches of his children accused the others of taking it even though a few years after the war, once Thomas Hines was back in Kentucky, the Bickertons hired an investigator to try to find it, but they never did. They were still offering a reward, so your granddad was pretty sure if it was in the family, someone would have turned it in. Everyone was desperate for money back then. Of course, whoever had it could have tried to sell it, but few people could have paid what it was worth back then, plus they would have risked exposing the thief." She raised her pencil-thin eyebrows. "Who knows what really happened to it? I doubt it ended up in the Hines family."

Tess couldn't imagine what the connection could be to the brooch reappearing if it wasn't the Hines family. It was too much of a coincidence. It seemed they were back at square one. Unless...

"Does the surname Gidden mean anything to any of you?"

Granny shook her head.

"Could you have any relatives by the name? Or family friends?"

"Not that I know of," Granny said.

"I've come across that name," Keeley said. "It seems like recently…"

Tess didn't want to fill in the blanks for Keeley. She wanted to know exactly where she had read or heard it.

Keeley snapped her fingers. "Didn't a Gidden work for the Bickertons? I've found that name a few times in a couple of different places. In some documents at the museum and—" She rubbed the side of her head as she blushed. "In the old newspapers on the microfiche. He went missing after the brooch was stolen."

"That's right," Tess said. "That's what we came across too."

"And you think he might be related to us?"

Tess nodded. "I wondered if he might be. Or have some sort of connection. He was from Kentucky originally."

Keeley turned to Granny. "Are you sure the name Gidden doesn't mean anything to you?"

Granny shook her head. "I'm not familiar with that name. Except maybe I've seen it somewhere…like at a store or something."

Nathan interjected, "There's a paint company with a similar name. But that's Glidden, not Gidden."

Granny laughed. "Well, I don't know any Glidden *or* Gidden."

Just as Tess was ready to say goodbye to Granny, the nurse returned. "Good news. The doctor says he'll discharge you tomorrow—as long as you do well over night."

Granny clapped her hands together.

"Great!" Val exclaimed. She turned to Tess and LuAnn. "Would it be possible for us to bring her back to the inn? Until I have a plan in place to take her home?"

"Of course," both women said in unison. Tess thought through the reservations and was sure they could manage it.

Val pulled her phone out of her bag and held it up. "I'm going to call your dad," she said to Keeley and Nathan. "And see if he can come out and help."

Nathan crossed his arms. "Good luck."

Keeley elbowed him. "Give Dad a chance."

"He'll be too busy," Nathan said. "There's always something more important."

Val shook her head at her son but didn't say anything. Instead she waved goodbye to Tess and LuAnn and stepped out into the hall.

***

As Tess drove out of the parking lot, LuAnn turned back toward the hospital. "What is it about that family that makes me want to do whatever possible to help them?"

Tess stopped as an ambulance left the hospital. "I know what you mean. All of them are so endearing. Granny's so cute I want to hug her. Val is such a great daughter-in-law and mom, and really genuine. She seems so in touch with both of her kids, and it's obvious how much she loves them."

LuAnn agreed. "And then the whole historical connection is fascinating too."

"What a blessing they decided to stay at our inn."

LuAnn laughed. "But we would have been spared all the drama around the brooch if they'd stayed somewhere else."

"Maybe not. Maybe the inn is the connection to the brooch—not the Hines family." Tess quickly glanced at her friend as LuAnn's eyes grew wide.

"Yes, there's always been that possibility. Perhaps we need to start exploring that angle more."

Tess turned onto the main street. "Because we've pretty much dead-ended the Hines connection, right?"

"Right," LuAnn agreed. "Do you think we can accommodate the family for a few more nights?"

Tess grimaced. "I hope so. Let's check when we get back. If not, I was thinking maybe I could sleep on a cot in your room and give Granny mine. Val and Nathan could sleep in the common area again."

"Sounds good to me." LuAnn patted Tess's arm. "It would be best for Granny to come back to the inn."

Late that afternoon, as Tess worked on juggling the reservations to accommodate the Hines family, Keeley, Val, and Nathan arrived back at the inn. They'd stopped by the museum, and Keeley had a box of artifacts to change out the items in the curio cabinet, plus an empty box.

She used the key Tess had returned to her to unlock the door.

As Keeley did her work, Val said, "We'll need two rooms, if possible, for the next few days. I hope Robbie can make it. He's not sure..."

"We have two vacancies on Tuesday but only one on Wednesday. But it seems things work out, right?" Tess said. "Let's wait and see."

"Sounds good." Val added, "I know I've said this before, but we appreciate you, LuAnn, and Janice so much. You three are the best."

Tess simply smiled at Val—the woman who put her life on hold to care for her mother-in-law. The woman who managed to work on the road while putting Granny Hines and Keeley and Nathan first. The woman who seemed so understanding of her husband's absence as something he couldn't help— instead of resenting him for it.

Val thanked her again, and then she and Nathan went and sat in the café. She had a magazine, and he was playing some game on his laptop.

Once Keeley had finished her work, she picked up the box of items she was returning to the museum. Tess leaned both elbows on the counter. "Do you think there could be a chance that there's a connection between the Hines and Gidden?"

Keeley shook her head. "I'd never heard that name before I saw it in the *Marietta Times* from 1863."

"How about on one of your ancestry programs? Has a Gidden ever popped up?"

Keeley shook her head. "Not on our branch of the family anyway." She put the box on the front desk. "But I can double-check." She pulled out her phone and tapped the screen a few times. "No. I'm not seeing anything here." She paused a moment as she stared at her screen. "Wait, this is really weird. A Perry popped up. Perry Cooper. That's the name of the guy who was stalking us, right?"

Tess nodded.

Keeley's eyes grew wide. "He's a fifth cousin."

"When was the connection made?"

"Wait. I haven't checked in a while." She hit a button on her phone. "Look at that. He popped up about three weeks ago."

"How odd," Tess said.

Keeley kept looking at her screen. "Oh, wow."

"What is it?"

"His mother's maiden name was Gidden. Frances Gidden Cooper. She was born in Bowling Green, Kentucky, and died last year."

Tess spent the next half hour trying to reach Perry on his cell phone while Keeley, Val, Nathan, LuAnn, and Janice sat in the café, talking and drinking lemonade. Finally, Perry answered. "Sorry," he said. "I was driving. What's up?"

Tess bit her tongue from saying, *You tell me.* Instead she explained that he'd popped up as a cousin on Keeley's ancestry app.

There was a long moment of silence.

Finally Tess asked if he was still there.

"Yep," he said. "And it's time for me to come clean. I'm still in the Marietta area. I'll be there in a few minutes."

CHAPTER TWENTY-TWO

Ten minutes later, Perry opened the door of the inn and walked inside. He had his backpack slung over one shoulder, and he wore his trekking shorts and a T-shirt that read, *May the facts be with you.* He and Keeley were two peas in a pod. And cousins to boot.

Tess walked around from the backside of the front desk and led him into the café to join the others.

"I owe all of you an explanation," Perry said. "And an apology."

"I'll get you some lemonade," Janice said.

A few minutes later they were all gathered around the long harvest table in the café. Perry wrapped his hands around the cold glass and turned to Keeley. "I was the imposter that tried to infiltrate your group, like I said. But I'm not really an imposter—I really am your cousin. A really distant one, but still, your cousin."

Keeley groaned.

"My mother was a Gidden—her great-grandfather was the son of the Gidden who worked for Mr. Bickerton. And her great-great-grandmother was a Hines, a daughter of Xavier's." He sighed. "It's all really confusing."

Keeley leaned back in her chair. "So you did follow us here?"

"Absolutely. I was one hundred percent determined to be here at the same time all of you were."

"Why?" LuAnn asked.

He ran his hand through his thick hair. "This is hard." His clear blue eyes met each of theirs. Tess's heartbeat accelerated. It was difficult to imagine such a kind man being a thief, but the evidence was beginning to pile up against him. She leaned toward him, longing for him to come clean.

LuAnn opened her notebook.

Perry took a long drink of lemonade and then placed the glass back on the table. "I'm ashamed to admit this, but I broke the glass to the curio cabinet. And then—" He inhaled. "I planted the brooch."

That wasn't what Tess had expected.

Keeley sputtered, "But why?"

"And how did you get the brooch?" Tess squeaked.

He spread out his long fingers on the tabletop. "I inherited it."

"From your mother?" Tess asked. "Frances Gidden Cooper?"

He nodded. "I didn't find it until after she died. Once I did my research, I was sure it was the missing Bickerton brooch." He explained that even though it seemed ancestors from both the Hines family and the Gidden family were involved in the theft of the brooch, he thought Gidden held most of the blame. "I can't prove it, but my guess is Gidden arranged for Xavier Hines to steal the brooch. I think from an employee at the inn."

Tess gasped. "Why do you think that?"

"There was an old letter that I found among some documents that belonged to my grandparents—I doubt my mother ever read it." He leaned down, unzipped his backpack, and pulled out a manila envelope. Then he took out a pair of archival gloves, put them on, and took a letter from the envelope, placing it on the table. "It's from Xavier Hines, and the ink is dim, but I can read it."

Janice sat up in her chair. "What does it say?"

"It's dated August 3, 1863." He leaned over it. "'*Gidden, I left the object where you told me to. Don't forget what I've done for you and what you owe me. I hear you were able to get the woman blamed. That's okay with me, just as long as you keep me out of it.*'" Perry looked up.

"'The woman?'" Janice glanced from LuAnn to Tess. "That must be Prudence."

Tess answered, "It matches her journal entries."

"What journal?" Perry and Keeley asked in unison.

Tess explained and then said, "I'll show you once we sort all of this through."

"What happened to Xavier Hines?" LuAnn asked Perry.

"He was killed during the Siege of Petersburg, in Virginia, in the summer of 1864. His oldest girl ended up marrying Gidden after the war." He looked straight at Keeley. "That's how I'm related to all of you."

"Weird," Keeley said.

Tess thought so too. "So why didn't Gidden sell the brooch? Or get the reward?"

"The brooch was too famous by then. Bickerton had done everything he could to get it back. Gidden would have had to go to Europe to sell it, and he didn't have that kind of money. Or fortitude. He ended up joining the Confederacy when he went back to Kentucky. I'm guessing he stashed the brooch first though. He lost an arm at the very end of the war, at Appomattox, and after the war he married and had three children. The oldest was my great-great-grandfather. I'm guessing the brooch was passed down through the generations," Perry explained. "My mother was an only child. She probably found the brooch among her mother's things and didn't realize its value. When she cleaned out her parents' house after they died, she was living in Arizona. I'm guessing she packed up a couple of boxes to take with her. I found the brooch in with other costume jewelry and pieces of china. The letter was tucked between some documents she'd kept from her parents— receipts and things like that."

Tess wondered how many heirlooms ended up being discarded because no one knew how much they were worth.

"What made you realize its value?" LuAnn asked.

"When I researched the Gidden and Hines families, I came across the story of the brooch. At first I thought I was projecting my research onto my life—but the more research I did, the more I was convinced I'd found the missing brooch."

LuAnn twirled her pen with her fingers. "So why didn't you take it to the police then?"

His face reddened. "In retrospect, that would have been the best thing to do. But I didn't. I just wanted to get rid of it—I knew it belonged here in Marietta, but I wasn't sure if it truly belonged to Irene Bickerton Martin and Thelma Bickerton. I knew there was speculation that the Hines family had the brooch, so I thought I could make it look as if someone in that family planted it. Once I found out about the family reunion, I tried to be included in the reunion, and failed. So after that I booked the last room in the inn." He paused.

LuAnn leaned toward him. "And then?"

"I broke the glass and planted the brooch. I thought that would be the end of it. I figured the police, with the help of Maybelline and Margaret, would figure out who the rightful owner or owners should be." He shook his head. "But then the brooch was stolen and everything turned upside down."

"What do you know about the brooch being stolen?" Janice asked.

"Nothing. Absolutely nothing." He nodded to Tess as he took out his cell phone. "I was at Buffington Island that day. I have the photos to prove it. I already showed Tess..."

"Yes," LuAnn said. "She told us. But you could have just downloaded some pictures of Buffington Island onto your phone."

He held up a selfie of himself with the monument in the background.

"Or not," LuAnn said and then smiled. "But you could have hired someone to steal the brooch. Or been working with someone."

He nodded. "You're absolutely right. I could have—but I didn't."

Keeley, who'd been uncharacteristically silent, cleared her throat. "Why should we believe your story? You haven't proven yourself very trustworthy."

"I get that." He grimaced, his eyes full of pain. "I guess the only way to prove I didn't steal the brooch back is to find whoever did."

CHAPTER TWENTY-THREE

Perry was staying at a hotel in town, but he came over the next morning after breakfast was finished to brainstorm who might have stolen the brooch. Maybelline allowed Keeley to come over to see if she could contribute any information. They all gathered around a table in the café dining room again. Robin manned the front desk.

"Where's Nathan?" Keeley asked as she sat down.

She texted her brother. Then her phone dinged, and she said, "He'll be right here."

A minute later, his footsteps thundered up from the basement. As he appeared, he said, "I was helping Thorn." He grinned. "He let me go in the Underground Railroad tunnel again."

"What?" Keeley put a hand on her hip. "Why do you get to have all of the fun?"

"I'll show you later," Tess said. "As an intern at the MURM, you deserve to see it."

Perry's eyes were bright with hope. "Maybe I could see it also? It would be a great addition to my research."

Tess smiled at him. "I think we could arrange a tour for the Hines/Gidden family sometime before you leave."

"Let's get started." LuAnn opened her notebook. "We now know who planted the brooch but have no idea who stole it."

She updated Keeley, Nathan, and Perry on what she and LuAnn and Janice had explored and discussed before.

Tess glanced from Keeley to Perry to Nathan. "At first we were looking for a link between the historical story and the current story, through the Hines family. But now we know the brooch was passed down through the Gidden family. Does anyone see what we might be missing as far as a connection?"

Keeley turned to Perry. "Are there any other relatives we need to know about? Anyone who might have been expecting to inherit the brooch?"

He shook his head. "Like I said before, my mother was an only child. And it seems like my grandfather never passed on the story of the brooch to her."

"All right." LuAnn tapped her pen on the table. "We'll keep the possibility of a historical connection on the list. What are some thoughts on the modern mystery?"

Janice picked up the thread. "The question is, who knew about it, saw its value, and had to have it?"

"Or," Tess added. "Who, with access to it, would benefit the most?"

"Well." Janice's eyebrows shot up. "The only people so far who have benefitted from the brooch being taken are Jim and Linda Walsh."

"In what way?" Perry asked.

"They're selling costume brooches inspired by the stolen one. And now bracelets and necklaces too," Janice explained. "It's all really gaudy and cheap."

Keeley rolled her eyes. "That's so tacky."

"Actually," Nathan said. "It's brilliant. But it makes me wonder how dedicated the guy is to his profession."

"What do you mean?" Tess asked.

"Well, he's a jeweler right? Trained in fine jewelry."

"Yes," Tess said. "He attended a gemology school in Switzerland."

"It is sort of tacky"—he glanced at his sister—"that he'd exploit the theft of an item like the brooch. It would be like an art dealer selling cheap replicas of a stolen painting."

Tess understood exactly what he was saying. She'd felt uncomfortable with what Jim and Linda were doing, but she hadn't been able to express it as well as Nathan just had. She glanced around the lobby. "I believe we should take this conversation into the kitchen, behind closed doors." They didn't usually allow anyone in the kitchen, but they had more tourists than usual wandering into the inn, thanks to all the brochures Linda was slipping into the swag bags.

LuAnn and Janice agreed. Winnie had gone out to pick up a few ingredients for the soup of the day, so it was the best place to talk.

Once they'd all resettled, LuAnn tapped her pen on the table and said, "So the big question is, did Jim and Linda stage the theft?"

Keeley tapped the tabletop. "Obviously, there was at least one other person involved if they did. Maybe they planned to sell the brooch and split the money."

"But who would do that?" Tess asked. "Who would take such a risk to steal an item that can be traced like that?"

Nathan hit his forehead with the heel of his hand. "I've read about this sort of thing. There's a whole market out there on the black web. Someone's probably already paid for it with Bitcoin. Someone in Singapore or Hong Kong. It's just like stolen art—an obscenely wealthy person out there is happy to have a masterpiece behind a bedroom door—you know, in a really big bedroom. Bigger than this inn. Someone could be happy to only wear the brooch in private. They'd still be willing to pay a ton of money for it."

Tess couldn't imagine such wealth.

"They're fine having it be a secret. Maybe they only wear it at home. Or someplace where they're sure no one will recognize the piece."

"Thank you," Keeley said in a sarcastic voice, "for that bit of information."

"Actually, that's very helpful," Tess said. "How would they ship the brooch? Certainly not by mail."

"Someone would come and pick it up," Nathan said. "Not the buyer. But one of his or her people. They wouldn't trust it to anyone else."

LuAnn jotted down some notes and then said, "So we need to brainstorm who would work with Jim and Linda on this, who would have been willing to actually steal it."

"I'm guessing it could be anyone," Tess said. "A paid actor. An acquaintance. Maybe Jim and Linda weren't going to split the money with him. The person wouldn't have needed to know what was going on. They could have been totally in the dark."

"But what if they weren't?" Perry asked. "Who could it have been? Do they have a son? Or another relative in the area?"

"Not that I know of," Tess said.

"Do they have any business partners?" Nathan asked.

"Good question." Tess exhaled slowly. "I didn't ask about that. But we should find out about any business backers too. Oh!" She raised her hand to her mouth. "Why didn't I put this together earlier?"

"What?" Janice asked.

"Frank Bryant." She explained to the others. "He's a local small-business investor that I've worked with. He said one of the businesses he works with, Fundae Ice Cream Shoppe, took an upward turn. It does seem to be doing better, but what if he was being deceitful? What if it was Uptown Jewelers that had really turned around?"

LuAnn tapped her chin. "That doesn't mean he was in on the robbery."

"I know," Tess answered. "But it's worth investigating."

"Any other connections between the Walshes and this guy Bryant?" asked Perry.

"One." Tess leaned forward. "Both Jim and Frank went to Ohio State at the same time."

"So they might have a shared history?"

"It's a possibility. Although Ohio State is a huge university," Tess answered, just as the front door dinged, signaling some-one had come into the inn.

"I've got it." Tess jumped to her feet and hurried out the door of the kitchen. A man with dark hair and a goatee closed the front door carefully behind him.

He turned and saw her, and a grin spread across his face. "I'm Robbie Hines."

Tess froze.

"I'm looking for Val. And Keeley and Na—"

Chapter Twenty-Four

Before he could finish his sentence, Keeley came flying through the door. "Daddy!" She flew into his arms.

Robbie hugged her long and hard and then let her go. "Where's your mom?"

"Up at the hospital."

"How about Nathan?"

She nodded toward the kitchen. LuAnn and Janice stood in the doorway.

Robbie lowered his voice. "Is he still mad at me?"

Keeley shrugged. "I don't know—he won't talk about it." She turned to Tess. "This is our dad. And this is Tess, LuAnn, and Janice, innkeepers extraordinaire."

Tess shook Robbie's hand. He didn't appear to be the neglectful husband and father that she'd anticipated.

Next he greeted LuAnn and Janice too. Then he called out, "Nathan?" He took a step toward the kitchen. "I'm here."

As Robbie reached the door, Nathan stepped through, with his arms crossed.

Robbie stared at him for a moment. He appeared as if he wanted to give the boy a hug but instead he patted him on the shoulder. "How about if you show me how to get up to the hospital and surprise Mom and Granny? I have an Uber waiting outside."

Nathan's jaw seemed to be clenched. "Granny's getting out this morning."

"That's why I'm here." Robbie patted Nathan's shoulder again. "Let's go spring her out. We can talk on the way." Robbie put his arm around Keeley and pulled her close again. "You too."

She shook her head. "I need to get back to work. Maybe you can come by later."

"I'd love that." He slung his computer bag over his shoulder. "Come on, Nathan. We can talk on the way."

The boy shook his head. "I'd rather stay here. The Uber driver will get you to the hospital. I'll see you when you get back."

Keeley elbowed her brother. "Knock it off."

He simply gave her a look of death and headed toward the stairs.

Keeley sputtered, "He's impossible."

"He needs some space," Robbie said. "That's all."

"You spoil him." Keeley's eyes narrowed. "So does Mom. You'd never let me get away with acting like that."

Robbie smiled at her and then, with his voice low, said, "I'll talk about this with you later." He turned to Tess, LuAnn, and Janice. "It's great to meet the three of you. I'll be back with Val and Granny as soon as I can."

"We'll be here when you arrive," Tess said. "Ready and waiting."

She watched as the father and daughter headed toward the door, arms locked around each other. She couldn't help but note Robbie's full head of dark hair. Val and Robbie seemed so young, and yet she knew how quickly the years sped by.

When they stepped back into the kitchen, Perry asked who'd arrived.

"Robbie Hines," Janice answered. "He's headed up to the hospital, and Keeley's going back to the museum."

"What about Nathan?" Perry asked. "Did he go with his father?"

Tess shook her head, not wanting to say any more. "He went up to his room."

"I really like that kid," Perry said. "He's sharp as a tack."

Tess agreed. He was also troubled about something.

The four of them continued to discuss their options.

LuAnn doodled the brooch on a page of her notebook, shading in the sapphire and ruby stones. "How about if I call Frank Bryant and ask him about investing in a local business? And see what he says."

"That sounds like a great idea," Tess said. "If he doesn't mention the jewelry store, maybe ask him about it, because it's been in the news. Say you're looking for a local business to invest in, but use an alias in case he's researched me and the inn."

"I'll drop the Lu and just use Ann."

Perry pushed back his chair. "Do you need me any longer?"

Tess shook her head. "But can we call if we think of anything else?"

"Of course." He stood. "I'll stick around until tomorrow." He headed toward the lobby but then stopped and asked over his shoulder, "Mind if I play your baby grand one more time?"

"Please do," Tess said. "We'd love that."

The three women sat at the table for a few more minutes as Perry began to play. It was a classical piece.

"Beethoven," Janice said, "'Moonlight Sonata.'"

Winnie returned from running her errands as they listened. "Oh, my," she said. "That angel is back in town."

Tess smiled at her. "Isn't it beautiful?"

"So, so, so amazing," she said. "It makes me want to sit down and weep."

Tess felt the same way, and she wasn't sure why. It wasn't a sadness, exactly. More like the feeling she got after reading a good book. Or seeing a particularly moving film. And when she saw Keeley and Robbie walk out the front door, linked together. It was beauty, all right. She wiped her eyes as she said a prayer for Nathan. Whatever was going on with him and his dad, she prayed God would help them work it out.

Janice leaned forward across the table and whispered to LuAnn and Tess, "Why don't the two of you go up and make the call. I'll help Winnie and Taylor get lunch started."

"Good idea," Tess said.

When they reached the lobby, the music reverberated off the ceiling. It truly did sound as if an angel were playing their baby grand.

"Let's take the stairs," LuAnn said.

On the third floor, voices down the hallway stopped them. Thorn and Nathan. Tess kept walking, not wanting to eavesdrop, but as she followed LuAnn up to the fourth floor, she heard Thorn say, "You need to talk to your dad about how you feel."

"I don't do that," Nathan responded.

"Then it's time you learned how."

Tess said another prayer for Nathan and for wisdom for Thorn. And for Robbie. He seemed like the kind of man who would listen. But hopefully he could tell Nathan how he felt too—and model for the young man what he needed to do.

LuAnn put the call on speakerphone. It rang several times, and just when Tess figured no one was going to answer, Frank's receptionist did. She said Frank was out of the office, but she'd be happy to take a detailed message. LuAnn explained she had heard of Frank's investment company. "I was wondering about his process of finding local businesses to invest in," she said. "I'm relatively new to Marietta and would love to contribute to the local economy—and make a profit, in time."

The receptionist assured her Frank would call right back.

"Should we get back to work?" LuAnn asked.

"Let's wait a few minutes." Tess walked over to the sink and pulled out the cleanser and sponge from under the counter.

"What are you doing?" LuAnn asked.

"Cleaning."

LuAnn rolled her eyes. "Relax for a moment."

"I can't." Tess sprinkled the powder in the sink and began to scrub. As she rinsed out the sink, LuAnn's phone rang.

She put it on Speaker as she answered. "Hello."

It was Frank.

The two chatted for a few minutes, and then he got down to business. "I've got a couple of local businesses that are doing really well right now. Of course, if you decide to invest in my company, it's not like you can choose the businesses. It's a package deal."

"Of course," LuAnn said. "I completely understand that. I've had my eye on one particular business, just because it's been in the news. I'm fascinated by what they're doing."

"What business would that be? The new ice cream parlor?"

"Well, that one is doing well too." She chuckled. "I have friends who had to wait half an hour to get a table."

"They just finished a back patio to accommodate more people." Frank's voice was full of pride. "My idea. It really swung things around."

"Great!" LuAnn's enthusiasm was as clear as a riverboat horn. "That's what I like to hear. How about the jewelry shop? What's it called?" She hummed. "It has 'Jewelers' in the name."

Frank hesitated and then offered, "Uptown Jewelers?"

"That's it," LuAnn said. "I walked by there the other day, and it was really hoppin'. What in the world is going on there?"

"You haven't heard?" Frank's voice was incredulous.

"About?"

"I thought everyone in Ohio had heard about that place. It's been in the newspaper. On the local news. Even on the national news."

"Goodness. And to think I thought I was up to speed." She laughed.

"I guess not. Uptown Jewelers was robbed. On July fifth. An expensive, antique piece was taken."

"Oh my," LuAnn gushed. "But it seems like people would be staying away from the place, not lining up to get inside."

"Well, the owners took my advice."

Tess's heart began to race.

Frank continued, "Let's just say they made one of the best entrepreneurial moves I've ever seen."

"Is that right?" LuAnn's eyes grew wide. "So they're one of the small businesses you invest in? That's done really well?"

"Let's just say they've turned things around."

"I see," LuAnn said. "I was wondering, could we meet in person? Sometime soon?"

"Of course. This afternoon would work. I run on my lunch hour, so how about around one thirty?"

"Run? In this heat?"

"On the treadmill, at the gym," he said. "It's a good, consistent time for me to get it done."

"One thirty it is then," LuAnn said.

"Perfect." After Frank gave her the address, LuAnn said goodbye and ended the call.

"Good grief," Tess said. "He'll meet with you in person but not me?"

"Weird, huh?"

"Very weird," Tess answered. "And he works out now? He must be trying to lose weight."

"So he's a big guy?"

"Yeah, I'd say so. Not tall but definitely good-sized. Let's just say, I got the impression he liked to eat. In fact, Jeffrey once said the guy wasn't that into golf, but he definitely could shoot a par three when it came to the club restaurant."

LuAnn stayed upstairs while Tess headed to the basement to retrieve a gallon of toilet bowl cleaner to fill the containers in the housekeeping closet.

The lobby was silent now. Obviously Perry had left and taken his angelic music with him. Janice stood at the counter and gave Tess her signature sweet smile. "I have good news, bad news, good news. Which do you want first?"

Tess wasn't in the mood for games, but Janice was so cute she couldn't disappoint her. "How about in that order. Good. Bad. Good."

"All right. The honeymoon suite is now vacant for tonight."

Tess clapped her hands together. That was good news. "Val and Robbie can stay in it."

"Exactly."

"What's the bad news?"

"Well, *someone* had to cancel. The couple who were celebrating their fifth anniversary."

"Oh, that's sad. Why?"

"Well, that's the other good news. The wife is pregnant."

Tess clapped her hands together again. "There's nothing better than a baby."

"Exactly." Janice beamed. "And they've been trying since their wedding night."

Tess's heart lurched. She could imagine the pain of dealing with infertility for five years.

Janice nodded. "They've gone through all sorts of treatments, but success at last. And twins to boot. Of course, she's sicker than a dog."

"Aww." Tess had horrible morning sickness with Jeff Jr. "That explains why they canceled. Poor thing."

Janice nodded in agreement.

"Except for the morning sickness, it sounds like it's an all-around good situation though."

Janice tilted her head and laughed. "You're absolutely right. Everyone's a winner."

Tess felt a sincere joy for the couple. But she also thought of when she'd held her baby girl for the first time. As an adoptive mom, her heart expanded bigger than any ninth-month big belly she'd ever seen. God created families in all sorts of ways, and she knew, without a shadow of a doubt, that His best for her was Lizzie. Just the thought of her beloved daughter filled her eyes with tears.

The women were busy in the café, but LuAnn snuck out just after one for her appointment with Frank. Tess didn't see

Nathan at all. He didn't come down for lunch or to hang out with Thorn or to leave the inn.

Tess focused on helping Winnie clean the kitchen, expecting LuAnn back anytime. Finally she arrived just after three, a little out of breath. "Sit with me for a few minutes," she said to Tess.

They sat at the far table in the café. "I thought you said Frank Bryant was a big guy."

"I did. I mean, like I said, not tall. But round."

"The Frank Bryant I met was as slim as could be. As slim as Nathan."

"You're kidding."

"I'm not," LuAnn said. "I saw a photo on his wall of him at some Christmas party where he was a lot heavier."

"But now he's as thin... as the thief."

LuAnn nodded. "Yup."

"But why would he risk it? Anyone could have seen him."

"Except, according to Frank, the traffic through the jewelry store was only a couple of customers a day at that time. But it does seem he would have been on the lookout for you, considering you're one of the owners of the inn where the brooch made its mysterious appearance."

Tess pursed her lips and then said, "I had to tell him I was one of the owners, so he wouldn't have known it at the time of the robbery. And I doubt whoever the robber was got a good look at my face before he shoved me."

LuAnn frowned. "Jim wouldn't have thought to tell him you were the one bringing the brooch in," she said. "He had no idea Frank knew you."

"Maybe we should be watching the jewelry store," Tess said. "Maybe Nathan was right that they might be selling the brooch on the black market."

"What exactly would we look for?" LuAnn asked.

"Someone suspicious?" Tess stood up. "Let's send Janice. She's pretty intuitive."

Janice was happy to get a dish of ice cream and a window seat at Fundae and stare across the street at Uptown Jewelers. She texted Tess and LuAnn every ten minutes to say only touristy-looking people were going in and out of the shop. She'd finished the ice cream and was now on her second cup of coffee. Tess was beginning to think the entire endeavor was futile.

An hour into their sting, Val opened the front door, and Robbie helped his mother into the inn. From the smile on Granny's face, she looked as if she were coming home. Or perhaps it was the fact that Robbie was at her side.

"Good news," Tess said. "The honeymoon suite is available."

"That's great." Val stepped quickly to the counter but then turned back to Robbie. "I think Granny and I should stay in there."

"I won't hear of it," Granny said. "You two have too little time together."

Val shook her head at Robbie, and he nodded. Then he leaned down close to his mother's ear. "We'll figure it out later. Right now, we'll get you settled down for a nap."

As Robbie and Granny shuffled to the elevator, Val leaned on the counter. "Have you seen Nathan?"

Tess shook her head. "He hasn't been down since this morning."

A wave of sadness clouded Val's eyes. "When his dad arrived?"

Tess nodded.

"Nathan wanted to work with his dad this summer, but Robbie wanted him to travel with us and have some fun. Robbie worked hard his entire life, since the time he was a pre-teen." Val spoke softly. "He thinks he's shielding Nathan, but he's keeping him from what he loves best instead."

"Which is?"

"Programming. And working with his dad." Val suddenly appeared exhausted. "So instead of appreciating his dad sparing him, he resents Robbie. Even though I'd say he's had a good time here. I know I'm glad he came."

"So am I," Tess said. "He's an amazing young man."

Val stood up straight. "Thank you. I really appreciate it. Not everyone sees that in him . . ." Her voice trailed off.

"Then they haven't gotten to know him well enough."

Val smiled. "That's exactly how I feel." She glanced toward the elevator. "I better go get Granny settled. I know she's tired."

A few minutes later, Janice sent another group text to Tess and LuAnn. *A bunch of tourists just exited the jewelry store—but there's a guy that's been hanging around outside for the last ten minutes looking in the window. He waited until the group left before he looked in the window again and then went in the store. I went to look in the window and it doesn't look as if anyone is in there at all except Linda. What should I do?*

Tess wasn't sure. She didn't want Janice to get caught up in anything dangerous. She decided to err on the side of caution.

Call Randy, she texted back. *See if he'll come check it out.*

Before Janice could text back, Tess got a text from Nathan. *Come up to my room NOW. URGENT!*

She couldn't imagine why he wouldn't text his parents, but she couldn't ignore his text either. Maybe something had happened with Granny. She bounded up the stairs, dialing Nathan's number as she did.

"Hello." His voice was flat.

"Do I need to call 911?" she asked. "Is Granny all right?"

"Granny's fine. And, yes, call 911. Have them send an officer over to Uptown Jewelers."

"What in the world?" She reached the second floor and started down the hall. Nathan's door was open. She stopped.

He sat at the desk with his laptop open.

"Call," he said, pointing at the computer, then holding his thumb and index like a telephone receiver.

She dialed as she stepped behind him. On the screen was a view of the back room of the jewelry store. Jim Walsh, Frank Bryant, and another man were gathered around the table.

Nathan zoomed in. Tess leaned forward, squinting as she focused on the black-and-white image. For a moment she couldn't believe her eyes, but it was plain as day. All three men were staring at the Bickerton brooch.

CHAPTER TWENTY-FIVE

Tess needed to know how Nathan had footage from Uptown Jewelers on his laptop, but first she had to call the police, and then she had to get over to the jewelry store.

"I'm on my way," she called over her shoulder as she rushed out of the room. "We'll talk when I get back!"

She tried calling Randy on her way down the stairs but he didn't answer. She left a message and called 911. She told them what was going on as she ran out of the inn and down the steps.

She hit End and rushed down the street, waving to Janice, who was standing outside of Fundae.

Janice reached Tess's side. "I called Randy, just like you said," she said breathlessly. "He went in the jewelry shop and then came out and went around behind the building."

Tess grabbed her arm. "Somehow Nathan has a camera or something in there—we saw Frank and Jim and some other guy looking at the brooch. How about the two of us walk into the jewelry store as calmly as we can, and you engage Linda in conversation."

Janice linked arms with Tess, and they made their way to the front door. "What will you say?"

Tess gulped. She wasn't sure. "I'll think of something."

Janice pulled open the door, and Tess entered first. Linda's face lit up when she saw them. "Two of my favorite people. Welcome!"

By the sweet expression on Linda's face, Tess really doubted she knew what was going on in the back room.

"Jim's in an important meeting," Linda said. "But he should be done in a few minutes."

Tess panicked for a moment as a feeling of déjà vu flooded through her. What if the suspicious guy pushed his way out and got away with the brooch, but this time Janice was injured?

She took a deep breath and opened her mouth to say something—anything—but before she could utter a word she heard Randy yell "Freeze!" and the back room's door was jerked open.

A man stumbled out of the room and headed for the front door. Tess gasped, fearing he'd get away, but the front door flew open and another police officer stood with his feet planted and his shoulders wide, blocking the doorway.

"You don't have a warrant!" Jim yelled from behind her. "This is an illegal search."

Randy rushed past Tess and grabbed the man by the arms. "This isn't a search. I simply came to ask you questions. But I just saw the brooch that was stolen from here." He put handcuffs on the man and read him his rights. Then he turned to the police officer. "I think you'll find that Frank Bryant left the building out the back entrance. I need for you to radio in and get a search out for him. Find him and take him to the station."

"Honey!" Linda stepped around the counter. "What's going on? Did that man find the brooch?"

Jim's face reddened, which surprised Tess. She was beginning to think he had no shame. "Linda, stay back at the counter," he said. "I don't want to involve you in this." He turned his back to her—and to Randy and Tess too.

Linda took a step backward, a confused look on her face, and then retreated behind the counter. Tess couldn't help but feel sorry for her.

Randy cleared his throat and said to Jim, "I'm taking you and your wife in also."

"I need to speak to my attorney," Jim said.

"Of course." Randy reached out his hand. "In the meantime, I need the stolen item."

"The brooch?" the handcuffed man said. "I need it too. I just paid for it. I uh...I thought this was an aboveboard transaction."

"Have you already transferred the money?" Randy stepped forward.

The man nodded.

"Then I'll need a record of that." He turned to Jim. "And of course, the brooch too."

Jim pulled the brooch from his pants pocket, and Randy took it from him. Tess was sure she detected a sigh from Jim. She felt the same way but for a different reason.

Randy glanced at Tess and then Janice. "I need the two of you to join us." He looked more closely at Tess. "I'm especially interested in knowing why you're here, Mrs. Wallace. Let's go, Mrs. Walsh."

"But it's not time to close up," she said. "I don't want to miss any customers."

"Close the shop, honey," Jim said. "It won't take long once we're at the station to sort this all out. You'll see."

⁂

After Randy took statements from Linda, Janice, and Tess, they were all free to go. But he kept Jim, the black market guy, and Frank, who was handcuffed and waiting at the station when they arrived.

When they reached the inn, Tess's heart was still racing. "Do you think Randy will stop by after he finishes interrogating the three men?" she asked Janice.

"He will," she answered. "You had to tell him the truth about why you were in the shop, and I'm sure he'll want to talk to Nathan."

As Tess put her purse in the office, Nathan came bounding into the lobby from the staircase. "Did they get 'em?"

Tess grinned at him. "They did." Then she sobered. "Nathan, how did you see into their shop?"

His face fell. "Umm." He shrugged. "It's not like it's going to be a secret, right? That police officer that came in the room. What's his name?"

"Randy Lewis."

"Yeah. He's going to be over soon with questions."

"Probably," Tess said.

"What's going on?" LuAnn asked, coming down the stairs.

Nathan wove his hands together and cracked his knuckles. "I hacked into the jewelry store security camera."

For once LuAnn seemed speechless, and Janice was at a loss for words too.

"Did you tell your parents?" Tess asked. "They should definitely be with you when you're questioned."

Nathan wrinkled his nose. "Nah. I don't want to stress them out."

"Either you tell them or I will," Tess said. "They need to know."

He shrugged. "If you insist. They're upstairs with Granny. Keeley's up there too." He pointed to the staircase. "I'll follow you."

"I'll call if Randy shows up," Janice said to Tess. "And I'll get LuAnn up to speed."

On one hand, Tess was grateful to Nathan for getting the information they needed. But on the other hand, she feared he might be in big trouble. Hacking into a security system was definitely a crime.

Tess led the way up the staircase to the second floor and then down the hall. The door to the honeymoon suite was open, and a peal of laughter filled the air. Tess couldn't help but smile, expecting it to be Keeley, but when they reached the doorway, she realized it was Val. Granny was propped up in bed with a tiara on her head, holding the remote control like a magic wand, and Val sat on the edge of the bed next to her.

Robbie stood off to the side, a smile on his face, while Keeley perched on the end of the bed. She was the first to notice Tess and Nathan in the doorway.

"Hey, Nathan." Robbie stepped forward. "Did you decide to join us?"

He shook his head. "I just have something I need to tell you."

"Oh?"

"Yeah. I hacked into a jewelry store security camera. There was a policeman there, and he's going to want to talk to you." He turned and bolted down the hall.

Robbie and Val seemed stunned. Granny appeared oblivious as she waved the remote around.

But Keeley leapt off the bed and took off after him, brushing by Tess. "Nathan, wait!"

"I don't want to talk about it!" Nathan's door slammed down the hall.

"I don't get it," Val said.

Robbie pulled out his cell phone. "I'm calling our lawyer."

Val turned to Tess. "Why did he do that?"

"To catch a thief," Tess answered. "The men who stole the brooch, to be specific."

"I don't understand," Val said.

Robbie spoke into his phone. "This is Robbie Hines. Put me through to Max, please."

Tess glanced toward the hall, wondering if Keeley was getting any more information.

Val scooted off the bed and stepped to Tess's side. "What exactly did Nathan do?"

"He hacked into the Uptown Jewelers' security camera. He helped solve the crime, but…"

"I get it now." Val ran her hand through her hair.

Both women turned to Robbie as he explained the situation to their lawyer. After a pause, he said, "Okay. Got it. I call the police station and say we want to talk with them."

There was another pause.

"All right. I'll phone you from there." He ended the call and then appeared to be looking something up online as he said, "What's the name of the officer who was at the jewelry shop?"

"Officer Randy Lewis," Tess answered.

Robbie placed the call. He explained who he was and why he was calling. "I'll bring Nathan right down," he said, followed by a pause. Then he said, "Are you sure? You're not too busy down there?" After another pause, he said, "See you soon."

As he ended the call, he met Val's eyes. "Officer Lewis is coming here to question Nathan."

"That's good," Val said. "Nathan will definitely do better in a place he feels safe."

When Randy arrived, Janice sent him up to the women's common area on the fourth floor where Nathan, his parents, and Tess had gathered.

Once they'd all sat down, Robbie asked, "Is it all right if I put our lawyer on speakerphone while they talk?"

"That won't be necessary." Randy turned to Nathan. "Could you tell me exactly what you did and why?"

Nathan explained that they all wondered if the owner of Uptown Jewelers could have staged the theft of the brooch, so he decided to hack into their security camera. "It was really easy. I know it's a new business, but they're using outdated software. So I just got in through a back door and joined the control channel." He explained a few other technical things that Tess didn't follow.

After a moment of silence, Tess took a deep breath and then said, "What's happened with Frank? And Jim and Linda?"

"Linda wasn't involved. Perhaps she should have been suspicious, but she seems genuinely devastated by the accusations. I spoke with Frank and Jim, and my supervisor is currently interrogating them. And then he'll question the other man again."

Robbie folded his hands on the tabletop. "Do they know what Nathan did?"

Randy shook his head. "They don't know."

"Will the evidence against them be thrown out?" Robbie asked. "Because it was obtained illegally?"

Randy shook his head. "I was there because Janice called me about a person acting suspiciously at the jewelry store. I went into the store and asked Linda if there was a back entrance into their workroom. She told me there was and gave me permission to access the building through that door. I caught the men red-handed with the brooch. As far as I'm concerned, there is no need to enter Nathan's activities into the record. Chief Mayfield agrees."

He turned to Nathan. "Did you know when you hacked into the system that you were doing something illegal?"

Nathan cocked his head. "No. But it wasn't immoral. At least I don't think so. I just exploited their incompetence. Tess had pretty much figured out who committed the crime, but she needed evidence to confirm it. Justice needed to be served." He sighed and lowered his head. "I didn't think of it as illegal. Sorry." His voice was barely audible. "Are you going to arrest me? Will I be sent to the Ohio State Penitentiary?"

Tess realized she was holding her breath and let it out slowly.

Randy cleared his throat as Robbie said, "Raise your head, Son. Face the officer."

Nathan obeyed.

Randy smiled. "We don't need the evidence for a conviction, so we're letting Nathan off with a warning."

Nathan's shoulders slumped in relief. Then he smiled back at the officer. "Thank you," he blurted. His parents echoed his thanks.

Tess suddenly thought of something. "Randy," she said, "did you ever find out who made that anonymous call accusing me of stealing the brooch?"

"He hasn't confessed yet," Randy told her, "but I recognized Frank Bryant's voice when I was interrogating him. I'm almost certain he's your guy."

Randy stood. "I won't thank you for hacking into a security system, but I can say it's been a pleasure to meet all of you." Everyone else stood too. Randy shook their hands and then turned to Nathan again. "Perhaps you should consider a career as a police forensic tech. You'd do great."

Nathan smiled for the first time all afternoon. "I'll keep it in mind."

After Officer Lewis left, Keeley slipped into the room. "He didn't haul you away. Does that mean you're not under arrest?"

Nathan grinned at her. Keeley patted him on the back. He turned and put his arms around her. "You can hug me," he said.

"Ahh, baby brother," she said, tucking her head under his chin.

Robbie and Val put their arms around the children for a family hug that lasted until Nathan squirmed and said, "Enough, already!"

The next morning, as Val and Robbie got Granny ready for the day, Nathan ate his breakfast while Thorn read the newspaper. Tess looked over his shoulder. The lead story was the recovery of the brooch. Randy credited Tess, LuAnn, and Janice with solving the mystery, and no mention of Nathan was made.

"What happens with the brooch now?" Nathan asked.

Tess glanced at LuAnn, who was on her way to the kitchen. Earlier that morning LuAnn had spoken to Brad, and Tess was wondering the same thing. "Since there's no way of knowing who the brooch truly belonged to when it came over from England, the Bickerton and Dawson heirs—Brad, Grant, Thelma, Irene, Charlotte, and Leo, Irene's son—have decided to share the inheritance. The Ohio Historical Society is working on an exhibit about Morgan's Raid. They're thinking about loaning it to be displayed in the exhibit."

"Wait." Tess raised her eyebrows. "All of them?"

LuAnn nodded. "None of them wants to sell the brooch. So this seems the best thing to do with it for now."

"Got it." Tess rested her hand on an empty chair. "Why the Ohio Historical Society?"

"Because they have the security to protect it. They'll figure out what to do with it after the exhibit ends." LuAnn smiled. "I think they're handling it all really well, considering."

Tess agreed. She followed LuAnn into the kitchen where Winnie was humming "Moonlight Sonata." It had stuck in her head too.

LuAnn picked up the basket of muffins from the counter and turned to Tess. "Do you have any idea how Frank's arrest will affect your finances?"

Tess sighed. "Well, I doubt in any way positive, but I sent him a certified letter last night to cash out my account, which I know he won't be doing. But his trustees will have to. Hopefully I won't lose too much." She perked up. "But if there's one thing I've learned in the last few weeks, it's to trust God. Right?"

LuAnn smiled as she headed to the door with the muffins.

As Tess followed LuAnn out to the lobby, a large bang startled her. It was too late for fireworks. Thorn jumped too. A second bang startled her again. But this time Thorn remained untroubled. "It's just a car backfiring," he said, as calm as could be.

Nathan grinned at him and gave him a high-five. Tess doubted Thorn would ever get completely over his pain, but it seemed he was making progress.

As Nathan put his hand back down, his grin turned into a frown. "When Mom told me we were visiting Marietta, Ohio, it was the last place in the world I wanted to come. But I'm really glad I did. I'm going to really miss this town, and the inn, and all of you too."

Tess reached up to give him her own high-five, and he gave her a big, hearty slap. "We're going to miss you too," she said. "I hope you'll come back and see us." She wrapped her hand around his for just a moment. "And I mean that, absolutely."

"Of course you do," he said, letting go of her hand. "If I can, I will."

The next morning Robbie and Nathan packed their rental car while Keeley, Val, and Granny sat in the lobby on the couches. Janice worked around them, taking down the red, white, and blue bunting.

Tess sat down in a chair across from Val and asked, "What are your plans from here?"

"We'll drive to Chicago and pack up Granny's things. Then she and I will fly home, while Robbie and Nathan rent a truck and drive her things out to California."

A sensation of joy rose in Tess. "And then?"

"She'll live with us," Val said. "It means my assistant will need to do more, but it'll be worth it." She wrapped her arm around Granny and pulled her close. Granny grinned from ear to ear.

Tess turned to Keeley. "What about you?"

"I only have another week here for my internship, and then I'll head home too. I'll have a couple of weeks before I start school." She reached over and patted her grandmother's hand. "It will be good family time. I can't wait."

Granny just couldn't stop grinning.

A few minutes later, Tess stood on the sidewalk beside Keeley and waved as the rest of the Hines family drove away. She thought of Prudence all those years ago. The brooch had been lost, then found. And now, lost and found again. Prudence hadn't been concerned about the brooch but about the people surrounding her. That was what was most important this time around too. The Hines family, in particular. And Perry Cooper. And Linda. The woman would definitely need a friend and extra care now.

With a simple, *So be it*, Prudence had given her worries and fears to the Lord. Tess thanked the Lord that she'd learned, once again, to do the same.

Dear Reader,

As a history major, I'm thrilled to be writing for the Secrets of Wayfarers Inn series. For this story, I especially delighted in the Civil War research and felt as if I'd stumbled on a gold mine when I chose to research Morgan's Raid. I'd read about the event before, which took place the same time as the Battle of Gettysburg, but I'd never delved into the details of it. (See the "insight" below for more information.)

As I read through books and online accounts of the raid, the character who fascinated me the most was Captain Thomas Hines. He was a spy for Brigadier General Morgan and first scouted the route of the raid. Later, once Morgan, Hines, and others were imprisoned in the Ohio State Penitentiary, it was Hines who—according to some accounts—came up with the idea of how to tunnel out of the prison and escape.

Who was this Thomas Hines, I wondered? And what would his current-day descendants think of him?

I came up with a group of fictitious offspring, whom I came to adore almost as much as I did our innkeepers—Tess, LuAnn, and Janice. But I needed something to link the current story to the past. What could it be?

Stolen loot was common during the Civil War and certainly during Morgan's Raid. Gold, jewelry, and other valuables "went missing" and were never recovered. And so I conjured up a valuable brooch, stolen from our dear Thelma and Irene's ancestors, that is absolutely fictitious.

Spinning *Red, White, and True* turned out to be a delightful experience for me. The time I "spent" in Marietta, with both Prudence and her family in the past and Tess, LuAnn, and Janice and the Hines family in the present, was thoroughly enjoyable. I hope you, dear reader, will share my delight as you read the story! Enjoy!

Signed,
Leslie Gould

About the Author

Leslie Gould is the #1 bestselling and Christy-Award-winning author of over thirty novels. Besides writing, she also teaches part-time at Warner Pacific University. Leslie and her husband, Peter, enjoy traveling, research trips, and hiking. They live in Portland, Oregon, and are the revolving-door parents of four grown children and two cats.

Morgan's Raid

During the Civil War, from June 11-July 26, 1863, Confederate Brigadier General John Hunt Morgan led 2,460 cavalrymen on a thousand-mile raid that originated in Tennessee and crossed the Ohio River into Indiana. The raid coincided with both the Gettysburg and Vicksburg campaigns, and Morgan hoped it would draw troops away from those battles and frighten the North into demanding their soldiers return home.

After raiding Indiana, the Confederate soldiers entered Ohio on July 13 and destroyed bridges, railroads, and government stores across the southern part of the state. On July 17, the Confederate soldiers raided Marietta. Citizens of the area felled trees across roads to slow the invaders and did their best to protect the town. Damage, thankfully, was minimal in Marietta compared to other areas; but in Ohio alone, Morgan and his men raided over 4,000 homes and businesses.

When Morgan and his troops attempted to recross the Ohio River and return to the South, he was arrested, along with several of his officers. They were sent to the Ohio State Penitentiary, but they escaped in November of 1863 by tunneling out of the prison and taking a train to Cincinnati. They then crossed the Ohio River to safety. Morgan was later killed in 1864 during a raid on Greeneville, Tennessee.

Winnie's Red, White, and Blue Berry Tart

Pastry Ingredients:

1¼ cups	flour
½ cup	butter (cut into small pieces)
3 tablespoon	ice water

Custard Ingredients:

¾ cup	granulated sugar
½ cup	flour
1/8 teaspoon	salt
2 cups	whole milk
2 large egg yolks	
2 tablespoon	butter (cut into pieces)
1½ teaspoon	pure vanilla extract

Fruit Topping Ingredients:

2 cups	raspberries
2 cups	blueberries
¼ cup	raspberry jam (melted)
	powdered sugar

Pastry: In a medium-size bowl, cut flour into butter with a pastry blender or two knives until the mixture resembles coarse crumbs. Add ice water. Mix until dough comes together. Gather dough into a ball, flatten, wrap in waxed paper, and refrigerate for 30 minutes. With your fingers, press the tart dough evenly into the bottom and up the sides of a nine- or ten-inch tart pan. Freeze for 20 to 30 minutes until very firm. Heat oven to 425 degrees. Prick bottom of tart shell at one-inch intervals with a fork. Line snugly with foil. Bake 12 to 15 minutes until crust is set and just beginning to brown. Remove foil and bake until crust is golden brown, 10 to 12 minutes more. Cool completely.

Custard: Combine sugar, flour, and salt in medium saucepan. Whisk in milk until smooth. Bring to a gentle boil over medium heat and, whisking constantly, boil for 4 to 5 minutes until mixture thickens. Remove pan from heat. Whisk egg yolks in small bowl, then gradually whisk in one cup of the hot-milk mixture. Pour egg yolk mixture back into the saucepan and, whisking constantly, simmer for 2 to 3 minutes until slightly thicker. Remove pan from heat. Add butter and vanilla and stir until butter is melted. Place plastic wrap directly on the surface of the custard to keep a skin from forming. Refrigerate until cool, about one hour.

Assemble: Spread chilled custard onto prepared crust. Top with fresh fruit. Brush fruit with melted jam and sprinkle with powdered sugar. Serve immediately or refrigerate up to 24-hours.

Read on for a sneak peek of another exciting book
in the Secrets of Wayfarers Inn series!

THE SECRET INGREDIENT
by Janice Thompson

"Go, Winnie! You've got this!" Janice Eastman's voice rang out above the crowd of onlookers at Marietta's Rising Star baking competition. "You're the best!"

Embarrassed at her sudden outburst, she put a hand over her mouth and then pulled it away to speak to her friends standing nearby. "I can't believe I just did that. Must be the heat getting to me." Or maybe it had more to do with the excitement of the day. Rooting for a good friend at a large competition like this was all new to her.

"It was a little out of character for you, Janice." Tess Wallace wiped the moisture from her brow with the back of her hand. "But I'll agree about the heat. It's really getting to me too. And the humidity's not helping."

"Why anyone would choose to hold a baking contest out side during the month of August is beyond me." LuAnn Sherrill fanned herself with a program and strained to see around the woman in front of them who was wearing a pink, wide-brimmed hat. "Can you even imagine how hot it is on that stage, what with all of the cameras and ovens and lights? I'm surprised they haven't had to call 911 for any of the competitors yet."

Janice nodded and lifted the hair off of her neck in an attempt to cool herself down.

LuAnn fanned herself with her hand. "Where is Robin with those water bottles?"

Tess leaned to the right to see through the crowd. "She left ages ago. I hope she didn't get distracted at the cake display booth. I saw the most delicious looking German chocolate cake over there with coconut pecan icing. I can almost taste it now."

Janice could almost taste it too, but she had more important things to think about right now. "Focus, ladies. We're here to support Winnie, not add more carbs to our diet."

"Speak for yourself." Tess chuckled and licked her lips.

Janice turned her attention to the stage where several tables were arranged in perfect rows, giving the audience an excellent view of the individual competitors. Each baker had a station equipped with a stove, table, ingredients, mixer, and utensils. Winnie Washington, Janice's close friend and the inn's renowned cook, looked up from her station and offered a confident smile.

"She must be feeling pretty good about how things are going." Janice's gaze shifted to the large banner featuring the colors of the Rising Star Flour logo. It hung over the stage, advertising the event with great fanfare. Every now and again a hint of a breeze caught the edge of it, causing the deep blue and orange letters to ripple ever so slightly.

The emcee—a short, jolly man representing the company—
made his way from station to station, microphone in hand,
interviewing the participants. Not that any of them looked
particularly thrilled with the interruption. Like Winnie, they
seemed pretty focused, including an unfamiliar blonde with a
bright pink apron. Janice didn't recognize the woman, but she
was very well put together, if such a thing could be judged from
her hot pink and lime green apron.

"Winnie's hanging in there, like it's not fazing her at all."
LuAnn chimed in. "And don't be embarrassed about cheering
for her, Janice. You're proud of her. We all are."

"If anyone can pull off a win, Winnie can." Tess paused and
then laughed. "It's even in her name."

"Winnie's already a winner in my book," LuAnn said. "And
I'm not just being punny."

Janice laughed at her friends' remarks and then turned her
attention back to the stage. Winnie seemed to have things well
in hand. She peeked in the oven and gave a thumbs-up, signi-
fying that her pie was nearly done.

"How much longer do you think it will be?" Tess asked.

LuAnn glanced at her watch. "Ten minutes until the buzzer
goes off for the pie baking competition. I'm glad they got the
bread category finished earlier. I'm still tickled pink that she won
that one."

"My bets are on her to win in the pie category, too." Janice
added.

Tess fussed with her hair, which had gotten a little fuzzy in
the extreme humidity. "I agree. And I'm just glad this day has

come at last. I've put on four pounds since she started trying out all her pies on us in preparation."

Robin arrived carrying four bottles of water. "You wouldn't believe how much I paid for these." She passed one in Janice's direction. "It's absurd what they charge for a bottle of water these days."

LuAnn took a sip, then sealed the cap and then held it against the back of her neck. "There. That should help cool me down. I hope I don't faint."

"I'm worried about Winnie. I'm so excited that Georgia is up there helping her." Janice waved at the petite young woman, but Winnie's assistant was too busy to notice. Oh well. "For someone who was a total stranger to us just a few days ago, she seems to fit right in."

"Agreed." Tess nodded. "I like her. She's a real sweetheart. Fun to have around the kitchen."

"Yes, and she's proving to be quite a baker," LuAnn added. "I'm so glad she asked Winnie to mentor her before she heads back to college. It's going to be a shame to lose her at the end of the month."

"I agree. And I'm grateful to Winnie for giving her a place to stay while she's here." Janice's gaze shifted to a man with a notepad and pencil in his hand. He moved from competitor to competitor, asking questions and jotting down notes on a gray notepad. "I don't think I know that guy." Janice pointed at the tall, thin man—probably in his late twenties—with a balding head. "The one taking notes and pictures. Looks like a pretty expensive camera he's got hanging around his neck."

LuAnn appeared to be taking the guy in. "Oh, that's Hank Clive. He works for the *Marietta Times*. Brad told me he just took over for one of their beat reporters. I think he's from Kentucky, maybe? Something like that."

"Gotcha." Janice shook her head. Nothing about him seemed familiar, but if Brad Grimes trusted him, he must be okay.

LuAnn seemed to be preoccupied with the contestant in the pink and lime green apron. "Do either of you know that woman?"

"Sandie Ballard." Robin took another swig of her water and held her fan up to her face. "She just opened a bakery a few blocks from the inn. I can't believe you haven't heard. Everyone in town is talking about it. They even did a blurb on the radio about it. It's called the Better Batter."

"The Better Batter?" Janice pondered the name. "Interesting."

"Maybe, but trust me when I say everyone's talking about her." Robin released a loud sigh. "I've heard her shop is adorable. Do you think we'll lose customers to her?"

"Nah. What's she got that we haven't got?" Tess asked.

All of the ladies turned at the same time to gaze at the woman, who looked like something straight out of a magazine.

"I can think of about thirty things, but I don't have time to make a list right now." Janice sighed. "Anyway, we'll keep doing what we do, and she can do whatever it is that she does."

At that very moment, a resounding laugh reverberated across the crowd as Sandie chatted with one of the judges.

On the stage, Winnie opened her oven and pulled out her pie. Although too far away to see for sure, Janice thought it looked fine, just the right shade of golden. Before long, the other contestants had their pies out of the oven as well.

Minutes later, the buzzer went off. Then the judges made their rounds to sample the wares. Janice whispered a prayer when they got to Winnie. Judging from the look of sheer bliss on the female judge's face, she had this one in the bag.

When the judges finished their work, the emcee called all of the participants to join him center stage in a long line. He started with third place, which went to an elderly man named Harvey for his lemon meringue pie. Next came the second-place award, which went to Sandie Ballard for her southern caramel pecan pie. Now, for the moment of truth. The emcee cleared his throat, then reached for the trophy, which he held aloft in his left hand, while speaking into the microphone in his right. "We've got our pie category winner, folks! Winnie Washington of Wayfarers Inn takes the prize for her coconut meringue pie!"

A rousing cheer went up from the crowd. The emcee handed Winnie her trophy.

"Ms. Washington has taken both the pie and bread categories, which makes her our top baker. She will represent our fair county at the state competition in Columbus at the end of the month. If she takes the prize there, she will win a lifetime supply of Rising Star products." He pressed the microphone into Winnie's face. "Do you have anything you'd like to say?"

"I…I…I…" Winnie shook her head. "I'm just so honored. And so stunned."

A rousing cheer went up from the crowd. Janice watched as Winnie took her spot center stage and gestured for Georgia to join her. The shy young woman eased into place next to Winnie, but looked as if she'd rather be anywhere else but in the public eye. Why she felt so out of place was beyond Janice. Georgia was made for the stage.

Winnie bolted off the stage with Georgia on her heels. She headed right for the Inn Crowd, who offered exuberant congratulations. "Thanks. I just can't believe it." Winnie shook her head. "I thought I was a goner at the halfway point. I looked in and the filling in my pie was lopsided. I had to give it a nudge to level off, but it worked just fine." She turned to Georgia and gave her a tight hug. "And I couldn't have done it without you. Seriously. Thank you."

"You're so welcome." The young woman looked elated. Never mind the fact that she had flour in her dark curls and a smudge of white meringue on her cheek. "I can't remember when I've ever had so much fun. Though, I thought I might faint from the heat at one point. I still can't believe they held a contest like this outdoors in August."

"Well, speaking of fun, they're about to give away samples of all the goods. I say we head to the cake booth and fill up on our favorites." Robin took off through the crowd toward the cake table.

"Well, I guess we've lost her." Tess laughed. "I'd rather start with pie samples, myself."

Janice agreed. "Yes, let's make the rounds and sample the wares, shall we?"

They walked together to the stage, where the bakers offered tantalizing bites of the pies they had just baked. Janice took a couple of nibbles of lemon meringue, which tasted delicious. Before long, she ended up in front of the unfamiliar blonde.

The woman extended her hand and smiled. "Hello, ladies. I'm Sandie Ballard." When the woman released her hold on Janice's hand, she reached for a business card at the end of her table. "I just opened my shop, the Better Batter, this past week."

"And you're already giving our Winnie a run for her money in the pie category." Janice took a little taste of the yummy sample. "For pity's sake, you've got chocolate and caramel mixed in with these pecans."

"I call it my turtle pecan pie." Sandie beamed. "You can buy the pecan turtle at my new bakery. It's my Tuesday special." She pointed to the stack of pink and lime green business cards on the front of the table. "Take as many of those as you like and hand them out. The more, the merrier."

Janice took one and pressed it into her purse.

Tess licked her lips. "I think I'd forgotten how many different types of pies and cakes there are in the world."

Janice cleared her throat in an attempt to send a quiet message to Tess: "Stop fraternizing with the enemy." Not that Sandie Ballard was really an enemy, but there was no point in sending the café's customers to a new shop, after all.

"Hey, let's head over to the cake table." Tess nudged Janice with her elbow. "I want to get a taste of that cookie butter cake that took the prize." She took off toward the cake table with Janice on her heels.

The women made their way to the cake samples, and before long everyone was nibbling.

"This cookie butter cake is the finest thing I've ever put in my mouth," Tess declared. When she finished it, she clasped her hands together and grinned. "Say, all of these baked goods have given me an idea. What if we put together a little marketing campaign to help the inn capitalize on Winnie's win?"

"What sort of marketing campaign?" Janice asked as she took another bite of cake.

"Oh, I don't know. Did you see the big banner advertising today's event? Maybe we hang something like that over the front door of the inn to share the news of Winnie's win."

Janice shrugged. "Okay. That doesn't sound too extreme."

LuAnn's eyes flashed with sudden excitement. "What if we offered a free loaf of bread to the first twenty people to book a room at the inn."

Winnie looked a bit perplexed by this notion. Janice felt a little confused, herself.

"Local people, you mean?" she asked. "Or will out-of-towners get the loaves of bread when they arrive for their stay? If so, Winnie might be giving away bread for months to come."

LuAnn shook her head. "Why not both? The rooms have to be booked between now and Tuesday. That way the baking won't drag on forever. They book a room, they get a loaf of bread. It's that simple."

"We haven't had a lot of locals book rooms," Tess argued. "People don't often stay at an inn in their own town."

"But don't you see?" The pitch of LuAnn's voice rose. "This could change all of that. Book a room at Wayfarers Inn and we'll give you a hot-from-the-oven loaf of bread, straight from Winnie's oven. But you have to jump on the offer quick, or you'll miss out."

"Sounds like a lot of work."

"I don't mind, Janice." Winnie's voice sounded from behind them. "I bake so frequently, anyway. Sounds like a fun way to entice people, the locals included, to try out the inn."

"Perfect." Tess paused and looked around. "I'll see if I can track down that reporter. Maybe he'll add this information to his article."

Winnie pointed off into the distance. "Speaking of the reporter, I see he's still talking to Sandie Ballard." She took another bite of her cake.

Janice gave the woman another glance. "Right. Looks like he's got her posing for a photo with her red ribbon. Oh, look! She's holding a loaf of bread for the picture. Fun."

Winnie stopped eating her cake, and gave the man another look. "He tried to get my picture earlier when I caught him rooting around backstage before the event."

"Rooting around?" This took Janice by surprise.

Winnie shrugged. "Well, you know. Going from baker to baker, asking about their ingredients, and so on."

Janice pondered Winnie's words. "That does seem strange."

"Not really. Some of the contestants seemed a little put off by him—until he explained that he was a reporter. Then a couple of them put on fake smiles and started talking about themselves like they were superstars. That's when he approached me and asked to take my picture."

"Did you let him?" Tess asked.

"Yes, but I had sweat pouring down the side of my face, thanks to the heat. I'm sure I looked just lovely. Nothing like that beauty queen over there." She gestured to Sandie.

Janice patted her on the arm. "Beautiful or not, she couldn't beat our Winnie."

"But she still got second place, so that should tell you something," Winnie countered. "Apparently she's really good."

"But nobody, and I mean nobody, can beat our very own Winnie Washington from Wayfarers Inn." Tess spread her arms wide, as if showing off a banner. "Marietta's own Rising Star! I can see it now. Maybe we'll even use the Rising Star colors, just to make a point. How does that sound, Winnie? Can we start spreading the word about the free loaves of bread?"

"Sure. I'll need a lot of help in the kitchen but I can probably get them baked on Monday, ready for pickup on Tuesday morning."

"Perfect! I'll let Hank know right away." Tess took off toward the reporter, a woman on a mission.

Janice could tell Winnie was enjoying the flattering comments. And why not? She certainly deserved all the accolades this day could bring.

A NOTE FROM THE EDITORS

We hope you enjoy Secrets of Wayfarers Inn, created by the Books and Inspirational Media Division of Guideposts, a nonprofit organization that touches millions of lives every day through products and services that inspire, encourage, help you grow in your faith, and celebrate God's love in every aspect of your daily life.

Thank you for making a difference with your purchase of this book, which helps fund our many outreach programs to military personnel, prisons, hospitals, nursing homes, and educational institutions. To learn more, visit Guideposts Foundation.org.

We also maintain many useful and uplifting online resources. Visit Guideposts.org to read true stories of hope and inspiration, access OurPrayer network, sign up for free newsletters, download free e-books, join our Facebook community, and follow our stimulating blogs.

To learn about other Guideposts publications, including the best-selling devotional *Daily Guideposts*, go to ShopGuideposts .org, call (800) 932-2145, or write to Guideposts, PO Box 5815, Harlan, Iowa 51593.

Sign up for the
Guidepasts Fiction Newsletter
and stay up to date on the books you love!

guideposts fiction
Inspiring reads chosen just for you!

What's New

Mysteries of Lancaster County

Welcome to Bird-in-Hand, Pennsylvania, a quaint village in the heart of Lancaster County's Amish Country. Here, amid rolling green hills and well-tended farms, where the Classen sisters, Elizabeth, Martha, and Mary, reunite after inheriting their family home. Together, they operate Secondhand Blessings, a charming gift-and-thrift store, housed in the old homestead's barn. Little do the sisters suspect as they stock their shelves with Amish handcrafted gift items, antiques, and yummy baked goods that they're also filling their rustic store with a host of mysteries and surprises. Learn More

Reader Favorite

Mysteries of Martha's Vineyard

On the historic island of Martha's Vineyard, Massachusetts, recent widow Priscilla Latham Grant inherits a lighthouse. She's no sooner settled into her new surrounding than she comes face-to-face with wave after wave of adventure—which include rediscovered family, new friends, old friends and head-scratching mysteries that crop up with surprising regularity. Learn More

From Our Editors

Tearoom Mysteries

Take a picturesque New England town... add some hidden treasures... a few suspicious characters... and a good measure of faith and friendship and you've brewed up Tearoom Mysteries!

Come explore at your leisure this charming village with its lovely mountain lake surrounded by wild blueberry bushes. Just like the people who come to Elaine and Jan's tearoom, you'll find yourself feeling relaxed. Learn More

A perfect blend of faith, family and fun!

You'll get sneak peeks of new releases, recommendations from other Guideposts readers, and special offers just for you . . .
and it's FREE!

Just go to Guideposts.org/Newsletters today to sign up.

Guideposts®

**Visit Guideposts.org/Shop
or call (800) 932-2145**

Find more inspiring fiction in these best-loved Guideposts series!

Tearoom Mysteries Series

Mix one stately Victorian home, a charming lakeside town in Maine, and two adventurous cousins with a passion for tea and hospitality. Add a large scoop of intriguing mystery and sprinkle generously with faith, family, and friends, and you have the recipe for *Tearoom Mysteries*.

Sugarcreek Amish Mysteries

Be intrigued by the suspense and joyful "aha" moments in these delightful stories. Each book in the series brings together two women of vastly different backgrounds and traditions, who realize there's much more to the "simple life" than meets the eye.

Mysteries of Martha's Vineyard

What does Priscilla Latham Grant, a Kansas farm girl know about hidden treasure and rising tides, maritime history and local isle lore? Not much—but to save her lighthouse and family reputation, she better learn quickly!

Mysteries of Silver Peak

Escape to the historic mining town of Silver Peak, Colorado, and discover how one woman's love of antiques helps her solve mysteries buried deep in the town's checkered past.

**To learn more about these books,
visit Guideposts.org/Shop**